Etched
in Lies

A. M. Hughes

**LODESTONE
BOOKS**

Winchester, UK
Washington, USA

First published by Lodestone Books, 2015
Lodestone Books is an imprint of John Hunt Publishing Ltd., Laurel House, Station Approach,
Alresford, Hants, SO24 9JH, UK
office1@jhpbooks.net
www.johnhuntpublishing.com

For distributor details and how to order please visit the 'Ordering' section on our website.

Text copyright: A. M. Hughes 2014

ISBN: 978 1 78279 956 6
Library of Congress Control Number: 2015948072

A CIP catalogue record for this book is available from the British Library.

Design: Stuart Davies

Printed in the USA by Edwards Brothers Malloy

We operate a distinctive and ethical publishing philosophy in all
areas of our business, from our global network of authors to
production and worldwide distribution.

For K & E with all my love

Etched in Lies

Chapter 1

When she really put her mind to it, Dylan could ignore just about anything. Open textbooks, papers and pens littered the booth where she sat, but she gazed through the large picture window at the people walking down Main Street. Around her, people came and went with the dinner rush, but she didn't pay them attention either. This was the perfect place to get some homework done before she was forced home. Unless, that is, she was being hounded by her best friend, who just flew into the restaurant, a whirlwind of chaos, heading straight for her.

"Dylan," Megan whined as she plopped into the booth, snatched a piece of pizza and inhaled the aroma.

Dylan focused on copying the next homework problem into her notebook and almost resisted grimacing. She knew where this was going.

"It's been months. You need to move on," Megan continued, fully accustomed to these defense tactics as well as the fact she was one person who couldn't be ignored forever.

"Who says I haven't?" she muttered, instantly distracted by a paper cut slicing across her index finger and the blood seeping to the surface.

The squeal of shoes next to the booth drew Dylan's attention to a guy studying her. She knew she had never seen him before, and though at first glance she was intrigued, the fact that he was staring at her only served to ensure her interest in him would stop right there. Determinedly, she gazed back at her homework as a drop of blood landed on the Algebra problem.

She kept her head down as she reached for a napkin, listening for the guy to walk away. Her sanctuary was turning into a prison. To the side was a guy who, for whatever reason, was studying her. Yet sitting in front of her, Megan was even more dangerous. If Dylan gave even the smallest hint that she was listening, she wouldn't get her homework finished. Ever. She didn't want to hear Megan's rants anymore.

And who said she hadn't moved on? Dylan played with the idea as she stared at the blood smeared across the homework problem she just finished. Though she would never verbally admit it, she knew Megan was at least partially right.

In defiance, she doused the last slice of pizza in hot pepper flakes, something Megan couldn't tolerate, and unsuccessfully hid a smirk as she chomped down. Reaching for her drink, she noticed the only proof a paper cut had even existed was a thin line. She studied her finger, barely aware that Megan had started speaking again. As she watched, the line on her finger faded, leaving no proof that a minute ago there had been a severe paper cut. No cut healed that quickly.

Megan slammed her hand on the table and shook Dylan's attention away from her finger, though the cut still tugged at her mind.

"All I'm saying"—Megan munched on a piece of crust and leaned forward, determined to make her point—"is that you haven't even given any guy a chance."

Dylan resisted the urge to bounce her head off the table and closed her eyes, willing a calming breath into her lungs. "None of them could keep up with me. For one of them, I even had to dial 911 after he collapsed a quarter mile into the jog." The irritation grew in her voice with each word.

"Jog. Right," Megan snorted. "Those were dates, not races."

Shrugging, Dylan bit her lip as she remembered the last guy. He had let her pick the activity and had been willing to go for a run with her. They had done one lap around the school. He had stopped. She had continued, no longer hearing the wheezing gasps for breath coming from behind her; and it was only when she glanced back that she saw her date limping quickly in the opposite direction. She had done her best to keep her laughter in check.

"You better not be going back into hibernation on me."

She snuck a peek at Megan. Her friend wouldn't buy any retort. Bruno's was as close to a cave as Dylan could manage, but she didn't care. She liked it here.

Megan glared at her phone as it began to chirp. "I have to go." She dropped the still ringing phone into her bag without answering it. "We'll talk more later."

It wasn't a question.

Dylan returned to her homework offering a noncommittal nod of the head, but she pushed it away the moment the door shut. Megan's words bothered her. Was it really so horrible that she didn't want to date anyone? Sure, Megan always chose attractive guys, but there hadn't been anything below the surface besides hormones. And stupidity.

She took another bite and gazed through the large picture window, wondering what Megan would do next. As she watched Megan walk in front of the window chatting with a few guys, she didn't notice grease drip down her arm. She nearly choked when Megan winked at her.

"Son of a..." She ground her teeth. Soon, she would have to give up another night. Haphazardly, she wiped the grease sliding towards her elbow, shoveled another bite into her mouth, and grabbed her drink.

Still chewing, she slid out of the booth and turned towards the counter. No one was supposed to be standing a foot away from her, let alone the guy who had stared at her earlier. She flinched, the empty plate and half-finished soda inches from his shirt. Both watched the soda slowly slosh out of the cup and splash across his chest.

She flicked her gaze to his shirt and back to his face as he closed his mouth with an audible snap. He looked down and then allowed his eyes to travel slowly back up.

"Shit," she managed around the pizza shoved in her mouth, and put everything down adding another stain to her Algebra homework.

Praying for the ground to open and swallow her whole, she searched desperately for a napkin not covered in pizza, or blood. Without luck, she turned towards the counter.

"Jimmy, throw me a towel." She mentally chastised the shake in her voice.

"What'd ya do this time?" Jimmy called as he came out of the back and tossed one to her. "I swear you're the sloppiest person I've ever met."

Pursing her lips to keep the retort silent, Dylan turned her attention back to the guy. He hadn't moved as the soda spread down his shirt. She held the towel out to him, finally swallowing the rest of the pizza in her mouth.

"Um, sorry."

"No worries. You didn't see me coming."

Desperate to hide the blush creeping up her face, she looked away. Out of the corner of her eye, he shrugged and finally took the towel. He blotted the spot soaking up some of the moisture before wiping his hands clean. He tossed the towel back on the counter before looking back at her.

"Jack Poesy," he said, holding his hand out to her.

"Dylan Lord." She smiled and shook his hand. She looked at him again. "I haven't seen you around before, have I?"

A smile crept across his face, but he shifted nervously. "We go to school together."

Her cheeks reddened. It was a very real possibility that this guy did go to school with her. She walked around with blinders on, and liked it that way. People didn't bother her, and she didn't bother them. "Am I really that observant?"

He shrugged and leaned against the booth. "I'm good at not being seen, if I don't want to be. But why would you know me? We don't exactly hang out in the same crowd."

She eyed his outfit trying to figure out where he belonged. He definitely did not look the part of a geek. He wore a simple T-shirt that was somehow fitted without being too clingy and a faded pair of jeans, and work boots that were too clean to be used to work. The muscles in his forearms flexed when he stuck his hands in his pockets. He could have passed for an athlete, but he wasn't.

Tucking a strand of her short bobbed hair behind her ear she shot a look over and made eye contact with Jimmy, folding pizza boxes behind the counter. With a slight raise of her brow, she told him not to come over. She was very glad she wasn't alone with this guy who made her jittery and had barely said anything.

"So, you know who I am?"

He smiled. "I've seen you around school a few times when you're not busy running everywhere."

Something in his voice had the hairs on her neck tingling. While it was true she was always running late, which was quite ironic considering she was one of the best runners on the track and cross-country teams, there was something about him that made her want to look away. A chill climbed her spine and goose bumps broke out over her arms.

"Yeah, well speaking of..." She picked up her plate and drink and took it over to the counter, intent on getting away from him. "I've gotta run."

The paper cut across her finger opened again, and she quickly stuck her hand in her pocket. She hadn't planned to leave. She turned back just as Jack closed his eyes and took a deep breath. He mirrored her movement and stuck his hand back in his pocket.

"That wasn't very nice, Dylan," he said, his voice just above a whisper when he opened his eyes and held her gaze.

Goose bumps multiplied. She crossed her arms defensively, stepping back and bumping into the counter. "What wasn't?"

"Lying to me." He stepped towards her and spoke very deliberately, his voice rising slightly, implying she already knew this answer.

"Whatever," she huffed, and moved past him towards the papers that were still scattered around her booth. "Everyone lies."

"No, not everyone lies." Jack shook his head. "The truth is everyone is going to hurt you, but you have to find the ones worth suffering for."

Straightening slowly, the papers in her hands slipped back onto the table.

"What?" Jack fidgeted, the air of confidence surrounding him beginning to crumble.

She shook her head. "Just trying to figure out what's going on here."

"W-what do you mean?"

"Did Megan put you up to this?"

Her anger started to boil as she imagined several different and highly creative ways to get even with her best friend for setting this up without even a warning. Spinning away she muttered and reached across the table to get a few more papers. "I swear to God I'm going to kill her. Maybe I don't want to date anyone right now—"

Her words were cut off when Jack spoke again, his voice soft just as it had been a moment ago. "I'm here because I want to be, not because anyone forced me to, or asked me to, or whatever it is you think happened. No one set this up."

Dylan could feel her anger drain and humiliation start to rise. In her mind, it had been logical to assume this was all Megan. His voice forced her to look at him. She saw a shy smile creep back as he took a small step towards her.

"Why don't you come with me?" he said with a shrug. "We could go somewhere and talk."

"I'm busy." He flinched, but she refused to acknowledge the increasing sting of her own paper cut.

"Please stop lying to me." Concern shaded his voice.

"I'm not," she insisted, and watched him flinch again, hoping she wasn't visibly flinching herself.

"Fine." Defeat was clear in his voice. "You don't have to come with me, but very soon you will wish you had."

"Doubtful."

She shuffled a stack of papers, determined to ignore him since talking wasn't working. She didn't look away from her papers even as his footsteps quietly and slowly moved away. The chime on the door made her cringe.

"I am glad I met you, Dylan," he called solemnly. "But I am sorry to say you won't be glad you met me."

With the soft click of the door, she sank back into her booth, the stack of papers scattered on the table. She took a deep breath, willing her nerves and her hands to stop trembling.

"What was that all about?" Jimmy gathered her plate and threw it a bin.

She shrugged but didn't look at him, still not completely sure what it had been about. Quietly, she cleared her throat, hoping her voice would be calm. "Just some moron from school, I guess, who doesn't have anything better to do than mess with people."

She looked out into the parking lot. Jack stood by a parked car looking back at her. "What is his problem?" she blurted out.

"Want me to go take care of him?" Jimmy asked. "No one messes with my favorite customer."

"I'm only your favorite customer because you are obligated to tell your sister that."

Jimmy shrugged, his attention already moving past her. "Here comes the boss."

In the parking lot, Bruno extricated himself from his car and waddled towards the restaurant. "Should I get the wheelchair now or make him walk all the way here?" Already she could see him panting.

"Be nice." Jimmy threw the towel back at her. "And clean up the soda you spilled on the floor."

"I don't work here. Isn't that your job?"

Jimmy laughed. "You're here enough. If Bruno catches you here much more you know he's gonna find you a job bussing tables."

"I am a paying customer, thank you very much."

Jimmy raised an eyebrow. Dylan followed his gaze, bit back a chuckle and looked at the open books and papers that littered the table where she regularly ate her dinner. She loved it here. Her spirits dropped immediately when she realized she would have to head home soon.

Bruno gasped as he came through the door and smiled. He looked over at her booth. "It's nice to see that my restaurant works just as well as a library as it does a pizza shop."

She shot him a little grin. She had heard it before from Bruno. *His shop blah blah blah...not a place to do homework blah blah blah...needs to eat more.*

"You need to eat more." He leaned against the counter. "You're all skin and bones."

Dylan narrowed her eyes. They chuckled and she silently cursed her mother. It wasn't her fault she was the spitting image of her mother at this age. The only difference between their tall, thin figures were the streaks of red added to her sun-streaked brown hair before the start of the school year.

"And on that note, I'm leaving." She threw the towel back at Jimmy and started to organize all of the papers scattered across the booth.

"Tell Mom I'll be home late," Jimmy called over. "I have a paper due tomorrow that I haven't finished yet."

A drop of blood fell from her finger and splattered next to the grease stain already on her homework. She grabbed a napkin and wrapped her finger before she looked over at Jimmy.

"I'll tell her." She slid her books into her bag and headed for the door. "See you later, Bruno."

He cleared his throat as he puffed to regain his breath.

Her smile faded when the door shut with a jingle behind her.

A girl got out of a car and stood next to Jack. Though they were several rows away, Dylan knew they were talking about her. She stared back and watched Jack hold up a finger.

Unwilling to acknowledge him, she hurried away. It wasn't until she reached home that she realized what finger he had held up: his right index finger. The very finger on which she had multiple paper cuts throbbing.

Chapter 2

Shouting woke Dylan before her alarm the next morning. Climbing out of bed, she desperately tried to ignore the argument she had heard so many times before. On a sigh, she acknowledged the pattern; every morning that started with yelling ended up being fabulously awful for her. A silent prayer passed her lips as she willed this day to be different.

Pausing to hit her alarm, she pulled her hand back sharply. The paper cuts were worse. Her entire finger was red. Thin lines were still clearly visible.

"What the hell," she muttered as she searched her running bag for some Neosporin and Band-Aids.

She took both with her into the bathroom. Dylan let the water run before she was ready to step into the shower. The white noise of the falling water and hum of the pipes helped drown out the yelling and momentarily calmed her. But they were only temporary fixes, and she knew that.

Eventually dressing, she chocked the continued pain in her finger to the day and headed to wake her younger brother, Tony. On the way, she found herself pausing outside Jimmy's room. Though he didn't usually stay at home during the semester, she was surprised to see his bed empty when last night he said he would be home. She shook her head and walked into Tony's room carefully avoiding the dirty clothes and video games that littered the floor.

"Let's go." She nudged Tony's shoulder before walking over to turn down the music he always played, letting the argument filter into the room. "Time to get up."

Tony tossed his pillow over his head and rolled over. "Go away."

Sticking to their routine but no mood to play with him, she turned towards the door and skipped a couple of steps. "You have five minutes to get up or I'll be back. With water."

With a glance back, she smirked as Tony shot straight up in bed. He knew she wasn't lying. She had used water before to wake him. Cold water. She headed back to her room to get her running bag and homework and passed Tony already in the hall as she headed downstairs to finish getting ready for school. She ruffled his hair in passing causing it to stick up even more like a cockatoo.

Marla and James Lord's argument faded when they heard the stairs creek. Dylan dropped her bag and books on the kitchen table without looking at her parents. Sadly, this too was part of the routine, and she hated it.

"Morning." Her mom's overly chipper voice grated. Her mom was always like this when they were caught fighting.

Her father got a cup of coffee left the kitchen. She heard the weather report drift in from the living room and her father grumble as he slumped into his chair, the springs groaning under his weight.

"Breakfast?" Her mother didn't wait for a response before she reached for a bowl.

Dylan shook her head. "Just a granola bar. I have a meet tonight."

"Okay." The bowl snapped back into the stack.

Silence filled the kitchen and Dylan fiddled with the pile of mail.

"Why do you guys always fight?" She hadn't meant to ask, but couldn't stop herself.

Her mother's shoulders sagged as she turned away. "Your father and I love each other very much..." her mother began, but Dylan wasn't listening anymore.

The pain in her finger increased with each word. She looked down at her hands still holding the stack of mail and watched the Band-Aid fill with more blood.

"Whatever."

She grabbed her stuff and headed into the living room to wait for Tony, not acknowledging her mother still speaking behind her.

Her finger was a bright red, the color darkening and the pain swelling with each breath she took. Tony stomped down the stairs, snapping Dylan out of her observation. Not waiting to make sure he followed, she grabbed her stuff and quickly headed for the door.

Five minutes later, she realized Tony wasn't behind her.

"Of course it would be like this," she huffed, and gritted her teeth as the pain in her finger flared. Spinning back, she paused and watched Tony run towards her, the zipper of his backpack opening further with each step.

"Thanks for waiting for me," he sulked as he frantically tried to keep his school bag from spilling all over the sidewalk.

She snatched a paper the wind had grabbed and glared at her brother for a moment before her expression softened. She took a deep cleansing breath and watched him struggle with his bag.

"Sorry," she managed on the exhale. She wasn't angry with Tony, and had no right to take out her frustrations on him. "Do you have everything? We have time if you need to go back."

Tony knelt down and opened the bag taking everything out and checking it. She held the paper out for him. Slowly Tony took it, not making eye contact with her.

"Think I have it all," he finally replied.

"You have your homework? Books? Lunch money?"

His shoulders sagged. She knew the answer before he spoke.

"Here." She reached into her pocket and gave him some money.

He smiled as he shoved the money in his pocket, then resumed stuffing everything he had just checked haphazardly back into his bag, his shoulders already lifting. She ruffled his hair again and helped him up as a little stab of pain shot up her arm. With a stiff nod, she walked with him to school. A quick glance across the street warned Dylan her day wouldn't get better.

Jack stood on the other side of the street talking on a cell phone. Though he wasn't looking at her, she knew he was there for her benefit. She hurried away, barely paying attention to the fact that her little brother had to run to keep up with her.

"Fabulously awful," she repeatedly mumbled after she walked Tony into the elementary school and then headed the last few blocks to the high school alone.

Her mood didn't improve when she made it to her locker. Jack was leaning against it.

"What is your problem?" She spoke through clenched teeth and shouldered Jack out of the way.

"I just wanted to prove to you that I went here." He carried the same relaxed smile he had worn a little the night before.

"Wonderful." She grunted forcing her bag and books into the locker before grabbing stuff stacked on the shelf, refusing to look at him as she continued to speak. "You've made your point. You look very natural blocking my locker. Can you leave now?"

She slammed her locker shut but refused to turn.

"I need to talk to you."

"Not gonna happen." She spun around and headed away from him. She hadn't forgotten how foolish she had felt last night and did not want a replay of those events again today, but he kept pace with her.

"Let me rephrase." He sounded confident and a little cocky as he spoke. "You need to talk to me."

She stopped dead in the hallway. Jack stopped with her, but shoes squeaked and shuffled as others fought to make their way around them.

Forcing herself to remain calm, she turned slowly and spoke with what she considered an ample amount of patience. "Jack, I have a meet after school. I don't have time to worry about whatever delusional confession you have waiting for me."

He nodded. "How's the finger?" His gaze dropped to her armload of books clearly seeing the bloody Band-Aid that she was holding straight out rather than against the books like the rest of her hand.

"What's it to you?" Her patience was already fading.

"Everything." Jack's face remained calm as he reached into his pocket. "I told you..." he paused and locked his gaze on Dylan "...you would regret meeting me, but unfortunately, we don't have a choice."

"There's always a choice, Jack." No longer able to hide her exasperation she rolled her eyes.

Jack slowly shook his head. He folded a piece of paper and slipped it into the book at the top of her pile. "When you're ready to talk, call me."

Jack walked away, while she cursed herself for admiring the view.

"What was that?"

Dylan cringed at the sing-songy tone in Megan's voice. She turned towards her, and watched her follow Jack's progress easily through the crowded hallway.

"Nothing," she mumbled, and headed for her homeroom, disregarding the increasing throb of her finger.

"That" — Megan laughed — "did not look like nothing."

"Do you know who he is?"

"Jack?" Megan sighed. "Of course I do. Junior. Definitely hot, but usually a loner. I think he was dating someone in our grade last year or something. Why?"

She could almost hear Megan calculating, trying to orchestrate a date. Choosing her words carefully, she answered, "I met him last night at Bruno's. He freaked me out because he knew me, but I had never seen him before."

"Oh." Megan drew the word out.

"Don't even think about it," Dylan snapped. "Besides, I assumed you had sent him and told him as much, so that avenue is shut forever."

Megan chuckled. "And now you wish it wasn't."

"Shut up," she mumbled under her breath.

"My experimental hermit." Megan hugged her. "Maybe if you didn't spend so much time running and a little more watching, you would have noticed him before."

She looked away. Megan was right. She only lived to run, and could count on one hand the vast number of friends she had, and watched as one of those people approached. Sadly she didn't even consider him a friend. Noah was only a friend through association. How her artsy best friend had landed Noah Greer, football running back, was beyond her, but Megan was happy, and therefore so was she. Dylan saw the smile stretch across Megan's face and knew the focus wouldn't be on her for a while.

She finally nudged Megan's shoulder to get her attention as Noah leaned in and whispered something that had Megan giggling. "You're still coming to my meet right?"

"Yup." Megan reached into her bag. Still giggling she shot a look at Noah.

Noah kissed Megan as the bell rang and left for his homeroom.

"I have a sign for you and everything." Megan jumped back into the conversation and unrolled a banner that read: *Dylan RUNNING for President.*

Dylan's smiled but it was short lived as she looked out into the hallway and Jack walked by. He paused, giving her a shy smile before walking away.

Megan looked at her friend. "Parents fighting again this morning?"

"It's turning into one of those days." She plopped down in her seat as the bell rang. Megan sat down on her desk and waited. "I was ready to leave for school fifteen minutes early but had to wait for Tony." She shot her a look as Megan tried mostly unsuccessfully not to laugh. "Then Jack, with whatever his issues are, keeps totally pissing me off. And I have the paper cut from hell."

She held up her finger to show Megan.

"Jeez what did you do? Slice it with a razor blade?" Megan tried to grab Dylan's hand.

Dylan shook her head and jerked her hand away. "I just picked up a piece of paper last night, and then this morning I don't know what I keep doing, but it hurts like a son of a bitch."

Megan walked up to Mrs. Nally's desk and grabbed several Band-Aids from the top drawer. Carefully, she pulled the old one off. Both girls saw it was more than a few small paper cuts. A clear cut ran across her fingertip.

"That looks deep," Megan said quietly, a hint of concern flavoring her usually carefree voice.

Dylan wrapped the new Band-Aids around it and spent the rest of homeroom staring intently at the cover of her book, knowing Megan was still surveying her.

The day did not get any better.

She was late for every morning class – an astonishing feat of stupidity and skill, even for her. Everywhere she looked, she saw Jack. Either he was heading into a classroom next to her, or he was passing her at her locker, or she was passing him at his. It was as if the universe really wanted to prove to her just how blind she was. Lunch, though, definitely took the cake.

When Dylan got up to return her tray she ran right into Jack.

Her face grew red as the remnants of her meal splattered all over his shirt and the ground. Yet Jack only sighed. "We really have to stop meeting each other this way." He straightened her tray and took it forcefully from her. "At this rate, I'll be out of clothes pretty quickly."

"I'm so sorry." She was mortified at a repeat of last night. But this time was worse. She stood there, willing her legs to move but unable to look away.

"Yeah, I know you didn't see me." He set the tray back down on the table. "But honestly I'm beginning to get a complex about how often you don't see me and I end up wearing food."

"I'm really not a klutz."

"I know you aren't, I just have bad timing." He reached into his pocket. "I noticed this fell out of your book in one of your mad dashes to class, and I wanted to return it."

"You just happened to notice," Dylan challenged, and raised an eyebrow.

Jack smiled and held out the folded note. "You really will want to talk to me."

People around her were laughing. She looked at his hand letting the anger cover her embarrassment. "I'd better go turn in my tray, unless you'd like more of a design on your shirt. I think there's a spot by the collar that I missed."

"Wait!"

She didn't admit she could feel him only a step behind her until her tray was safely placed on the kitchen's conveyor belt. "I thought I made it pretty clear last night and again this morning that I'm not interested." She clenched her fist as pain shot through her pinkie. She walked back to her table without looking at him. Her stomach lurched knowing he was still behind her.

Jack leaned in and whispered, his breath tickling the back of her neck, "You're lying again."

Dylan spun around, the little thrill she felt pumped through her veins. "And how would you know that?"

Jack grinned and he held up his pinkie finger where a small cut began to ooze blood.

Chapter 3

Even as she ran, Dylan couldn't get Jack out of her head. She had laughed at him as she walked out of the lunchroom, but the laughter had faded as soon as he was out of sight.

She had been so distracted that she had forgotten to get her books out of her locker for the next class. The bell had already rung by the time she convinced her algebra teacher to let her get her homework. Barely waiting for his response, she bolted from the room and skidded to a stop as she approached her locker. A small triangle of paper stuck out of the slot. It was from Jack. She knew it without even opening it. Only he would be ballsy enough to leave it after she had not read it twice already.

Checking to make sure she was alone, she finally opened the note and read the message: "When you're ready." There was a number written underneath. Her teeth ground together as she crumpled up the note and threw it over her shoulder before grabbing her books and running back to class. She didn't want to think about it anymore, but couldn't help wonder just what he wanted to say, and that bothered her most of all.

She gasped when she opened her bag at the end of the day to get her uniform only to find the crumpled note sitting in one of her sneakers. Not only did he not take a hint, but he had also broken into her locker. She remembered the look on Megan's face at the end of the day, and knew who had helped him get in there. Dylan slammed her locker shut, vowing to get even with her best friend later. She had a race to win first.

The wind hugged her as she sped around the course, happy to be running, happy to have time to think. The questions blazed through her mind. How did Jack get that cut? It was clear that he didn't have anything in his hands, and she very much doubted he was carrying a knife or anything sharp just to cut himself during lunch. And it matched her cut. Dylan shook the thought from her head already uneasy with where it might take her. But what was his issue? She had never before last night even spoken to him, or looked at him for that matter, and now he wouldn't leave her alone. Her mouth twitched as a new thought burst to mind. Twice she had spilled something on him. It made her feel better knowing that she was unintentionally getting even with him for bothering her. She caught the look of concern on a teammate's face suddenly aware how odd she must look grinning like a moron in the middle of a cross-country meet. She wiped the smile from her face and picked up her pace.

How did she get those cuts? Unable to control the thoughts bombarding her, she let them. She thought back to last night. Yes, she had picked up papers, but had she actually moved any of them at the moment she had been cut? The thought burned into her memory, and she knew without a doubt that she had not been moving any when it happened. She also knew she hadn't done anything to make them rip deeper this morning. And there was no way she had cut herself in the cafeteria. There had to be another connection.

She let the rhythm of her breathing sort the facts through her mind. The first cut was right after Jimmy said he had a paper to finish for one of his professors. The second was when her mother was saying how much her parents cared for each other. The third was when she was talking to Jack. What was the connection?

Jimmy didn't lie to her. They had a close relationship. He had always watched out for her. In the past few years when her parents had started arguing more consistently, it was Jimmy who took her and Tony to the park or out for ice cream to get out of the house. Of course, she didn't realize this until after Jimmy left for college and it was her turn to protect Tony.

The quick stampede of feet and a chorus of heavy breathing snapped Dylan back to the present. Cursing she sped up, but it was already too late. Three hundred meters ahead, she watched her main rival leave the woods and sprint towards the finish line followed closely by two of her teammates.

Barely out of breath, she jogged over to Megan who, as promised, still held the banner when Dylan finally crossed the line.

"Nice job," Megan tried to say cheerfully.

She could hear the hesitation in Megan's voice and barely acknowledged what she said.

That was not a nice job. That was a lousy job.

"Thank you, fabulously awful day," she grumbled as she waited with the rest of her team for the last runner to come in, pacing back and forth like a caged animal.

She had let Jack get inside her head and it had ruined her day. It had ruined the race. Her thoughts meshed together, jumbled. There was only one thing she knew. She had to get out of there. Now.

Movement out of the corner of her eye distracted her. Someone walked over to Megan. She refused to look, already sure she knew who it was. Purposely, she turned away, aware that she would be able to watch Megan and Jack in the reflection of the large glass windows that lined one of the school hallways behind her. It only took moments for her fist to clench, watching her best friend speak casually, bordering on flirtatiously with him. That is until she noticed Jack flinch.

Finally released, Dylan handed her bag to Megan, not even acknowledging Jack's presence. Running was her time to think, and she needed it now.

He flinched.

Scenarios flashed through her mind. Megan had been her best friend since they both learned to walk, and at this moment, She had no idea what he had asked, or how she had responded. She chastised herself for even thinking Megan would betray her. Whatever had happened or been said, she had to trust Megan was not just her own personal and highly unwanted matchmaker.

Dylan let her thoughts rumble as she ran through the park and headed back towards the school, ready to run another circle if she needed it. Her fingers still throbbed. She pushed herself harder, willing herself to forget about the cuts that weren't healing properly.

Slowly, painfully, her mind began to empty. Finally tired, she turned and headed home.

"What was with you yesterday?" Megan slammed Dylan's locker shut, shoving her bag into her arms.

She thought through her answer as she spun her combo. "I told you, it was a bad day," she managed as she stuffed the bag into her locker making more noise than usual as she felt pain slice through her forearm. She grabbed her arm and willed herself to remain calm. Megan's reaction told her she was failing miserably.

"What is going on with you?" Megan demanded, stepping forward to trap her against her locker.

Dylan slid the hoodie on to cover the bleeding. Fear flashed across her face when she let herself think about the answer. "I think I'm losing my mind."

"Not on my watch," Megan vowed, wrapping her in a tight hug.

Opening her eyes, she let out a groan as Jack walked towards them.

"He is really hot." She could hear the smile in Megan's voice.

"He is really pissing me off," Dylan snapped. Her next thoughts paused the same moment Jack did.

"Wait till I tell you what he said yesterday." Megan ended with a squeal when Noah appeared and wrapped his arms around her.

"What who said about what?" Noah looked cautiously between the two girls.

Megan wiggled her eyebrows. "What Jack said about Dylan."

21

Dylan swept her gaze from Megan to Noah and watched him narrow his eyes.

She spun around and stuck her arm in the locker, pretending to search for a pencil. "I don't want to know."

The pain from the new cut on her arm increased. She slammed her locker door and ran around the corner as Jack approached Megan and Noah. She looked back in time to see Megan smile and Noah force a chuckle at something Jack said. Megan blushed and slapped Noah. Jack shrugged, but she didn't stick around to try to read his lips. She turned and fled when all three of them glanced towards her.

She ignored everyone the rest of the day. She kept her head down and plowed through the crowded hallways grateful that Megan knew enough to let her be.

Gracefully, she tried to avoid Jack after lunch by rushing through the first door she saw. Unfortunately, she didn't realize where she was until a strange cough caught her attention.

Before she even fully knew what was happening, her face was turning red. The noise had come from a boy, standing in front of a urinal zipping his fly. She bowed her head and tried to force the door to open, but in her desperation to get out, didn't realize she was pushing the door when she needed to pull.

"Pull," the boy taunted from behind her.

Acknowledge his command, she pulled but didn't otherwise communicate as she rushed out. Spinning around to ensure the door had shut, she didn't see who was behind her until she crashed into a solid body.

"Where's the fire?" Noah chuckled, trying to steady her before she fell.

"At home," she gasped, the pain in her arm increasing.

Dylan ripped herself from Noah's grasp, hearing the door to the boy's lav opening. Come hell or a plague of locusts, she was leaving. By the time she had convinced the nurse that she was indeed ill and had to leave for the day, half an hour after stumbling into Noah, she swore laughter chased her through the hallways. She didn't take a deep breath until she was safely in her bedroom with the door locked and the blankets covering her head.

Chapter 4

Dylan bandaged her arms, threw on a long sleeve shirt and headed out into the drizzle. The rain didn't stop her from running, but the pain spreading through her hands and arm tried its best to do just that.

The humiliation of yesterday blazed clearly in her mind. Earlier she had listened to her best friend laugh at her bathroom story for half an hour before she hung up and turned the phone off. Shaking her head, she pushed harder, trying to distance herself from a moment that would not soon die away.

She thought about the boy standing, half-turned towards the urinals. It was bad enough barging in on one of the hottest boys on the planet who, until that moment, she was sure didn't know she existed. Reliving the details, she was forced to admit that had she been a different kind of person the feeling of mortification would have been non-existent. She would have laughed at walking in there, and would have calmly opened the door and left with a shrug instead of looking like a mouse stuck in a trap. Running into Noah right after was just icing. It was always just icing on her proverbial cake.

Dylan pushed harder, but slowed quickly as the pain radiated from her shoulders to her fingertips. Admitting defeat, she limped home, trying to step as lightly as she could to reduce the jolts that shot through her arms. A block later, she picked up her pace and crossed the street when she spotted Jack waiting under a restaurant awning. Chills ran up and down her spine as she shifted, trying to release the pressure she felt from someone's stare. Pausing at a corner, she checked behind her. The feeling of being watched faded. The street was empty.

"Finally." She smiled and rubbed her hands across her face, momentarily relieved that Jack had left her alone. The happiness lasted only long enough for her to feel a new throb open on her leg. As the sun began to fade she had almost convinced herself she was happy he had stopped following her.

She walked into school on Monday, determined to let the weirdness of the past week fade away.

"And how's my hermit today?" Megan leaned against the lockers as Dylan approached. "Are you done experimenting and ready to join the rest of us in the real world?"

"Bite me." Dylan nudged her as they walked into homeroom.

"So, that's a no." Megan frowned and looked past her.

"What?" she demanded, slamming her books down on her desk.

Megan shrugged as Noah walked in. "I just thought you would be in a better mood after spending some alone time with a handsome hottie."

"I haven't talked to Jack."

"And yet you knew exactly who I was talking about." Megan nudged her arm.

"It's not as though you've been subtle about trying to match us up."

Megan shrugged. "Oh, it wasn't me."

Noah shook his head. "I don't blame you, Dylan. He's a loser."

"Stay out of this. Dylan needs to live a little." Megan slapped Noah's arm.

"I'm living just fine, thank you very much. I refuse to go out with some crazy stalker guy"—she sighed—"no matter how good looking he is." She plopped into her seat. "He's finally gotten the hint anyway. I haven't talked to him since Friday."

"Good for you, Dylan." Noah gave Megan a kiss and headed to his homeroom.

She sighed as the teacher took attendance. This was what she wanted. She should be happy. Her thoughts ripped to the new slice of pain opening along the inside of her thumb. She sucked in a breath and listened to Carrie and Stephie whisper behind her. Their voices were low, she should have only been able to hear the repetitive consonant sounds, like a low hiss but she heard every word.

They were talking about Noah. He may not have been Dylan's favorite person, but he was being nice to her and he didn't need rumors like this. The longer they talked, the more pain she felt. She shot a quick look at Megan, hearing her best friend's name thrown into the fray. She didn't want to hear what they were saying anymore.

Not waiting for the bell, she rushed from the room. A hand shot out, halting her escape. Dylan forced herself to look at the hand that gently held her elbow before looking up into his face. The conversation followed her to the doorway where Jack had stopped her. Her own pain was mirrored in Jack's face. Closing her eyes, she shook her arm free and quickly walked on. Megan yelled after her, but she didn't stop to look back. The rest of the day, she tried desperately to convince herself that she couldn't have possibly heard what she did.

But she couldn't.

The constant throb in her thumb was an unwelcome reminder that this, whatever this was, was real. Sitting on the front steps of the school, she refused to let the fact she couldn't grip her laces stop her from getting ready for practice.

Though people were still coming and going, a particular movement caught her attention. Casually, Jack strolled across the parking lot heading right for Carrie and Stephie who were stretching before cheer practice. She narrowed her gaze, watching the girls laugh and talk easily with Jack. The laughter bounced off the building as Jack turned and headed back towards the school. Their eyes met. She opened her mouth to speak, but instead watched Jack turn away from her and slide into a car waiting for him. Grinding her teeth, she quickly tied her sneakers, only then realizing the pain was fading from her thumb.

Dylan studied her thumb as the last hint of a cut disappeared. She looked up in time to meet Jack's eyes as the car he was in turned out of the school's driveway.

The week progressed in the same strange manner. Phantom cuts showed up and faded, leaving only the slightest of lines that proved they existed. But even those lines faded by the next morning, leaving her to wonder if she was going mad. Jack smiled at her whenever she saw him, but didn't talk to her again.

By Friday, she was positive she lost her mind. Jack and Megan were laughing as she walked into the cafeteria. She slammed her books down and but didn't look at either of them before she went to buy her lunch. She walked slowly back to her seat, an almost empty tray in her hands. She stared at it, no longer hungry but also not ready to deal with Megan or Jack.

Too many things weren't making sense. Too many things didn't connect in any conceivable order. She had tried to figure them out. She had tried to run them out. She had tried to ignore them, but they weren't going away. With a sigh, she admitted the most troubling thought – she could no longer deny it.

She had to talk to Jack.

She looked over, knowing he would eventually glance at her as he too waited for her. He had promised she would need his help.

With a sigh and one small nod of her head, she admitted she did.

Chapter 5

He had agreed to meet her at Baby Bruno's. She would not go to his place, and she'd be damned if she'd let him step foot in her house.

Avoiding Jack, who was patiently tapping his fingers on the table, she looked around. There were only a few people in the restaurant early on a Friday night. She knew Jimmy wouldn't be working, which was a plus, kind of. She didn't really need to have him ragging on her about a date, which this was *not*. Dylan made that clear earlier, and then had been insulted when Jack dared smirk at her as she outlined the ground rules. There was about an hour before people started coming in from the football game. It meant this conversation had a time limit. She had timed it well, and they both knew it. A lighthearted attempt to hide a chuckle caught her attention. Bruno was standing behind the counter, not even trying to hide his humor when he winked at her and looked towards Jack before he headed into the storage room. Uproarious laughter muffled, but not silenced, by closed doors grated against her nerves, already frayed and tight.

"Let me see your hand."

Dylan didn't acknowledge Jack's request as she meticulously peeled her jacket off and folded it over the straps of her bag. She fiddled with the sleeve, smoothing out all the wrinkles, desperate to prolong the start. Certain she didn't want to know the end.

She slumped down in her seat and finally looked at him as he held out his hand, patiently waiting for her. She ground her teeth and resisted the urge to give him a finger before stomping away.

"Why should I?" she demanded, on the verge of a fully-fledged pout, crossing her arms roughly across her chest, unable to hide the flinch when her fingers grazed her side.

Jack sighed. "Just give me your damn hand."

She smirked and brought her hand up, glad to see that he

wasn't always as polite as he had seemed. Gently, he removed the Band-Aids. She sucked in a sharp breath as air hit the cuts and resisted the urge to close her eyes. Her noise and flinch brought his attention back to her face. A silent battle of wills raged. Though it was momentary, Dylan was positive time slowed when they stared at each other.

Relaxing, Jack went back to looking at her hand. He studied it for a minute, turning it over in the air, pulling her arm further across the table and pushed up her sleeve. She bit down to hold in a whimper as Jack ran his fingers along the cuts on her arm.

"Can I have my hand back now?" she snapped, annoyed mostly that she didn't know what he was doing. She tugged her arm, but Jack only tightened his grip slightly. She stopped immediately only barely beginning to understand that Jack was stronger and tougher than she had given him credit.

"In a minute," he mumbled, his attention still fixed on her hand. Shifting his hold, he reached into his pocket and pulled out something. "Now you have to hold still. This won't hurt, but it will feel weird."

"What will?" She studied what he had removed from his pocket. It was a narrow cylinder shaped piece of glass. It was about the size of a small tube of Chap Stick. "What is that?"

"Shhh." He threw her a quick glance and looked back at her finger. "Hold still."

She tried to pull her hand back but he grasped her more tightly. Her pulse radiated through the cuts and she lost circulation in his grip.

Jack looked up at her one more time. "Please." He whispered it, still not releasing his grip on her hand. "Hold still."

Dylan ordered her arm to relax and he looked down at her finger. Slowly, Jack placed the cylinder against it. The coolness of the glass caused her flinch, but she did not feel any pain. She shifted uncomfortably as her finger began to hum and the glass started glowing. Starting white, it turned pink eventually fading to a brown before it stopped glowing.

"Feels better, right?"

Audibly, she snapped her mouth shut only just aware it was hanging open. With a twitch of his lips, Jack moved the piece of glass over her fingers and up her arm, stopping at every cut. Each time, she felt it hum and the glass glow before the pain disappeared. When he released her hand, she bent and flexed her fingers that only a moment ago were red, swollen, and cut.

"You should have talked to me last week; it wouldn't have been that bad." He spoke casually as he put the piece of glass on the table rolling it under his palm.

She stared at Jack, unable to close her mouth even though she knew it was gaping open. The skin on her fingers still hummed slightly when she made a fist and rubbed it along her thigh.

"How's she taking it?"

The words she wanted to say were lost as she looked up to see a girl she had seen several times during the week plop down in the booth next to Jack.

"Dylan"—Jack gestured with a nod of his head—"this is Vi."

"Vi?"

"Vi Suttler." She grabbed Dylan's hand and shook it with more force than anyone would have expected from a girl with a voice so soft. "It's nice to officially meet you." Vi looked over at Jack, when Dylan only continued to shake Vi's hand. "Is she usually like this?"

Jack shook his head. "Nope. Usually she is quite forceful and outspoken."

Though his words were casual, she knew Jack wasn't as comfortable as he had been a few moments ago. Tension had edged back into his voice, and hearing that, she turned her attention to the new person at the table.

She gazed at Vi whose blond hair fell in waves over her shoulders. She kept pushing her long bangs out of her hazel eyes as she leaned back in the booth. Dylan felt jealous of this girl she didn't know. She would have given her arms for hair like that. Noise filtered into the restaurant as Dylan stared at Vi. She shook her head and looked from her to Jack. He rolled the little piece of glass between his fingers absent-mindedly and watched her. Dylan gazed at his hands before he put the thing back in his pocket. She clenched her hand again. The pain was gone, and she was happy for it. She had no idea what had just happened. In addition, she had no desire to find out.

Now, all she had to do was make herself believe that.

Dylan looked over her shoulder. A crowd of football fans stormed in, cheering and pumped from the team's obvious win.

"And that's my cue." She didn't look at either Jack or Vi as she unfolded her jacket. "Vi"—Dylan shot her a half-hearted wave— "a pleasure to meet you, I'm sure."

She threw Jack a glance as she draped her jacket back over her bag. "Thanks for fixing me, Jack, I guess. And now if you don't mind, I'm leaving." She slung her bag over her shoulder. "Wait," she said, seeing them moving in their seats, "let me rephrase. I'm leaving alone." Her smile turned into a wicked little grin. "You don't like it? Tough."

She saluted Bruno as she walked out. Vi called her name, but she didn't look back. She was half a block away before they caught up with her.

"Wait," Jack snapped as he grabbed the back of her shirt. "Just a second."

Dylan spun around. "Why?" She looked at Jack and could see Vi only a few steps behind him. "Why do I have to wait? I already said thanks for whatever you did, but magic time is over. It's time for me to go back to the real world."

"But we have to talk," Jack pleaded with her. She stared at him, determined to walk away as quickly as she could. He looked back over his shoulder. Dylan saw Vi nod to him and watched him reach into his pocket. "Fine," he mumbled and rubbed the back of his neck as he pulled out the glass tube again.

"You don't want to talk to us? You don't want our help?"

"I never asked for your help." Dylan lowered her voice and stepped towards Jack, aware that people were noticing the scene play out.

"But you need it," Jack said, without looking at her. The tone of his voice, deeper, more ruthless, stopped her retort. "You need to hear us out." Jack was unable to look at her. "Until then, you can have these back."

With a swift movement, Jack skimmed the glass over her fingertips. Immediately the pain returned. One at a time, the cuts on her fingers and thumb reopen and blood trickled down her arm.

"You...!" Dylan gasped. "It's been you doing this to me the whole time? What did you just do to me!"

"It hasn't been us." Jack crossed his arms.

Vi walked up and stood beside Jack, putting her hand protectively on his arm. "We gave you back the lies you are so determined to carry." She held out a piece of paper to Dylan.

She looked to Jack. He shook his head and sighed. "When you're ready to hear what we have to say, call." He took the paper from Vi and placed it in Dylan's bag.

Vi walked away.

"Just don't take too long, okay?"

Jack's shoulders dropped as he spun towards Vi.

Dylan stood on the sidewalk and watched them disappear into the crowd who came from the game before looking back down at her hand. "What the hell did he do to me?"

She reached into her bag and pulled out a tissue, and carefully wrapped it around her finger before she pulled her sleeve down to cover the cuts on her arm.

"Fabulous," she grumbled, and turned to head for home.

"Dylan," she heard someone call.

She exhaled as Megan carelessly ran through the busy intersection and stopped in front of her. "One of these days your luck is going to run out."

"But it hasn't yet." Megan dismissed Dylan's concern with a flick of her wrist. "I've been trying to call you for the last hour. Where have you been?"

Dylan reached into her bag and fished out her phone. The screen flashed as she hit the button. "That's weird. It was on." She scrolled through her recent calls seeing Megan had called several times.

"What is going on with you lately?"

Dylan shook her head. "I have no idea, but I just want to go home and crash. Maybe tomorrow will be better."

"Do you want to know what Jack asked me today?"

"No."

Dylan knew she most definitely did not want to know that. She made a fist and felt her fingers throb. She hadn't wanted to know what they had talked about last week, and nothing had changed. As they rounded the corner, Dylan could already see that it wasn't going to be a pleasant night.

Megan grabbed her arm. "Come stay at my place."

"That's not fair to Tony."

Megan shrugged. "Bring him. He can hang out with Brian and we can totally ignore them all night."

She nodded. This wasn't the first time she was glad Megan had a little brother that was the same age as her own.

"What about Noah?"

Megan frowned then shook her head. "We haven't had a girl's night in for a while. He'll understand."

Dylan raised her eyebrow and looked at Megan, ignoring the sting that opened on her pinkie finger.

"Okay, he might not understand, but whatever." She dismissed this with a wave of her hand. "We need some alone time too. Right?"

She shook her head as the pain in her pinkie finger receded. She smiled and squeezed Megan's arm as they walked into the house. Her parents were in the kitchen. They had long since resumed whatever argument they had started that morning. They didn't even notice her when she walked past them and climbed the stairs to her room.

She emptied her running bag and threw it at Megan to pack while she went into her brother's room and grabbed Tony.

"Let's go," she mouthed to him as she pulled his ear buds out.

Tony finished destroying whatever monster he was fighting before he answered. "Where we going?"

"Megan's for the night."

Tony logged off his game and shut his computer down. "Good. I wanted to show Brian my new game." He grabbed it off his dresser while Dylan grabbed him a pair of pants and a clean shirt, which she shoved in the bag with her own stuff. Megan was waiting at the top of the stairs for them. Dylan gestured to her and Tony to be quiet and indicated the front door. Megan and Tony crept down the stairs. As soon as they were safely out of the door, Dylan took a deep breath and headed down the stairs herself, making sure to hit the last steps, which creaked loudly. As she knew they would, the voices in the kitchen stopped before she hit the bottom of the stairs.

Dylan strolled confidently into the kitchen. "Tony and I are going to stay over at Megan's tonight." She willed herself to remain calm as she walked over to the kitchen counter. Her father nodded and her mother managed a smile.

"Have fun, sweetie," her mom said as she turned her back to Dylan and began cleaning the counter top. She could hear her father mumbling, but wasn't paying attention as her mother spoke again. "I love you."

She flinched as her pinkie began to throb again. She looked down and watched blood seep to the surface. "Yeah, okay."

She turned and quickly walked through the living room and slammed the front door.

"You okay?" Megan asked, seeing her pained expression.

"I'm fine." She masked a smile as pain radiated through her palm.

Megan carried on walking, and chatted with Tony. Dylan paused. In the light coming from the living room, she could see a slash run along the palm of her hand.

"I'm fine," she said again, and watched the blood run more freely. "I forgot something. I'll be right back." Dylan clamped her mouth shut to stop from groaning in pain. She dashed back inside and up the stairs. Closing the bathroom door quickly, she examined her hand. She dug through the medicine cabinet and finally found a bandage large enough to cover her palm, but she hesitated to put it on.

Something had to change. People were talking about her in school. Some of the girls on the cross-country team thought she was cutting, and the guidance counselor just happened to swing into many of her classes during the day to talk to different teachers and students. She thought she knew the truth, but if something didn't change, she also knew that wouldn't be enough.

She studied her reflection in the mirror.

"I'm fine." She looked down as a new cut sliced through her palm. She flexed her fingers as the blood pooled. Tears stung her eyes as she looked back into the mirror.

"I'm not fine," she whispered so quietly she didn't hear herself say it.

Yet, instantly, she felt the cut on her palm stop throbbing and saw the cut close. Some of her fingers were still bleeding.

"What the hell?"

"What's taking so long?" Megan's voice made her jump as she threw the Band-Aid into her pocket.

She turned her back towards Megan and quickly wiped her face and hands with a washcloth. She shrugged. "I guess my day is just getting better."

Megan wasn't fooled, but was grateful her best friend didn't call her on it. "Well it will once we get out of here. Are you coming?"

She nodded and silently followed Megan out of the house. It took two blocks, but Megan was right. Now that she was away from the craziness of her home, and Jack was nowhere to be seen, she was feeling better, at least a little better.

She forced a smile and listened to Tony explain the game to Megan with more enthusiasm than he had in a while.

Her smiled faded when a car passed by. A car she has seen a few times since last week. A car driven by Vi.

Chapter 6

Dylan sat up, momentarily disoriented by the bright colors and weird noises of Megan's room. Finally remembering she had spent the night, she relaxed, her heart still pounding. The last moments of a dream quickly faded and were gone. Sunlight poured in through the window. Tony and Brian's voices carried from the next room. There was an ease in their muffled conversation that had her relaxing further.

"About time you woke up." Megan stood in the doorway holding two cups of coffee. "I was getting ready to use your water method if you didn't move soon."

She looked over at the clock. "It's eleven?"

Megan handed a cup over. "Yup. You must have been tired. What with all the snoring and talking in your sleep."

"I do not talk in my sleep," she said, already bringing the cup to her lips.

"And yet you don't deny snoring."

Dylan took a gulp of the coffee and immediately felt better. Warily, she glanced at Megan over the cup. "What was I saying?"

"Something about cuts. And you kept telling Jack to get the hell away from you."

She threw a pillow at her friend. "I so did not say that."

"Oh you so did!" Megan ducked as the pillow sailed out of her room.

She looked down and shook her head. "Not that it matters anyway. After last night I probably won't have to worry about it."

Megan snorted. "Doubtful. He's serious about you. We just have to work on knocking down that huge brick wall you surround yourself with." Megan smiled and took another sip. "We'll get there, but for now, get up. We're going to go get some food. There's no sense in doing demolition on an empty stomach."

Dylan's stomach rumbled as she stood. "I'll be ready in five."

"You have fifteen." Megan walked out of the room.

Thirty minutes later, they walked to Baby Bruno's, laughing and talking the entire way. Tony and Brian ran across the parking lot and hurried inside. The girls followed, not rushing to catch up.

A chill raced up Dylan's back; the laughter caught in her throat and she paused. Someone was watching her. Surveying the area, she noted a car alarm across the street start blaring and a mother struggled to get her kids into the car. She turned back towards Baby Bruno's in time to see the door swing shut and quickly open again.

Megan emerged; a slightly wild, slightly amused grin danced on her face. "Wanna go somewhere else?"

"Why would we go somewhere else?" She knew the answer. She watched Megan raise an eyebrow, a confirmation. "Oh hell no. He is not taking Bruno's away from me."

"You can't kick him out." Megan could barely speak through the laughter.

"Watch me," she seethed and reached for the door, but paused. "No, you know what?" She spun back to Megan. "Let him stay. Just because he's here doesn't mean I have to talk to him."

Even as the words left her lips, she knew they were just for show.

Her heart pounded awkwardly for the first time ever entering Bruno's. The reason lounged calmly in a booth at the back of the pizza shop. Without her permission, their eyes met. She forced her eyes to sweep past him as if she hadn't seen him and barely stopped a groan from escaping when she found Tony and Brian. Of course, they had chosen to sit in the booth directly in front of Jack.

"If I make it out of here in one piece, I'm gonna kill our

brothers."

"Just do it at your house. My mom will kill me if I get blood on the carpets."

Elbowing Megan, she headed for the counter. "Make us a fresh one, okay?" She grabbed a few glasses sitting on the counter.

"One's coming out in a few seconds. I'll bring it over." Jimmy nodded at her as he flipped dough into the air.

Knowing she could no longer prolong it, she trudged to the table and pushed Megan further onto the bench. She didn't look at Jack as she sat down, determined to ignore him. But she could hear him clear his throat as she fidgeted in her seat.

"Just go talk to him," Megan whispered.

She shook her head but didn't turn to look at Megan. "Thank you for looking. Now he knows I actually saw him."

"He already knew that." Megan sighed. "No time like the present to start trying to knock down that wall."

"Stomach still empty," Dylan replied out of the corner of her mouth, trying her best with only her tone to threaten Megan with a very painful death if she didn't stop immediately.

"Try not to make a mess today," Jimmy joked as he placed the pizza on the table.

Behind her, Jack coughed in a sorry attempt to cover a laugh. She fisted her hands under the table and plastered a smile on her face. She would not let Jack have this effect on her. Shaking any thoughts of him from her head, she focused on her little brother.

She grabbed her own straw to shoot it at Tony, but it hit her glass, tipping it slightly. Trying to compensate, she jerked her arm and watched soda splashed out of the glass and landed right on Jack's pants.

"Seriously!" she moaned, simultaneously trying to sink under the table and get away.

Megan, Tony, Brian and Jimmy laughed. Her temper flared.

"Okay, I'm beginning to think you're doing this deliberately,"

Jack said calmly.

His voice was enough to get her moving. She elbowed passed him and headed for the door. As soon as she was on the sidewalk, she ran. She ran by a group of women shopping, and flinched when three new cuts opened on her fingers, but she didn't stop. She felt more pain appear as she passed by a woman talking to a toddler. The further she ran, the clearer she could hear Megan shout her name and the boys laugh at the mess she left at Bruno's.

She rounded another corner, finally able to think clearly. She shouldn't have run away and cursed herself for it. That wasn't like her. No one chased her out of Bruno's. She stopped in front of Megan's house. She knew they'd be back eventually, but she didn't want to wait. She wanted to hide. She dug her phone out of her pocket, shot a quick message to Megan asking her to see that Tony got home okay, and flipped it to silent. Sliding the phone back in her pocket, she felt the few slices that had opened on her hand in the mad dash away from Baby Bruno's begin to close.

Unable to even process what was happening, she filed it away. It was something else she would deal with. Later. She needed time to straighten out the crazy things spiraling through her head. She walked home and didn't answer her phone the rest of the weekend.

She sighed as she headed to her locker on Monday morning.

"Seriously, Jack. You need to find someone else to bug. I thought you had gotten the message when you left me alone last week."

Jack took a step back.

"What?" she spat.

His lips curved, almost involuntarily. "Just making sure you don't have something else you want to throw at me."

She yanked open her locker, determined to forget about that past week.

"How are the hands?"

She looked down to where several fingers were now covered in Band-Aids. "They hurt. What did you do to me anyway?" "I didn't do anything." Jack shook his head. "And I'm not going to explain that to you in the middle of the hallway."

"Whatever." She knew that wasn't exactly the truth. She knew whatever was happening was connected to him, but she had spent the weekend convincing herself it was all just bad luck and fluke accidents.

"What are you doing after school?"

"I have practice, Jack."

Jack rubbed his neck. "And after?"

She shrugged. "Probably going to do my homework."

He took a step towards her and dropped his voice to just above a whisper. "You really need to talk to me."

She spun away and began rooting around in her locker for a pen. "You really need to get away from me," she shot back, annoyed to hear her voice shake.

"I know you're hurting right now." Jack took a deep breath. "Stubbornness will only get your so far before it starts to hurt you." Dylan stiffened and looked further into her locker. Jack inched closer and whispered into her ear. "I can't help you until you let me."

She spun back to snap but he had already walked away with his hands shoved in his pockets. She slammed her locker and headed in the other direction.

Pain spread through her hands all week. Running was impossible because the movement of her arms sent spasms through her body. She couldn't focus on her homework. She couldn't hold anything to eat. Yet, she did everything she could to avoid Jack whenever she saw him walking through the halls, his last words echoing in her mind. The added attention she was getting from everyone else reinforced her desire to deal with whatever this was without him.

People she didn't know were glancing at her in the halls. Her teachers were calling on her in every class, the concern clear in their expressions. She had spent three fun filled hours with the guidance counselor and school psychologist, and she had been right. They didn't want to believe her, but then again, she could barely believe herself.

Her once prized status of invisibility was clearly gone.

By Friday, she wanted to commit herself into a hospital.

She walked into the bathroom and winced flipping on the light. "This is getting ridiculous," she grumbled.

She knew she was right, but she didn't want to admit what she had to do.

Megan's off-key singing floated down the hall from her bedroom. She couldn't help but smile as Megan mercilessly butchered the song. She focused on that as she tried to cover all the cuts, but other noises were bombarding her. Clearly, she could hear her father listening to the news in the living room below. The broadcaster's voice floated up to her. As the women on the TV spoke, Dylan cried out. A new cut opened across the back of her hand.

"What's the matter?" Instantly, Megan stood next to her.

She threw her hands in the running water, biting the inside of her cheek as the soap stung the new openings. "I thought I saw a spider." She flinched as the cut that had formed a moment ago grew. "You sure Noah won't be mad?" she said, intentionally changing the subject

Megan rolled her eyes at the not so subtle subject change. "He's fine. We're playing Hunterton Valley and he won't be home until late. You already know he's swinging by after the game."

She knew Megan was still staring at her. She also knew Megan had noticed that she had yet to take her hands out of the running water. "We'll be waiting down stairs." Megan's voice was layered with concern and skepticism.

Tony hesitated outside the bathroom door, his expression

clearly clouded and as concerned as Megan's. She didn't want her little brother to look at her like that. She turned off the water and stared at her own reflection.

She barely recognized herself anymore. Where once there had been an ease and determination was now a barely controlled agony and fear. She didn't want to admit it, but Jack was right. She had to hear whatever he had to say, and hopefully, he would pull out that magic wand of his and make her hands and arms stop throbbing.

"Okay, Jack," she whispered as she put another Band-Aid on her hand and threw the empty box in the garbage already overflowing with others, "you win."

Chapter 7

"Your hands are worse." There was certainty in his voice.

"Yes." Her voice shook, barely above a whisper.

"Are you ready to listen to me now?"

"I don't know." She spoke honestly and listened to the silence on the other end ready to believe the call had been disconnected.

"Fair enough," he finally said. "Where do you want to meet?"

"I don't know." She bit her lip, still not completely sure this was a smart decision. "I'm heading to Megan's."

"I'll meet you there." He hung up without waiting for her to reply.

She stared at her cell for a moment before getting the rest of her stuff and descending the stairs again. Megan and Tony were waiting for her on the sidewalk. Seeing her, Tony started walking down the block. Megan cocked her head and stared at her before they followed.

"I knew it." Megan's cocky grin had Dylan ready to call off the whole thing.

The smile spread even further across her friend's face when Jack walked down the sidewalk towards her. Megan had it all wrong. This was not some secret meeting. This wasn't even about hanging out with a friend. This was about getting her hands to stop bleeding long enough for her to hold a pen or brush her teeth. She didn't smile at Jack who stopped and leaned nonchalantly against the mailbox.

Megan poked Dylan with her elbow. "You should have asked me what Jack wanted to know." Dylan turned towards her friend, not sure she understood where this was going. "Remember I asked if you wanted to know and you said you didn't. You should have wanted to know."

"Why?"

"Because I wanted to know where she lived so I could talk to you," Jack replied quietly.

Jack looked down at her hand. She followed his gaze as a drop of blood fell to the sidewalk. Jack motioned Megan inside with a flick of his chin.

"Door is open when you two are finished." Megan smiled as she steered Tony towards the house.

They stood silently and watched the house. "I hoped you would eventually talk to me. And I thought it would be somewhere you felt more comfortable." Jack rubbed his neck, watching Megan open the front door. "You have a great friend there."

"You're telling me this because you think I didn't know that already?"

"Just acknowledging a fact." Jack took a step towards Dylan. "You ready?"

"Where are we going?"

Jack looked at the house and watched Megan's head appear out of a second story window. "Somewhere we can talk with some privacy."

She took a step away from him. "A few less witnesses so when I scream it won't be heard?"

"I won't hurt you." He spoke slowly and looked down at her hand. "Do you have more pain since I said that?"

She shook her head.

"Then you know I'm telling you the truth." Jack stepped closer and looked straight into Dylan's eyes. "I'm not here to hurt you." He gently took her wrists.

Jack took a step down the sidewalk and laced her arm around his elbow. She threw a glance over her shoulder. Megan waved encouragingly through the window.

Two blocks over, Jack led the way into Washington's Park, and a small wooded area. Lights lined the path leading to a gazebo. Jack led her towards it. He dropped her arm as they stepped in. He walked across and sat down on a bench in a shadowy corner.

She stood in the middle and studied him. Though she could hear people laughing from around the area, she felt alone.

"Show me your hands," he said, and pulled the glass cylinder out of his pocket.

Defensively, she balled them into fists, biting down, determined not to show how much it hurt. Jack spun the cylinder in his hand.

"What is that?" She stepped forward, curiosity getting the better of her.

Jack held it up in his hand. "This"—he resumed spinning it gracefully between his fingers—"is a dissimulator." She took another step towards him and watched the light that surrounded the gazebo dance through it. "Technically, a dissimulator is a liar or someone who is deceitful."

Dylan snorted. "Thanks for the vocabulary lesson," and she plopped down next to him.

Jack continued as if she hadn't spoken. "But this"—he held the glass between two fingers so she could see it clearly—"cleans a Fide of lies, and allows them to keep working."

He looked up at her but didn't move. "Let me see your hands, Dylan," he said quietly.

Jack reached out, took her hand and waited, never taking his eyes off her. Slowly, she opened her hand. He peeled the Band-Aids off her fingers, and then turning her hand over, removed them from the back of her hand. He moved slowly, allowing her to see what he was doing.

With the lightest of pressure, Jack placed the dissimulator against the finger he had healed once. Both watched the glass glow from white to pink to brown and back to white as it had before. Jack moved to her pinkie and both watched the glass glow a brighter red before it too faded. The glow faded white before turning sky blue. Jack repeated the process on her other hand and arm; the glass filled with colors as it healed each cut.

Finally, Jack placed the dissimulator across the back of her hand. She made a fist and felt it vibrate lightly against her skin. She rubbed her hand on her jeans then carefully reached out to take the dissimulator. She held it in the light and saw that the glass filled with smoky gray wisps. Sighing, she handed the glass back to Jack.

"Are you ready?" he said quietly as he turned to look at her.

Dylan stared at him. She was definitely not ready for whatever he was about to tell her. She could feel it. She knew this wasn't going to be something she wanted to hear. Jack ran his finger along her healed hand. She looked down at his fingers and watched them trace along the hint of a scar where the cut had just been.

No sound came out as she mouthed, "Yes."

She winced as she a new cut opened up on her finger. Her hand became tinged with blood and Jack laughed.

"It would appear you aren't, but I have to tell you anyway."

"What just happened?"

"You lied to me."

"But why? How would you know? How does it happen?"

Jack shrugged and leaned back. "Because I'm a Fide." She was about to speak but Jack shook his head. "And you are too."

She got up with a laugh and started walking away.

"I'm not lying to you," Jack said, grabbing her arm.

She hadn't even heard him get up.

"How do I know that?" She yanked her arm out of Jack's grasp.

He straighten his shoulders, took a deep breath and closed his eyes before he spoke. "I don't like you."

Instantly a cut open on her cheek and she saw one mirrored on Jack's face. Jack pulled the dissimulator out and ran it along the cut closing the wound. She brought her hand up and felt the smooth skin that a moment ago had burned and watched his cut close.

"That's how you know," Jack said, stepping even closer to her.

"Lies hurt us. Words are the most powerful weapons in the world, and sometimes it's easier to tell a lie. People are so accustomed to avoiding the truth. It's our job to find the truth. We must discover the truth and make people say it before it's too late for them and for us."

She looked into Jack's eyes and laughed. "Oh, you had me going. This is some trick."

Jack plopped down on the nearest seat and rubbed his neck, his shoulders hunched forward. "I knew I shouldn't be the one to tell you." He looked at her. "Vi did this so much better for me than I can for you." He sighed. "This isn't a joke or a trick. This is very real, and very important." She shook her head and tried to step back but Jack grabbed her arms and slowly stood. "Tell me a lie. If you don't believe me tell me a lie."

"I hate you." She spat the first thing that popped into her mind. Immediately, a cut open above Jack's brow. She gasped as the same cut open on her brow, blood dripped down her nose just as it dripped down Jack's nose. His mouth formed a little smirk.

"Now…" Jack's voice was barely above a whisper as he pulled her even closer. She could feel his breath on her lips. "Tell me the truth."

"I don't hate you?" Dylan spoke quietly matching Jack's level. She knew her voice filled with confusion.

"I don't want a question," he said, more desperately. "I want…I need to hear the truth."

She didn't know what to say. He stood too close, fogging her brain. Slowly he drew his thumb over the back of her hand as he held her in place.

"Please." His voice bordered on a plea.

Exasperated, she finally let the words out in a gush. "You've been a pain in my ass and I don't know what to do about it."

Jack took a deep breath and smiled. He raised his eyebrow. Where a moment ago had been a cut was now smooth skin. Dylan wiped her sleeve across his forehead and ran it down his nose removing the blood. The cut was gone. She wiped her sleeve over her face and stepped back to catch her balance. Her own cut was gone as well.

Jack took hold of her hand, not letting her move any further away. "Thank you for telling me the truth."

Dylan allowed Jack to pull her back over and they sat down together on the bench. He still held her hand. She could feel his thumb glide over the back of it, but she didn't pay attention to what he was doing. She was too busy trying to make sense of what had just happened.

"I need to go for a run." She spoke suddenly and stood up.

Jack still didn't release her hand. "It's ten thirty at night. You can't go for a run now."

"Why not?"

"There's more you need to know."

"What else is there? Are you going to squash my belief in Santa next?"

"Are you going to keep using sarcasm to push everyone who is trying to help you away?"

"Are you"—she poked a finger into his chest—"going to answer every question with a question?"

"Are you going to start believing me?"

Dylan snorted as her eyes skimmed over him. "Doubtful."

Jack ran his hands through his hair, releasing his hold on her. "Fine. Go for your run. I'll wait here for you."

She jutted her chin out stubbornly, pulled the elastic from her wrist, and threw her hair up. "I don't know how long I'll be."

Jack studied her before finally nodding. "Do you want me to come with you?"

She shook her head. "I like running alone." She turned to walk away but couldn't resist. "And you won't be able to keep up."

Jack grabbed her shoulders spinning her around to face him. "There is more you have to know, but I remember how disorienting it was when I learned everything. Dylan..." He paused as he ran a finger along her jaw. "You have to let me finish telling you everything."

She shivered at his touch and pulled away. She paused and let his words sink in for a moment before she nodded. "I'll come back."

"Then I'll wait for you. Just don't take too long."

She knew his eyes were on her as she walked away from the gazebo. Once on the sidewalk, she started to run.

Conversations stopped when she ran past. She tried to smile when people stared, but most of the time it wasn't convincing and she knew it. She also knew she didn't care what they thought. She was much more concerned with what she was thinking.

What had Jack done to her?

Could she really blame him for whatever this was? Maybe she needed to start with an easier dilemma. Did she believe him? It was easy to say yes when she had seen him heal her hand, had felt her skin rip when he lied to her, watched him bleed when she lied to him.

Okay, so she didn't hate him. That didn't mean anything. She didn't even realize she didn't hate him. How was that fair?

"Yeah, my mom's cool with it." The words hit her as she passed a group of guys from school and immediately a cut opened on her thumb. She stopped, now listening to their conversation. "She won't find out anyway." The cut deepened.

The guys laughed as she walked back towards them, taking her time to slow her breathing.

"She won't know what?" She tried to capture the casual way Jack had spoken to her the first time they met, but it fell flat. Instead of confident and cool, she sounded panicky and nosy.

They turned and looked at her. Her smile felt forced as she leaned against the building.

"What's it to you?" One swayed forward.

She smelled beer on his breath and forced herself not to step away. She kept the smile on her face.

"Just curious." She could hear the nerves jump through her.

"My mom's gonna be out of town tomorrow." He smirked. "So we're throwing a party. You wanna come?"

"Does she know about this party?"

He shrugged. "Nah." The other guys laughed.

The cut that appeared when she ran past a few moments ago faded away.

She could feel lies.

Great.

She wasn't even trying to listen to people's conversations. He had been barely speaking loud enough for her to hear him, but she had, and she had known he was lying before her thumb had sliced open. She couldn't deny Jack had been telling her the truth.

But that still left her with a head full of questions. Had Jimmy lied to her? What did Jack mean? Did he like her? What was she supposed to do with this? It's not like she could tell anyone.

It's not like she could be all, "Hey dumbass, I know you're lying so knock it off." Yeah, that would work really well. And if this kept up, she would land in the hospital because people would think she was cutting. People were already prepared to commit her for that, at least the adults at school who were paying attention.

She passed the bank and watched the clock flip to 11:10. A little steadier, she headed back to the park taking a longer route; she felt fairly confident she wouldn't have to run into anyone and therefore wouldn't have to hear any lies. She groaned, knowing there wouldn't always be a long way around people. She had to learn to control this thing. Maybe there was a switch.

Involuntarily, she smiled as she entered the park. Jack was still sitting there. She relaxed knowing he had kept his word and waited for her.

"How's the thumb?" He leaned towards her as she approached.

"Okay." She stepped forward, barely dealing with the thoughts flashing through her mind. "How could you know about that?"

Jack blew out a deep breath before answering. "I am here to help you learn to be a Fide." Jack shrugged. "Consider me your on the job trainer."

"Oh fabulous." Dylan rolled her eyes as she sank into the bench.

"Hey, watch the sarcasm. What that means is right now I feel what you feel." Jack saw the look on her face and backtracked quickly. "I feel the lies you feel. I don't *feel* what you feel." Dylan felt her cheeks getting hot. "I've felt every lie that you've said, or someone has said in your presence since we met that first night." He nudged her shoulder. "You saw that I felt it earlier when you told me you hated me. I felt it when I told you I didn't like you. And I felt it a little while ago when you heard someone lie, but I also know you heard the truth because your thumb doesn't hurt anymore." He held up his thumb. "And neither does mine."

There was a thin line where the skin still healed.

"You need to slow down. I'm having a lot of trouble digesting all of this."

Jack nodded. "So did I."

"I don't even know where to start."

"Ask me anything." Jack leaned back against the bench.

She thought through all her questions, not sure which to pick first. "Why me?" she blurted out, and immediately rephrased, "Why us?"

Jack turned on the bench. His eyes narrowed and she waited for him to speak, not registering that the reason she was feeling dizzy was that she was holding her breath.

When he finally did, Dylan barely understood the answer.

"Because we died."

Chapter 8

Dylan blinked twice before she stood, feeling the color drain from her face. Jack raised his hand to grab her wrist, but hesitated.

Her face went blank.

She turned and walked away.

The joke was over.

She left the park heading for home. Halfway there, she remembered she was staying at Megan's and turned around, knocking Jack over in the process.

There was no way in hell she was dead. Whatever game Jack was playing, she was done. She dug her nails into her palm. She didn't wince at the pain, but watched the blood slowly dribble down her wrist. Proof, in her mind, that she was very alive, and Jack had no clue what he was talking about.

"She's taking it well." Vi spoke lightly from behind her. Dylan's steps faltered for only a moment as the conversation continued. "Jack," Vi chastised, "there were better ways..."

"I know, Vi." Jack sounded defeated. "But I didn't expect her to ask *that* question."

"Well, you should have," Vi snorted.

Dylan spun around and watched both Vi and Jack stop when she did. She studied his face and felt her confusion grow as she saw concern etched into his features. Vi, on the other hand, looked shockingly unconcerned and studied her calmly.

Jack opened his mouth to speak, but closed it slowly and looked down at the sidewalk. Without saying a word, she turned back and kept walking, resisting the urge to run from them. She didn't stop until she was safely inside Megan's house, finally taking a deep breath when the lock on the front door snapped into place.

"Well." Megan drew out the word and walked towards her, a

bowl of popcorn in one hand and a beer in the other. "Did you have fun?"

Noah chuckled from the living room.

She shot him a look and walked passed Megan muttering. "I need a drink."

"Hi, sweetie." Mrs. Lewis smiled instantly lifting Dylan's mood. She was always so nice and so happy to see her; it was the total opposite of how it felt in her own home. "Having a good day?"

"Nope."

She held Mrs. Lewis's gaze for a moment and tried to soften the look on her face, but knew it was impossible at that moment. Megan walked in behind her, but Dylan didn't acknowledge her instead walking to the fridge. As she cracked open a beer, she turned and locked eyes with Megan. With only a look, she dared her to say a word.

Dylan closed her eyes and downed it, breathing heavily when she slammed the can on the counter more forcefully than she had intended. She looked at Megan's mom and bowed her head apologetically. Though it was clear that Megan's mom would rather have them drink under her roof, it felt wrong standing in front of her while she did. She didn't wait for Megan to speak as she grabbed another and walked into the living room. She plopped down on the recliner since Noah had claimed the couch.

Her gaze floated past Noah to the large picture window that overlooked the front yard. She shivered certain that Jack was still out there. She spun in the chair and raised the can to her lips, but Megan grabbed it out of her hand before she could take a sip.

"Hey!"

"What happened?" Her friend kneeled in front of her.

She had no idea how to answer this. The truth was out, and she feared Jack had at least been honest about the lying. She had seen for herself what happened when she lied. A grin danced across her face wondering just how much pain Jack would feel.

Looking past Megan, she studied a grin somehow similar to her own yet more menacing dance across Noah's face.

She started to speak but stopped as Mrs. Lewis walked through the living room and headed up stairs. She waited for the door to click shut.

"Nothing happened," she seethed, still humiliated.

She had been fooled, and she winced as pain sliced through her leg.

"Right." Noah's smile spread before he continued. "You were gone for a few hours. You come back, down a beer, and nothing happened. You barely drink at parties and now you're ready for another."

Megan nodded. "Not buying it."

Blood dripped down her calf. Pain flared when she shifted. A knock on the door saved her from another lie, but she knew, before Megan said anything, that it would be one of two people: Jack or Vi.

Out of the corner of her eye, she watched Noah's expression change and his eyes narrow.

"What the hell did you do to my friend?" Megan yelled. She got up and went to the door.

So Jack had the balls to knock on Megan's door. She could hear the calm tenor of Jack's voice and strained to hear his voice. She thought back to earlier. She hadn't even been trying to listen and had been able to hear others clearly. Why couldn't she hear Jack who just on the other side of the room?

"Stay away from my friend!" Megan yelled, and Dylan heard her slam the door.

Proud of her friend, Dylan smiled and drank from her beer can, hoping it would help shield her from some of the pain in her leg. It wasn't working fast enough.

"I'm gonna use the bathroom," she said, feeling the pain in her leg quickly intensify.

It didn't register that Megan hadn't come back after she had shut the door, or the fact that she had heard multiple people walking around, until that was, she was in the bathroom.

With the door shut, she reached for the light. A hand went over her mouth and she heard the lock click into place before she fully realized why she wanted to scream.

"You will let me finish." It was Jack.

Dylan pushed him away and went for the lock, but Jack grabbed her hands. She slapped him away. "What are you, crazy? What the hell are you doing in here? Get away from me. I don't want to hear anymore."

"If you don't like it, tough. You need to hear this, and you need to fix your leg."

She watched the muscles in his jaw clench. "How do you know about my leg?"

He shifted her hands so he was holding both with one hand and lifted his pant leg. "Because mine is bleeding too. What happened? What did you tell Megan?"

Dylan looked at his leg and tore her hands out of his grasp. "What did you tell Megan to get her to let you in here?"

"I told her a lie." Jack's words seeped out of him, anger clear on his face.

"Well, so did I," she spat back.

Dylan and Jack stared at each other in silence. He stepped over to the side, and sat on the edge of the tub. He took a deep breath before he looked at her.

"I told her that I told you I liked you, but you didn't believe me. So you went for a run to figure out if I was telling you the truth, but when you came back I was kissing Jenny Backler. I told her that I had to talk to you because I do like you and Jenny had been drunk and didn't know what she was doing, but that you hadn't let me explain before you took off."

"Jenny Backler? Really, you couldn't think of anyone better?"

Jack shook his head. "She was the easiest person for Megan to believe." He nodded towards her leg. "What did you tell her?"

She sighed as she walked over and closed the toilet seat. "She asked me what happened and I told her nothing had happened." Pain immediately eased from her calf. "This is technically true, the way her mind jumps to conclusions. Nothing did happen."

Jack shook his head. "Little white lies are sometimes the most dangerous." He hesitantly reached over and took her hands. "Dylan"—his voice quiet and sincere—"I can't lie to you. It's too dangerous."

"Does that mean you would lie to me if you could?"

Jack dropped his gaze to the tiled floor, but increased his grip on her hands. "If it meant that I would be able to protect you, then yes, I think I would lie to you."

"Jack." She stared down at his hands still wrapped around her own. Faint scar lines crisscrossed over the backs of his hands. "I wish you would lie to me. I don't think I can handle this." Her shoulders slumped. "I can't do whatever you are expecting me to."

"It doesn't work that way for you anymore."

They sat quietly for a minute.

"I can't take this back, can I? I can't change what's happening to me?"

Jack didn't answer her, but the answer was still clear. There would be no going back from this.

Finally taking a deep breath, Jack spoke. "Instead of me just dumping everything on you, why don't you ask me a few questions? We'll try and take this slow, okay?"

She chewed on her lip as she found a question she wanted to hear the answer to. "How long have you been...?"

"A Fide?" Jack finished her question with a smirk. "A little over two years ago. Right before I turned fifteen."

She fidgeted. "And who told you about all this?"

"Vi. She found me."

"How?"

"I tried to walk out of store with a game under my shirt.

When the buzzers went off, I lied. I told them that I had paid for it, but lost the receipt. Stupid, I know, to lose a receipt in the course of twenty steps. Vi had been outside in the parking lot and felt the lie when I spoke.

"They took the game then kicked me out of the store. Vi came up to me and asked what happened. I told her the truth and watched her smile. Then she lied to me."

"What did she say?"

Jack chuckled. "She could give me a ride home. That she had candy if I wanted any. I think I will always remember that first cut. I felt like she had just pulled out a razor blade from her bag and slashed it across my forearm."

She looked down at his arms.

"I thought she was crazy, but I didn't feel like walking so I let her give me a ride. I thought I was cool anyway, riding with a senior. I was lame."

"She went to Pine Glenn too?" Dylan chewed on her lip. Maybe Megan was right. She really didn't pay attention, but if Vi was a senior when Jack was fifteen, she and Vi wouldn't have been in school together, would they? Jack rubbed his thumb over the back of her hand. She took a deep breath to focus. "Did you take the news easily?"

Jack chuckled. "She explained everything to me as she drove me home. I didn't run away from her as you did, but I also didn't believe her, as you seem to believe me. I almost got both of us killed before I accepted the truth." He rubbed his hand along his chest before he grabbed her hand again.

"Oh, I'm not taking this well. I'm still trying to decide if this is really happening or not." She pulled her hands out of his and shook them as she paced the small bathroom. "How did you almost—"

"That story can wait for another time." He shook his head cutting her off. "Death isn't something I really wanted to talk to you about right now."

"About that. There has to be a mistake. I'm not dead."

"A Fide is created at the moment of a person's birth." Jack paused. She barely breathed and waited for him to speak again. "When I was born, the umbilical cord was wrapped around my neck. My heart must have stopped beating. Even if it was only for a moment that was long enough."

"That didn't happen to me." She sank back onto the toilet, realizing she knew very little about her own birth. "I know I was born early."

"How early?"

"A few weeks, I think."

Both sat silently for a moment. "Dylan, something happened when you were born. I don't know how or why, but it's the reason you arrived early. If it didn't, you wouldn't feel lies now."

Her head swam as she tried to process the information. She wanted very badly just to run away again, but she knew she had to stay. She knew she had to hear this.

"You were serious when you said lies could kill."

Jack nodded. "Very serious."

She let out a ragged breath. "I really don't know what to do." Jack waited for her to speak again. The silence stretched for a few minutes. "I want to know the truth, but I don't think I can hear more about this."

"Then ask me one more question for tonight. Anything you want, and we can talk more tomorrow."

Dylan looked into his eyes and saw the calm ease she had seen before. He waited for her to speak, but she wouldn't. She sat there and slowly shook her head back and forth.

"Dylan"—he brought a hand up and placed it on her cheek making her stop—"ask me."

She let out a nervous laugh and pulled her hands away from his. "I don't think I want to know the truth about this one." She stood and wiped her hand on her pants. "I'm not ready for it."

Dylan reached out for the door and listened to the lock click.

She paused for a moment, and spoke without turning around. "How are we going to explain this to Megan?"

"That is a little complicated, but we will tell her the truth."

"The truth? That I'm some kind of crazy lie detector and I couldn't stand to hear the truth so I ran away?"

Jack traced a pattern on her back and he stepped closer. "No. That I was a pain in the ass that wouldn't leave you alone until you would hear what I had to tell you."

Goosebumps covered her arms. Dylan kept her hand firmly on the doorknob to stop it from shaking. She turned around and stared into Jack's eyes. "And what's that?"

He stepped even closer and a smile appeared on his face. "I'm here because I like you."

Chapter 9

As she and Tony walked slowly back home, Dylan yawned. Last night had stretched on until the sun peaked over the distant horizon. She smiled, reliving everything.

When she had finally walked Jack to the door, she had seen Vi leaning against a street light on the other side of the road. Jack had hugged her before walking off the porch towards Vi.

"Well." Megan's voice had snapped her out of her reverie as she walked back in the room.

She walked towards the couch where Megan was curled up with Noah. She avoided looking at Megan, whose eyes were bright with questions. Noah scowled and grabbed for his beer. She wondered how she would answer truthfully.

"Well," Megan said again, more urgently. "Looks like you two patched up that little misunderstanding."

She fell into a chair. "Looks that way."

Megan tucked her legs under her so she was leaning towards Dylan. "I would have done the same thing. I mean, Jenny Backler? The scumbag. I cringe just thinking about all the guys she's been with."

She just stared at Megan, refusing to look towards Noah. She shivered remembering a similar story she had heard about Noah in homeroom. But it didn't matter. Her friend was on a roll. There was no need for her to talk. That meant there was no need for her to lie. She was lost in her own head, lost in the last few minutes.

"You know," Dylan interrupted, not sure where in the recap Megan was, "I'm mad at you for letting him in." She felt a small slice open by her elbow.

Noah chuckled.

"Really?" The disbelief was clear in her voice. "I figured you'd be happy."

She swayed eventually. "Okay, maybe I'm not mad at you

now, but I was. You had no right, Megan."

"Oh, if the roles had been reversed you would have let him in to talk to me. You should have seen the look on his face when he was on the porch. There was real pain there. I could see how much he wanted to make things right."

"I'm sure," Noah muttered.

She nodded in agreement. She was sure there was real pain there, but she wondered if it was the pain of her running distrust or just the pain of the lie. "But why the bathroom? Why didn't you sneak him upstairs or just bring him in here?"

"He said he wanted to talk to you where you wouldn't escape. It was his idea to hide in there."

"Well he got his wish." She took a drink of the beer she had opened earlier and forced herself to swallow. It was warm. "And what were you supposed to do? How were you going to get me in there?"

Megan shrugged. "The way you downed that first beer I thought you'd be running for the bathroom before too long."

"I can hold my drink just fine, thank you very much."

Megan sighed. "No I just mean you'd have to go. And if you didn't, I'd have thought of something I needed you to get for me."

She stared at her friend.

"You know," Megan said, lounging back into the couch and snuggling into Noah, "he almost made me come and interrupt you guys twice. I had no idea what was taking so long. I kind of figured you'd just punch him and walk out."

"I tried, but he grabbed my hands and wouldn't let go."

"So what's the deal with you two? A few days ago you didn't even know he existed and now…"

She shrugged. "He said he likes me, but I honestly don't know what the deal is."

Megan walked out of the living room and grabbed a drink from the kitchen, calling as she went. "Oh, he definitely likes you. But what about you? Do you like him?"

"Maybe?" The cut on her arm reopened.

"Don't lie to me. I saw the look on your face after you closed the front door. You definitely like him."

Dylan silently admitted defeat. "I know I thought he was cute when I spilled soda down his shirt the other night, but it sort of pissed me off how he kept popping up around school. Then later when he was talking to you at my meet."

Megan shrugged and sat back on the couch. "I think he was just trying to prove to you that he did live here. He told me you didn't even know who he was when you guys bumped into each other at Baby Bruno's."

She thought about this for a minute. Was it possible that he really was just trying to prove that he wasn't lying? She felt the cut on her arm start to throb lightly.

"Wait. Megan, how do you know him?"

"I think we were in the same study hall last year or something." She dismissed this with a wave of her hand. "Honestly. You really can be so blind sometimes. I bet if I did a lineup of people from school, nine out of ten you wouldn't even recognize."

"Now that's not fair. I know quite a few people."

"And how many of them do you actually talk to? How many people's names do you know? You are an experimental hermit. How many people do you hang out with besides me?"

"And me," Noah chimed in, less than enthusiastic.

She smirked at him, but she knew Megan had a point. Still, her mind stuck on a thought and it brought the focus back to Jack. "But I don't get it. We never even talked before last week. Doesn't that strike you as odd?"

Megan took a long gulp of her drink, making her wait. "The way he tells it he has been interested in you for a while, but too afraid to talk to you."

She shook her head. "The last thing I associate with Jack is fear. Just the way he stands there with that calm ease of his. It's really quite unnerving."

"Oh yeah, you definitely like him."

She shook her head and the cut sliced a little deeper. She sighed and bowed her head. "Yeah, I guess I do. He's been a giant pain in my ass, but I do like him."

The cut stopped throbbing as soon as she spoke the words.

"What guy isn't a pain in the ass?"

"I'm not," Noah muttered defiantly.

"You have a point." She held out her beer and Megan tapped it with her own. "So, he really likes me?"

She heard Noah sigh as he got up to get another drink. Megan looked at her stunned but Dylan didn't pay attention. Something nagged at the back of her mind. It was all too quick. Too convenient. Too perfect. The way her parents used to be. She shivered as fear climbed her spine.

She would not let some hot mysterious guy sweep her off her feet.

Megan cleared her throat and brought her out of her thoughts. "Not everyone is out to hurt you."

She took a sip of beer, trying to minimize what Megan just said and to give herself a moment to steady her voice. "I never said they were."

"Yes you did. With Eric. You pushed him away," Noah chimed in as he came back into the living room.

Both girls shot him a look. Noah shrugged, turned around and walked back into the kitchen.

Dylan turned her attention back at Megan. "We dated for over six months."

"And never once did you let your guard completely down." Megan sighed. "And it looks like you are already putting a wall up to protect yourself from Jack."

She took a long drink, forgetting the beer was warm, and avoided Megan's stare.

"I am the only one you've really let in. You don't have sixteen years for Jack to gain your trust, but I'm sure you'll easily push him away in a few days."

"That's mean."

"And that's why you love me. You know I'm right." Megan had reached over and grabbed her leg as she had stood to go and join Noah in the kitchen. "Just think about it."

Dylan had let her head fall back against the couch, listening to Megan and Noah's muffled laughter from the kitchen.

Tony's voice brought her back to the present. "What was with you guys last night?"

"What do you mean?"

"The yelling, the banging, the laughing. I really thought there was some kind of party going on down there."

"We were just talking."

His steps slowed as their house came into view and she wrapped her arm around his shoulder. "It'll be okay."

"I hate it when they fight." Tony trudged forward.

"So do I." Dylan nodded. "But maybe they won't be fighting when we walk in." The cut was opening. She was only being hopeful, but knew it was a lie.

"You don't believe that." Tony looked up at his sister.

"No I don't," she acknowledged. "But I can hope."

Both stopped when they saw their parents' cars were in the driveway. Tony sniffled as they walked towards the front door.

"Just go upstairs and shut the door, Tony."

"What are you going to do?"

"Something that should have been done a long time ago. Something Jimmy probably should have done."

"You aren't going to kill them, are you?"

She ruffled her brother's hair and smiled. "No I won't kill them." Movement out of the corner of her eye caught her attention. Jack walked towards her. "I'm going to talk to them. I'm going to tell them they have to stop fighting." She brought her focus back to her brother.

"Will that work?"

Hope flowed over Tony's face.

"I don't know. I'll be up in a minute."

"Thanks, Dylan." Tony hugged his sister before he opened the door.

She heard him running up the stairs as she turned and looked at Jack. "You're just always around, aren't you?" She smirked and met him halfway down the driveway. "You didn't follow me home from Megan's did you?"

Jack shook his head. "I happened to be in the area"—he coughed—"deliberately coming to say hello now that you know I'm alive an' all." He smiled. "And you probably think I'm completely crazy." He pulled her into a hug carefully, tentatively wrapping his arms around her. "How are you?" he whispered still holding her.

"The crazy is definitely debatable." She bit her lip. "And ummm, I'm not quite sure." Pulling back she looked into his eyes. A small smile accompanied her step backwards. "It's all very weird. And to top it off with knowing I can't lie." She shook her head trying to gather herself. "I mean I know I can lie, but I can also feel it. Definitely not pleasant. I don't know what's going on."

"You never let me finish telling you everything."

"I figured as much, but right now I have to take care of something else."

She jerked her head towards the house where they could clearly hear her parent's heated conversation. Jack's brows creased.

Dylan shook her head. "It's hurting Tony to live with it." She closed her eyes and forced herself not to shut him out. "I didn't realize how bad it was until Jimmy went to college. I didn't realize how much they actually argued."

"What about you? How much does it hurt you?"

Dylan stiffened not wanting to acknowledge he was right.

"I just told my brother I would talk to them. I can't take that back," she whispered, not meeting his gaze.

"I'll come in with you."

She shook her head. This was something she did not want him to witness. "That would only makes things worse." On an impulse, she reached forward and took Jack's hand. "I have to do this. I know you may not understand, but I can't keep running. Not from this."

She bit her lip to hold in the emotions as Jack pulled her into him. "Just be careful. There are still a lot of things I need to explain to you. There are a lot of things you don't know, and I'm afraid talking to them will really hurt you."

She tensed and looked towards the house. Jack's arms dropped from around her. "I am just hoping they will hear me."

She held up her hand pausing Jack's movement. "I need to do this Jack." Her words were barely above a whisper. "There are too many things in my head right now. I'm having a hard time telling what's real and what isn't. But the one thing I know is that they fight. Constantly."

"What about me?"

She shook her head, not ready to let her doubts out, but unable to keep them silent much longer.

Jack shoved his hands in his pockets and looked past her. "I haven't told you anything but the truth."

A small chuckled slipped through her lips as Megan's words echoed through her head. "Can't you see how difficult this is for me?" She threw her hands in the air. "You come out of nowhere one day and the next day...I don't know."

Jack stepped towards her. "You seemed like you believed last night. What happened?" Anger simmered as he looked at her.

"It felt like a dream and then..."

Jack echoed her words in a harsh whisper. "And then..."

Biting her lip, she stared into his eyes. Finally, she shook her head and spoke. "I woke up."

Chapter 10

They stared at each other for a long moment, before Jack simply turned and left without looking back over his shoulder.

"I don't like Jack," she told herself, and felt pain rip across her hip. Still watching Jack, she saw his step falter as he reached for his side. He paused but never turned around.

"I do like Jack." A small chuckle caught in her throat. She couldn't even lie to herself about her own feelings. Still standing there, she sighed and closed her eyes. *That's it, Dylan,* she chastised herself, *push him away. Just like Megan said you would. Just like you knew you would.*

Noise poured out of her house and seeped back into her consciousness.

She marched through the open door, slamming it behind her as she entered. She saw a pillow and blanket heaped at the end of the couch, and knew her father had slept there last night. She picked up the pillow and carried it to the kitchen. Without warning, she chucked it at her parents and watched it hit and shatter a glass that was on the table. Shocked, her parents turned towards her. She watched her mother's jaw drop and saw her father about to speak but she beat him to it.

"What is your problem? Almost every day all we hear is you two fighting, and I'm sick of it. Do you have any idea what this did to Jimmy? Do you wonder why he never comes home anymore? And what about me? Did you once think to ask how I've been doing at my meets? Or how school's going? No. All you do is yell at each other. And from the sounds of it, which, by the way, carries quite well through our house so Tony can hear even with his bedroom door shut, all your arguments are about a bunch of bullshit."

Dylan paused to take a deep breath. Her mother's face went ghost white while the vein in her father's forehead popped.

"No wonder I take Tony to stay at Megan's as much as I possibly can. Thank God she has a little brother Tony's age so he has someone to talk to. But even if she didn't, I would still take him! Your fighting is the reason Jimmy always took us for pizza, or ice cream, or to hang out at the mall as often as he could. I just didn't realize what he was doing until he left for college. I'm sick of it!"

She was screaming and could feel the heat flood her cheeks.

"I'm sick of watching Tony smile when we leave the house because he knows he doesn't have to hear you guys anymore. I'm sick of watching his pace slow when he knows he has to walk back through the door." She waved an arm at the front door. "I'm sick of pretending, like you guys do every morning, that there's nothing wrong with our family.

"This has to stop." She fought the tears that burnt her eyes, refusing to let them fall.

Before she could move, her mother ran over and hugged her. Dylan stood still and listened to her mother cry on her shoulder. She glared at her father who sat motionlessly at the table, his mouth clenched shut and the muscles in his jaw twitched. She wiggled out of her mother's grasp and ran upstairs. She quickly changed into a clean pair of pants and a hoodie, threw some money and her phone in her pocket, laced up her sneakers and headed for the front door.

The door shut behind her, but not before she heard a faint, "I'm sorry," emitting from her father. She didn't know if the apology was for her or for her mother and, right now, she didn't care. All she knew was she needed to get away.

Dylan let the tears fall as she wandered aimlessly around town. She paused outside Baby Bruno's and saw her brother working. She knew he had lied to her, but wasn't ready to deal with it. Jimmy waved to her through the large window. She simply turned and walked away.

Her phone rang, but she didn't want to talk to any of the

people that would probably be calling her. She didn't want to hear another lie from Jimmy, and she definitely didn't want to hear whatever excuses her parents were going to give her. She doubted it would be Megan and, right now, she didn't know what she could say that wouldn't be a lie. She wanted it to be Jack, but after what had happened earlier, she doubted he would want to talk to her either.

She sighed as she entered the park. A few people sat in the gazebo but none of them were Jack. She headed for a small playground by the far entrance.

Something was wrong. She didn't want to run. All she wanted to do was sit and let her thoughts overwhelm her. She lowered herself onto the swing and absent-mindedly pushed herself back and forth, her shoes scraping along the hardened, packed dirt.

Great.

Not being able to lie was messing with her defense mechanisms. She couldn't even pretend nothing was wrong anymore.

"How did I know I would find you here?" She flinched at the sound of the voice when she hadn't even heard anyone approach. Taking a calming breath, she looked up to see Noah standing in front of her. She had no idea how long she had been sitting on the swing and moved her legs experimentally, feeling pins and needles shoot through her limbs. Noah continued as though nothing had happened. "Do you realize half the town is looking for you and the other half is worried about you?"

She cleared her throat experimentally, determined her voice should sound calm and collected in front of him. "How did you know I would be here?"

Noah shrugged and sank into the swing next to her. "Something just told me you would."

There was the hint of something else in his voice, but she couldn't quite catch it. They swung for a few minutes; the only noise the squeak of the metal chains as they rubbed back and forth.

Noah cleared his throat. "You really let them have it then?" She tried to ignore the tone she could still hear radiating from him. "From what I hear it was nicely done."

"I should have handled it better." She recalled the looks on her parents' faces as she stormed out of the house. "Who did you hear it from?"

Noah's only answer was to raise an eyebrow.

She sighed. "Megan."

"You did the right thing." Noah stood and placed his hands on her shoulders, forcing the swing to stop and her to look at him. He leaned in and whispered in her ear, "You know you did." You did the right thing on all accounts."

She nodded as he walked away and a layer of fog drifted over her mind. Noah was right. She had done the right thing, both with her parents and with Jack. Megan was wrong. Putting up walls was the only way to keep from getting hurt.

She watched the late autumn sun set, and allowed those thoughts to solidify in her mind. She had been right. A chill filtered into the park, and still she didn't move, only shoved her hands deeper into her hoodie after she had pulled it tightly over her hair. Her phone kept ringing, but she just went back to swinging.

She felt the swing set shift again as someone slowly sat down next to her. She didn't look over.

"He really does like you." Vi's soft voice surprised her.

Dylan stopped swinging. "How did you find me? Did you ask Noah?"

"Noah was here?" Vi looked stunned.

She looked at her and nodded. "Yeah a while ago?" and with a shrug, she went back to swinging. "I lost track of how long I've been here."

She didn't notice the dead tone her voice had taken. Forgetting Vi was there, she went back to listening to the rusty chains moan against each other in the silence.

"Dylan..." Vi's voice brought her back again.

"Vi?" She could feel the confusion wrap around her. "What's going on?"

"You know the truth. You need to believe in it." Vi's soft voice was layered with impatience. "I need to hear the truth."

"The truth." She clicked her tongue.

Vi grabbed the swing and forced her to stop. Carefully, she placed her hands on Dylan's cheeks and waited for her to look up.

Dylan could feel her eyes twitch, desperate to look anywhere but at Vi, but unable to do it.

Vi whispered his name. "Jack."

She felt herself shudder. "Fine. He likes me. So what."

"So what?"

"He only likes me because he knows what I'm going through with this thing."

She watched the blood run down Vi's neck. She brought her fingers to her neck, feeling the wetness of her own matching wound. Shaking her head, she looked back to Vi.

"You can feel my lies too?"

"Only when you lie directly to me," Vi said softly. "You just lied. You know the truth."

"He does like me?" She could hear the honesty in her voice. "And it doesn't have anything to do with being a walking lie detector?"

Vi shook her shoulders sharply enough to make her teeth snap. "You need to speak the truth. Don't hide what you know in a question."

She pulled away from Vi and took a deep breath. "Jack likes me."

"About time you accepted the truth." She spun around and saw Jack leaning against the post next to her swing. He smiled down at her before he looked at Vi. "Thanks for the help."

Vi stood and brushed her jacket off. "Anytime...wait. Not anytime." Vi wiped her neck clean before she spoke again. "You need to start believing us. There are enough people out there lying. Or creating lies. We can't lie to each other."

Vi walked over to Jack and grabbed his hand. "This complicates things." Jack nodded as Vi looked over and smiled. "Have fun, you two."

Dylan watched her go before looking over at Jack who hadn't moved. "What's complicated?" she asked.

"I told you last night I would never lie to you, but right now may not be the best time."

She nodded and slowly got up. She still felt foggy. She took a hesitant step towards Jack but kept her head down. Her phone started ringing again and she pulled it out, seeing it was Megan. Still, she didn't answer. She looked quickly back through the other missed calls. Seven were from Jimmy. Nine were from home, and nineteen were from Megan.

She unlocked the phone and sent a text to Megan.

I'm not fine, but I'm with Jack. I'll call you later.

A moment later she read the response.

Got a hysterical call from your mom. Nice job there. 'Bout time it happened. Have fun with Jack.

She put it back in her hoodie. A shiver went up her spine as a cold wind blew through the park.

"That was Megan," she said, and took another small step towards Jack.

"What did you say to her?" Jack's voice was soft.

She raised her head. "I told her that I wasn't fine, but that I was with you. And I told her I would call her later."

"And what did she reply?"

She let a small smile touch her lips as she pulled out her phone and flashed the screen at him.

Jack reached out and grabbed the front of her shirt and pulled her the last step towards him. She hesitated but finally allowed herself to lean into him and felt his arms wrap tightly around her. She let out a jagged breath and sank slowly into him, letting him hold her as her legs turned to mush under her.

"Can I ask you a question?" he whispered into her hair.

She nodded but didn't trust her voice to speak.

"Why did you think I only liked you because we are both...how did you put it...walking lie detectors?"

She didn't pick her head up but answered into his jacket. It was easier for her to say without having to look at him. "Because you said something about being connected and that you could feel my pain. I just figured it had something to do with that, and that it wasn't really how you felt."

He pulled Dylan in even more tightly.

"That only makes it easier for me to like you."

"Easier. As in if we didn't have this creepy mind thing you wouldn't bother?"

Jack shook his head. "Easier. As in I don't have to lie if I have to go help someone."

"Like you're helping me now? You help other people?"

Jack winced. "Not exactly. Fides get very few new Fides to help train. There aren't a lot of us out there, I don't think." He looked around. "But as far as helping people find the truth" — Jack nodded — "I do that, and so does Vi, and so will you."

She took a deep breath and look back down at Jack's chest. Taking her hands out of her hoodie she wrapped them around his waist. A million questions sped through her mind.

"I don't know what to ask you. I know you won't lie to me, but I also don't want to make you answer something you don't want to."

Jack smiled. "Well, while you're trying to figure out in which order to bombard me with questions, why don't we go for a walk?"

"Where're we going?"

Jack shrugged. "I don't really have any place in mind. I'm

getting cold standing here."

They walked in silence for several moments. Dylan was the first to break it.

"How long..."

Jack glanced at her, waiting for her to finish the question. She took a deep breath and spat the question out before she could change her mind. "How long have you liked me?"

A shy, nervous grin danced at the corner of his mouth. "It was last year. You were running late to one of your classes and I watched you hurdle some poor kid who had dropped his books in the hallway. Your foot nicked his head and he smashed it off the floor. The look on your face was priceless. You ran over to him, grabbed his papers, shoved them in his hands, apologized quickly and took off again. You didn't see the way he looked at you after you left."

"How did he look?"

Jack stopped and turned towards her. He tucked a strand of hair behind her ear. With a little chuckle he said, "A little in awe and a little stunned..."

"They mean the same things, you know."

"Not exactly." Jack shrugged. "And that's beside the point."

She shook her head. "But why did that make you like me?"

"Because I saw you were living your life by your own rules. I saw you were a caring person, but also quite unobservant. You went through the halls with these blinders on. I tried to talk to you once, but you didn't even hear me. I saw how you were with Megan and the girls you ran with, and could tell you were kind. I saw how you were with your brothers and knew you cared. And I thought you would be the kind of girl I would want to spend time with. You were the kind of person I wanted in my life.

She stared at her feet, unable to respond to him.

"But then you started dating..."

"Eric."

Jack nodded. "And I knew I would have to wait."

"That's it?"

"Did you expect something more?"

"A crush that you waited almost a year to act on? I haven't been with Eric in—"

"Three and a half months, I know."

"Stalker much?" She elbowed him lightly.

Jack nudged her back. "Only when you weren't looking."

"According to Megan I'm always like that." She bit her lip. "I'm not good at this kind of thing, Jack." She paused. "You've heard what it's like in my house." She wanted to say more but couldn't find the words to explain.

Jack interrupted her with a smile and small shake of his head. "We'll figure it out."

Chapter 11

They walked down the road arm in arm. Though it felt surreal, she no longer doubted that it was. She was with a guy who wanted to be with her. A guy who couldn't lie to her, and even better, a guy who didn't want to lie to her.

"When did you realize I was a—"

"Fide?" Jack sighed. "A few weeks ago, just after your sixteenth birthday."

"How did you know...oh!" She rolled her eyes remembering the spectacle Megan had made of her locker that day. "Megan. Right." She paused, reliving the embarrassment that day had brought. She snapped herself back to the present. "So, how does that work? How did you know I was one?"

"At first I didn't. I thought maybe I just wanted to talk to you, but never had the chance. Then I felt a constant pull towards you, much like Vi had towards me."

"Did you and Vi..." she couldn't finish the question and shifted nervously looking past Jack.

"No. We're just friends. We've always just been friends." Jack squeezed her arm for emphasis but he was silent for moment. "It was actually Vi's idea to try and talk to you at the pizza shop."

"Why?"

"I knew you went there to hang out with your brother after practice. And that usually you were alone."

She jammed her hands into her pockets. "Did you purposefully wait for me to spill my drink on you so I'd have to stop and say something?"

Jack laughed. "I wish I had been that clever. It had taken a while to get up the nerve. It really was just bad timing."

"You needed courage?"

"To talk to a girl I've liked for a long time?" He looked at her with a you've-got-to-be-kidding expression.

She rolled her eyes and poked him in the side. "And what about in the cafeteria?"

"More bad timing."

They walked towards Megan's house and Dylan took out her phone. She saw there were several voicemails. She looked at Jack.

"I never told you what happened with my parents." She watched his expression tighten.

"It's your decision to tell me what you want."

She shook her head. "That's not fair. How can you give me that space when I won't give you the same?" She paused and searched Jack's calm expression. "I made you tell me why you liked me. That wasn't very nice, yet you aren't forcing me to tell you about my parents."

Jack shrugged. "I told you I would never lie to you."

"And you should expect the same from me."

"I do." Jack leaned in. "But just because I expect the truth, doesn't mean I will make you tell me something that is obviously still very raw. I had wanted to tell you everything I already have." Jack smirked. "Maybe if I had just told you everything last night…"

"I wouldn't have believed you."

"And what changed? Why do you believe me now?"

"I don't know." She chewed on her lip. She looked up at Jack and knew he was waiting for a better answer. "Jack"—she took his hand—"I don't know what changed, or if the change will stick, but I will figure it out, and when I do, I will tell you."

He smiled. "Then I'll wait for your answer."

"So how did you know? How did you know I would start feeling lies that night?" She stopped midstride. "Did you do this to me?"

"No." Jack shook his head as he eyes widened. "It was already happening, and worse things could have happened if I hadn't gotten to you in time."

"Like?" She paused. "Wait, what do you mean it was already

happening?"

"I mean that lies were already starting to affect you. They weren't slicing through, but they were irritating your skin." Jack looked up into the sky. "And I know this because I was affected too. I had a few areas that looked like bug bites and a rash. All of it could easily be explained by natural phenomenon, but I knew it wasn't natural, and Vi confirmed that it wasn't. She heard you telling Megan about a rash the new laundry soap had on your arms." Jack looked at her. "There wasn't a new soap, Dylan. It was starting. And I'm really trying to be honest with you, but I don't want to get something wrong." He sighed. "Can we have a sort of to be continued on this line of questioning?"

She looked at Jack for a moment before she nodded, offering him a weak smile, already dialing. She turned her attention towards the house and watched Megan's bedroom light flip on. She held the phone away knowing Megan was about to yell, and she wasn't disappointed.

"Oh my God! Please tell me everything is okay."

Dylan could hear Noah in the background. "Look out your window and judge for yourself."

She saw Megan and Noah yank back the curtains and she waved.

"I swear if you move before I get down there I will hunt you down and kick your ass, Dylan."

"We're not going anywhere," Jack answered calmly.

"This was a bad idea," she said, listening to Megan make her way through the house.

The door slammed behind Megan as she walked purposefully towards them. She watched it open a moment later and saw Noah stroll onto the porch before her attention went back to Megan. Dylan would have taken a step back, but Jack pulled her tightly by his side.

"Where the hell have you been? Do you know how many times I've tried calling you? Do you know how many times your parents called me? And Jimmy?"

She took a deep breath, trying desperately to find the right thing to say. "But Noah knew I was okay?"

That wasn't it.

"Noah?" Megan's head whipped around to look at her boyfriend who was still standing on the porch.

Noah shrugged and walked towards them; Jack grabbed her a little more tightly.

Dylan knew the fallout from earlier was coming, and it wasn't going to be pretty, but Megan's anger was temporarily shifted to her boyfriend. She was about to speak when her phone rang again. She cringed when she looked down to see Jimmy was calling her. Glancing quickly at Jack she answered.

"Thank God you're alive," he said, before Dylan even had the phone to her ear. The sound of relief in his voice carried over the argument Noah and Megan were having a few feet away. "You can't just disappear for hours after telling Mom and Dad off. They've been worried sick."

"Yeah." Dylan rolled her eyes. "I'm sure they were devastated." She winced as a cut opened on her leg. Out of the corner of her eye, she noticed Jack shake his head.

"That's not funny, Dylan." She heard the disapproval in her brother's tone. "I mean, don't get me wrong, that had to be done...it was something I probably should have done years ago, but then to just leave, and not answer your phone."

She let her shoulders sag a bit. She hadn't wanted Jimmy to worry. "I'm sorry, Jimmy."

"Where did you go anyway? We looked everywhere and couldn't find you."

"Obviously not everywhere or you would have found me quickly."

"Dylan."

"I just walked around for a while then ended up at the park, and met up with a friend."

Jack raised an eyebrow. She cringed.

"And you're going home tonight?"

Dylan shook her head. "I don't think so. I'm still so angry at them that I would probably just end up leaving." She looked at Megan who sighed and nodded her head. "I'll stay with Megan. Tell them I'll come home tomorrow sometime."

Noah slid back into the house. There was silence for a moment before Dylan spoke again. She could hear the sounds of trays moving and people talking, and knew Jimmy was at work. "Jimmy, the other night you said you had to go work on a paper, but I know you were lying to me. Where did you go?"

Dylan waited for him to speak. "I couldn't bear to hear them fighting again so I just crashed at Abby's."

"Who's Abby?"

She could hear Jimmy fidgeting. "She's my girlfriend. We just started dating a few weeks ago."

"Why didn't you just tell me the truth?"

He laughed. "I figured you'd twenty-questions me about her, and I didn't want to admit that I was leaving you and Tony alone with that chaos to spend time with her."

Dylan nodded. "Well the next time I see you expect twenty questions. You have been warned."

Jimmy laughed. "Come to the pizza shop tomorrow for lunch. You can meet her."

"Sounds like a deal and I'll bring someone for you to meet."

"Whoa. When did that happen? You know I get twenty questions in return. Wait do I know him?"

"You've seen him," Dylan teased. "But I have to go." She smirked knowing her brother wouldn't be happy with only part of the story. "Megan is waiting to yell at me."

"Don't you dare hang up without giving me more information!"

"Tomorrow Jimmy. We'll talk tomorrow."

She closed the phone as she looked up at Jack. "I hope you

don't mind that I told him."

Jack pulled her close. "I will never mind when you tell someone the truth."

Megan cleared her throat. "And now for that truth you just spoke of...I believe I have a right to hear what the hell happened tonight." She spun around, not waiting for Dylan or Jack and headed into the house.

Dylan grabbed Jack's hand tightly. "Can we tell her the truth?"

He shook his head. "It's better if she doesn't know."

"Why? She's my best friend." She just watched Jack shake his head slowly back and forth.

"This has to be one of those areas where you trust me for now. Vi has to explain this reason to you."

"Then what are we going to tell her?" she whispered as she looked up and saw Megan standing next to the door, waiting for them.

"As much as we can."

Her stomach twisted as she led Jack into the house.

"Megan," she heard from inside, "close the door. I'm not paying to heat the whole town."

"Hi, Mr. Lewis." She watched him hand a bowl of chips to Noah. "How are you doing?"

Mr. Lewis smiled. "Oh I'm fine, how are you?"

Dylan barely stifled a cry when pain sliced quickly through her lower abdomen. At the same moment, Jack grabbed her upper arm. He felt it too. She felt blood seep through her shirt, and onto the dark colored hoodie. It would only be a few moments before Megan saw blood. She felt Jack squeeze her more tightly, and knew immediately. Mr. Lewis was not fine.

She internally rejoiced when her phone rang.

"I'll be right back, Megan," she called, already turning and bolting for the door.

Jack followed her out, already pulling her shirt up as she looked at the phone. She had no desire to talk to her mom, who she saw was calling. The pain shooting through her abdomen was bordering on unbearable.

"I don't know what to say to her," she whispered through gritted teeth as Jack ran the dissimulator across the wound.

"You have to talk to her," he said through clenched teeth.

She nodded as she brought the phone to her ear, but the call had already rolled to voicemail. Taking a deep breath, she focused on relaxing her muscles. Her entire body was tense, from both the pain in her stomach and not being able to talk to her mother. Eventually she willed her muscles to calm and she realized what Jack was doing. She blushed as his hands ran over her stomach. He held her close to him. She slapped his hands away.

"I'm fine. Heal yourself."

He stood and looked at her. "This one won't heal completely, Dylan."

She watched as the pain faded from his face. She could still feel where the cut had formed, but instead of a radiating pain, there was a dull throb.

"What does that mean?"

Jack grabbed her arm and pulled her closer. She could feel his breath against her ear as he spoke so quietly, anyone passing by would think he was just kissing her. "It means he is carrying around a very serious lie – a lie he hasn't completely admitted to himself. We won't heal completely until he tells the truth. We have to get him to tell us..."

She knew Jack wanted to say more, but something stopped him. She grabbed his hand. "Or what will happen?" Jack wouldn't look at her. He abruptly turned and headed down the porch. "Oh no." She grabbed his arm and forced him to stop. "You don't get to not answer me. Isn't that the same as lying?"

"I have to talk to Vi." Jack didn't try walk away, but he wouldn't look at her either.

"You have to talk to me," Dylan whispered. "What will

happen?" She waited for an answer she knew wouldn't come. "You can't protect me from this, Jack; you have to be honest with me."

Jack turned and stroked his hand across her cheek as he brought his gaze up to meet hers. Dylan could see the answer coming, the answer that she didn't really want to hear, and she knew she didn't. "You know I will always only tell you the truth, right?"

She nodded, afraid that if she opened her mouth Jack would hear her voice tremble. She balled her hands into fists to keep her fingers from shaking.

Jack rested his head against hers and he grabbed her tightly. "If we can't get Mr. Lewis to tell us the truth, if his lie spreads far enough through our bodies, we will die."

Chapter 12

Dylan shook her head. She had not been ready for this. She replayed his response over in her mind and felt herself reeling. The proverbial piece of straw was bearing down on her, about to break.

She spoke quietly, holding onto one thought, unwilling to deal with the rest. "Lies can spread?"

Before he could respond, his attention was drawn to the sound of the front door opening.

"I'm still waiting for an answer," Megan huffed as she stormed through the door and joined them.

Jack squeezed her hand, willing her to keep it together as Megan came closer. She stared at him, hoping to see a smile or some sign that he everything was going to be okay; that nothing had changed in the last few minutes. All she saw was his jaw clench as he stared back at her.

"Well?" Megan's voice raised an octave, and threatened to rise higher.

"I don't have one." She looked at Megan and spoke quietly, trying to control the level of panic she could feel rising. Megan wouldn't accept this. "Not one that you'll believe."

Megan rolled her eyes. "Try me."

"It was just too much for me to deal with. Between Tony practically in tears as we walked up the driveway, and Jack" — she nodded towards him as the words spilled out — "and everything else I just...snapped."

"Just like that." Megan narrowed her eyes.

"We both knew they had it coming." She knew Megan wasn't buying her explanation.

"Yes they did, but since when don't you answer your phone when I call? Since when don't you call to tell me what you did?" Megan glanced at Jack. "Or what you're still doing?"

She flinched at the venom in her best friend's voice, but didn't snap back. She had to end this; she could feel herself getting weaker. "It just sort of happened and I had to get away." She glanced at Jack before she stepped towards Megan. "I wasn't thinking," she said as she grabbed Megan's hand. "I'm sorry."

The door opened again but didn't take her eyes from Megan. "Are you guys coming back in?" Noah stuck his head out of the door. Dylan could hear the irritation in his voice.

"I think I have to head home." She looked from Megan to Jack. "I need to make sure Tony is okay and everything." She hugged Megan. "Can we talk tomorrow? I promise to call after lunch."

Megan narrowed her gaze but finally nodded. Jack didn't wait for more as he grabbed her hand and walked away from the porch. Dylan looked back to see both Megan and Noah frowning.

"I've never not told her the truth," she whispered, trying to control the quivering of her voice. "While I know I didn't lie, this was the first time I intentionally withheld stuff from her."

"I feel like I'm always trying to apologize to you," Jack replied quietly as they walked through the deserted streets, "but I am sorry you had to do that to Megan."

She squeezed his hand, but didn't say anything. Jack rubbed the back of his neck and slowed further as they approached her house.

"Will it be okay if I come over in the morning and we can hang out before we go see Jimmy? We don't even have to talk about what's happening with being a Fide."

She looked up at her house, a weak smile dancing at the corner of her mouth. "I'd like that."

Jack pulled her into a hug. "Good night, Dylan," he murmured as he leaned down and brushed her cheek with a kiss.

She looked back to see Jack reach the sidewalk. The house was uncommonly bright and unusually quiet. Her parents were talking in the kitchen. They stopped and looked at her as she passed, but didn't say anything as she moved towards the stairs.

She stopped and peeked into Tony's room to see him playing on his computer. He didn't acknowledge her as she walked past. She didn't even turn on her light as she flopped on her bed. The emotions of the past few days caught up with her. A single tear slid down her cheek as she thought about how her life was changing. A second tear never fell. Exhaustion settled over her too quickly.

"I don't think she's waking up," Tony taunted. A few moments of silence followed. "We can always try her water technique."

She kept her eyes closed and listened to Tony plot his revenge, unsure how long this conversation had existed.

"We'll save that for worse case," Jack responded. She could hear the humor in his voice even though he was trying to be serious.

"Why?" Tony pouted. "She never does."

"Fair enough. We'll give her a few more minutes." Tony stomped out of the room and her bed shifted under additional weight. "You better wake up, or I'll lull you back to sleep with my newly acquired and vast knowledge of how to level a Worgen Mage *after* I let Tony dump a gallon of freezing cold water on you."

She snapped open her eyes, and sat up slowly in bed, letting a dizzy feeling pass.

She looked around her bedroom and cringed. Nice. She wished she had cleaned it before Jack saw it. School stuff littered everything except her desk, and her clothes were heaped in a pile on her dresser. She pulled the covers up a little further only to realize she was still fully clothed, as she had been when she passed out last night. Wondering what she must look like, she surreptitiously attempted to fix herself a bit. She stopped fidgeting with her clothes and hair when she spotted a polka dotted green and pink thong hanging on the edge of her hamper, and the matching bra hanging off the back of her desk chair.

When Jack glanced towards the chair and then down to the floor, she wanted to die.

Embarrassment flooded through her when she found her voice. "What are you doing here?"

Jack cleared his throat and forced himself to look back at her. "Remember? You said I could come over this morning? Tony has been keeping me entertained for an hour so far."

Tony stumbled back in with a full pitcher of water. "Oh, not fair."

They heard Dylan's mom walking up the hallway. Reaching the door she said, "You can go dump that in the bath tub and return that pitcher to the kitchen now, young man." She pointed Tony towards the bathroom. "And I'm glad to see you've decided to return from the dead," she said, turning to Dylan "We were beginning to worry."

Both Dylan and Jack flinched as matching cuts opened up on the side of their hands. Dylan carefully cradled her hand in her hoodie and lowered her gaze. She didn't want to hear any more lies from her mother. Tony stood there and pouted. They all watched as the water came dangerously close to spilling on her floor.

"Let me help you, buddy." Jack cleared his throat and jumped off the bed.

Tony trudged out of her bedroom with Jack right behind him. Dylan took a jagged breath and looked at her mother. "I'm so sorry about what I said last night."

Her mother stopped her quickly with a wave of the hand. "You were right. We've been fighting a lot and it's not fair to any of you. There's nothing to apologize for."

Something passed across her mother's face, but whatever it was, she quickly reined it in.

Her mom looked over as Jack walked back in and smiled warmly. Dylan winced. She had never gotten a look like that.

"I must be tired," she mumbled mostly to herself. "I know I

didn't sleep well this week. And then everything else."

"Well you push yourself so hard. Rest a bit," her mother said, shoving pillows behind her head, "and I'll get you something to drink."

A look of surprise crossed her face at both her mother's words and her tone. She almost sounded sincere.

Once her mother's footsteps padded down the stairs, she turned to Jack. "You look tired."

He nodded. "I didn't sleep much last night."

She frowned. "Was it because of me? Did I do something? Are you...?"

She didn't even know how to finish the question. There were too many thoughts floating through her mind. Sighing, she sat up and hid her face in her hands, not sure what she wanted to or should be saying. She flinched as Jack reached out and touched her hand. He pulled away from her and she heard him sigh.

"You have nothing to apologize for," Jack said quietly.

"Neither do you."

"I didn't apologize."

"But you want to, I can hear it. And I will not listen if you do. I asked the questions. I've barely slept since I met you, and then I had a fun ride on that emotional rollercoaster yesterday."

"And that's why I shouldn't have told you."

She pressed her lips together and turned to face Jack before she spoke again. "I want my boyfriend to tell me the truth. No matter how painful or unpleasant. It is the only way we"—a staggered breath escaped as she spoke—"can get through this."

Jack nodded his head, a smile slipping across his mouth at hearing her call him her boyfriend.

She cocked her head to the side. "Can you do one thing for me?"

He nodded again.

"Next time you need to tell me something big, make sure I'm sitting down first? I felt a little woozy after that last whammy you hit me with." She cringed remembering just how real everything had gotten last night.

She watched Jack's mouth form a thin line as he nodded his head solemnly. "Even if I have to hold you down myself."

"Thank you," she said. She reached out and touched his hand but avoided looking into his eyes. She could feel something intense radiating off him but she wasn't sure if she wanted to know anything else. "Okay," Dylan said hesitantly. "I really need to get moving. All that extra running and I feel like a doll stuffed under a car seat."

Dylan hopped out of bed in her hurry to shake the feeling something bad was coming. She began to raise her arms over her head but abruptly stopped as pain shot through her stomach. It took a moment to notice her shirt; the blood had dried on both her skin and the material. Pulling her shirt up she saw the mark left from Mr. Lewis's lie. Though it wasn't bleeding, it was red and bruising. She could see it had started spreading slowly over her abdomen and was making its way towards her lowest rib. Gingerly touching the skin, she felt the pain swell. She looked at Jack.

"Mine looks like that too." Jack spoke without looking up at her.

She felt herself blush remembering his hands on her stomach last night. She quickly turned around and pretended to look through the window. "Does Vi know?"

"Yeah, I told her." He pulled out his phone and typed a message. "I'm just sending her a message now, letting her know you are okay and finally awake."

Dylan could hear how tired he was, and began to fiddle with her trinkets on a shelf by her window, suddenly uncomfortable being in her bedroom with Jack. No one had ever touched her the way Jack had, even if it hadn't been sexual, she couldn't shake the visual, or the feeling of his hands moving along her sides. She also couldn't stop cringing at the reasons it had happened.

"Why don't you go get some sleep? You sound as tired as I feel. Call me when you wake up and we can do something."

She heard Jack shift on her bed.

"Why won't you look at me?" His voice was barely above a whisper, but she heard him as if he was standing right behind her. An exasperated chuckle slipped from Jack's lips. "Isn't the refusal to tell the truth what got us in trouble in the first place?" She knew he was right, though it wasn't exactly fair since he was doing the same thing withholding thoughts. She clenched her fists and bowed her head. She heard the spring in her bed creak as Jack stood. "Is it about me?"

Her head snapped towards her door as the soft scuffling of footsteps caught her attention.

Jack took a step back. "You may have been saved by your parents this time, Dylan Lord, but I want to know what has made your face so red."

She looked around the room. In the mirror, she watched Jack raise his eyebrow as he looked back at her. "That's cheating," she said, bursting into laughter as her mom came in with a mug of tea.

"What's cheating?" Her mom looked at her suspiciously.

Dylan shook her head and flung her hand in Jack's direction. "Jack is apparently honing his skills as a spy."

She relaxed and sat down at her desk and, at the same time, she discreetly threw the bra in the hamper before taking the mug from her mother. She watched her mother talk easily with Jack.

"Are you two going to hang around here today?"

Shaking her head, she sipped the tea. "I promised Jimmy that I'd stop by for lunch."

Her mom nodded. "I have to go shopping. I'll leave money for you downstairs." She looked over at Jack. "Will you guys be back for dinner?"

"I will be, but I think Jack needs to get some sleep."

"Okay, well you two behave. Your father is downstairs," her

mother added as she walked out of the bedroom.

"I have no idea who that was, or why she's dressed up like my mother."

Jack shrugged. "I think she's just trying to make up for earlier nastiness."

"Maybe, but a few niceties are not going to compensate for years of…" She bit her lip, forcing herself to stop. She didn't want to think about it. She shook her head as she grabbed a pair of jeans and a shirt and headed for the door.

Jack brushed her arm as she passed. "And where do you think you're going?"

"To get a shower," she responded in the same accusatory tone.

"I'm still waiting to hear what had you so embarrassed before."

She smirked. "You're the spy. See if you can figure it out."

"And if I guess correctly?"

She paused in the doorway and nodded her head. "Then I will tell you the truth."

She walked down the hall and shut the bathroom door loudly so Jack would know the conversation was, at least, temporarily over. Though she knew Jack was waiting for her, she did not rush with her shower. The hot water helped reduce the tension that had crept into her muscles.

Finally relaxed, she headed back to her room, but paused at the threshold. Jack was asleep on her bed. She quietly pulled a blanket up to his shoulders before heading downstairs.

Her father was in the living room watching TV. She sat next to him nervously drumming her fingers on her thighs.

"I'm sorry I flipped out on you guys."

He grunted but didn't say anything as he flipped through the channels. When he found one he liked, he put the remote down but didn't look at her as he answered.

"You were right. We've been yelling about the stupidest things for no reason whatsoever."

"But why?"

"I wish there was an easy answer, but I don't have one. We talked after you stormed out, and we will try to fix things."

"Thanks Dad." She leaned over and hugged him before snuggling back into her chair.

"So who is he?" He didn't even wait for her to get comfortable.

She froze. "Jack?" She shrugged. "He goes to my school." She knew this was coming.

"And?"

"And?" Dylan responded sure she knew what her dad wanted to hear but desperate to avoid the conversation.

"Where'd you meet him?"

"At Bruno's. I didn't even know he went to school."

"How old is he?"

"He's a junior."

Her father grunted. "And have you been sneaking around with him for a long time?'

She shook her head. "We've just started seeing each other."

"You like him." Her father grumbled something when Dylan smiled involuntarily. He picked up the remote and jabbed at it. The silence stretched on, interrupted by the quickly changing channels and the sticky key on the remote. "I guess you could do worse," he finally admitted.

"Gee, thanks, Dad." She patted her father's shoulder and walked into the kitchen, ready to get away from the awkwardness of the exchange.

Grabbing a glass of water, she leaned against the sink. Right now, she wondered if she could do any better.

Chapter 13

"You should have taken a longer nap." Dylan squinted at Jack as they walked towards Baby Bruno's.

He shook his head. "You promised your brother you would meet him."

"Yes, but I don't want him to meet a zombie."

"I am not that bad," Jack managed around a yawn, and swallowed a snort.

"What's so funny?"

"Just remembering something."

"Oh, that's mature." Dylan rolled her eyes. "I won't tell you so you won't tell me?"

Jack nudged her shoulder. "Oh I have a pretty good idea what made you blush."

"Later," she said, and pulled him across the parking lot and into Bruno's.

She saw Jimmy trying not to laugh as they walked around counter.

"Really?" Jimmy said quietly as he hugged his sister.

"Be nice," she whispered in response.

Taking a deep breath, she began, "Jimmy, this is Jack. Jack, I think you've met Jimmy."

They shook hands as Jimmy motioned over to the back booth. Dylan watched as a short, redhead walked up and hugged Jimmy. He smiled down at her but was forced back behind the counter as a few customers came in.

"You must be Dylan," she said in a southern drawl extending her hand. "I'm Abby."

Dylan gasped as a cut opened down her side. She turned towards Jack and watched his face harden.

He stepped forward, his voice low and strong. "Your name isn't Abby."

"Of course my name is Abby." She looked from Dylan to Jack. "What kind of game are you playing?"

She stared at the girl, slowly backing away from Jimmy. Jack shadowed her movement. She watched the girl's face go white as she ran for the door. Dylan followed her outside, grabbing her by the arm.

"Get off me."

"Not until you tell me the truth. Who are you and why are you lying to my brother?"

The girl burst into tears and leaned against the building. She felt Jack close behind her.

"I can't tell you who I am."

Stepping forward, Jack knelt down next to her. His calm voice washed over the girl. "There is no one to fear here." He placed his hand on her knee and waited until she looked at him. "Who are you?"

The girl looked dazed as though she were trying to hear him through a fog. "My name," she said slowly as if trying to find the truth that had long ago been lost, "is Rachel."

"Why did you lie?" Dylan's voice was layered in an anger she couldn't control.

"Because I have to," Rachel cried into her hands.

She watched Jack lean in and whisper in Rachel's ear. She nodded and cried harder.

Jack stood and took Dylan's arm and walked away a few steps. "She's in witness protection," he whispered into her ear. "She is scared out of her mind. She's probably been in hiding for a long time." He ran his hands over his face. "I ran into one before."

"And she just happens to like the brother of a human lie detector," she whispered back, the anger still clear in her voice, but now there for a different reason.

Jack nodded but looked into the distance. Dylan's gaze drifted to the parking lot and to Noah who was walking away.

"There's more to this than just witness protection, isn't there?"

Jack nodded, and squinted a bit more than he already was.

She looked back at Rachel. "We won't tell." She knelt down and placed her hand on Rachel's knee waiting until Rachel looked up at her. "Your secret is safe with us, but it would also be safe with Jimmy."

Rachel nodded and took her hand. "Thank you."

Drying her eyes, Rachel stood and hugged her before heading back into Bruno's. Together, she and Jack watched Jimmy take Rachel's face in his hands and kiss her. Jack grabbed her arm and they steered away.

"You're hiding something from me," she commented after a few moments silence, not needing to look at Jack to know she was right.

"Just thinking everything through."

"About Rachel?"

"That's part of it."

She shot him a glance. "And what's the other part?"

"Parts," Jack said, still without looking at her. "They're plural."

She silent watched him put things together. She could see his mind spinning as the muscles in his face tensed and relaxed. "Are you going to tell me?"

He shook his head and slowed his pace. "I'm not being a very good mentor, am I?" He looked around, searching for the right words. "I won't always make you ask me questions." He wrapped his arm around her shoulder and pulled her closer as he dropped his voice. "You know there are Fides – humans who seek the truth."

She thought about it for a moment. "That means there are people who seek out lies?"

"Not exactly." Jack shook his head. "People lie naturally but some people, called Feeders, create lies. They naturally draw people to them with their personalities but can spin lies that just about everyone, including new Fides, can believe."

"I thought we could sense lies."

Jack rubbed the back of his neck. "There's no easy way to describe the feeling, but Feeders can sort of cloak their lies so we don't notice all the time. An experienced Feeder makes it almost impossible to tell they are lying. This is very effective if we aren't aware a person is a Feeder."

"So..." She tried to think it through. "...not only do we have to get people to tell us the truth, but we have to do it with people around making it easier to lie than tell the truth?"

"I never said being a Fide would be easy, did I?"

She rolled her eyes and thought for a moment. "And let me guess..." She looked at Jack.

He shook his head. "It appears there is at least one Feeder back in Pine Glenn."

"Back? As in..."

"There was one here when I was becoming a Fide. They try to hide the truth and want you to lie. But there was a Feeder here more recently. Vi and I think only a few months ago."

The questions spilled out before she could stop them. "How do you know? Why? What do we have to do? What can I do? What should I do?"

Jack waited for her to stop. "Want to choose a question?"

She rolled her eyes, forced herself to slow down. "Why do they want people to lie?"

"For a Feeder, lies are power. The more lies, the more power they gain. To them, power means control. And that's bad. The more powerful they are, the harder it is for us to undo what they've done." Jack paused for a moment and squinted against the sunlight. "If we can't stop them, it will be almost impossible to know what's true."

She nodded. "How do you know they're here?"

He smiled for a moment before taking a deep breath. "I can feel them, just as I am sure they can feel me. That's how I know they're here. They're probably here because of you. They would naturally be drawn to a new Fide in the hope of turning them." She opened her mouth to speak but Jack stopped her. "As hard as this may be, we have to be honest with each other. And we have to get you used to finding the truth and speaking honestly as quickly as possible."

She nodded, knowing another truth needed to be heard. One that would be much harder to face. They walked in silence, listening to the wind blow through the bare trees.

"What happens to a Fide if a Feeder turns them?"

"That person will never know the truth. They won't become Feeders, because a Feeder knows the truth but doesn't care. You've heard of people 'living the lie?' Well, many of them were Fides who couldn't see past a Feeders lie. A Fide who is turned will never be able to distinguish the truth from a lie." He rubbed his neck. "And that means they will doubt everything they hear. From the local weather, to the lunch specials, to personal feelings, they won't be able to believe anything." Jack looked across the street unable to look at her. "Most of them end up alone and insane."

Dylan wrapped her arms tightly around herself.

Cautiously, Jack held her face in his hands. "I will do everything I can not to let that happen to you."

She squeezed one of his hands still on her cheek before dropping it.

"But this isn't just on you. I have to help you."

Jack nodded and took her hand. They walked in silence for several minutes.

"Do you know who it is?" Her steps faltered as another fact surged to the surface. "Wait, you said 'they'?"

Jack ran a hand through his short hair and rubbed his neck. "I have an idea. I've noticed a pull around certain people, but I don't want to be wrong, so I'd rather say anything yet. Vi is working on it too, and we can't just confront a Feeder and tell them to stop. It will most likely get pretty ugly before it gets better so…" He shrugged unable to answer.

Her phone beeped. She dug it out of her pocket and read a message from her brother.

"That was quick." Jack smiled and put the phone back in her pocket. "Your brother took that better than I thought he would if he's already texting you."

"He's always been a kind and understanding person."

"Much like his sister."

She wrapped her arms back around herself. "I'm not like him."

"You are more like him than you know," he said quietly.

She shook her head and focused on a topic she could pretend to handle. "I just can't believe Rachel told him so quickly."

"I think a Feeder was trying to get her to conceal the truth, so, when she met us, that power was snapped. That's why it made it easier for her to talk to Jimmy after we left."

"So now what do we do?"

Jack smirked. "You could tell me why you were so embarrassed earlier." Her face flushed as she looked away. "Or we could try and weasel the lie out of Megan's dad." She groaned. She hadn't given Megan a satisfying answer about what had happened yet and knew Megan was waiting for her to call. "Or," Jack said, "we can go back and get something to eat."

She pounced immediately. "Option three."

"I knew you would choose that." He shook his head. "Too chicken to tell me the truth and too chicken to face your friend."

"That sounds about right."

"You know you can tell me anything, right?" Jack grabbed her and forced her to stop and look at him. "And with at least one and probably more than one Feeder around I'm not going to be able to let you adjust to this as gradually as I may have before. You are going to have to tell me the truth, Dylan."

She bit her lip and looked around trying to find a clear explanation. "I go for runs so I can clear things in my mind. You know" — she kicked a pebble—"to figure out what I want to say and what I don't. All this feels backwards to me."

"Then I'll wait." A smile crept across his face. "But I won't wait for long."

"Is that a threat?"

The smile turned into a grin. "Absolutely."

They headed back to the pizza shop, but she wasn't paying attention. Her thoughts were spiraling out of control. She wanted very badly to run away, and clear her mind of her questions. She felt Jack grab her hand more tightly but didn't acknowledge it as she forced herself to find order and calm in her own head.

She knew very soon she would have to run.

Dylan expected Jack at her locker Monday morning, but he never showed. Megan, however, was there with Noah.

And she was livid.

She tried to explain, but Megan's rage only festered and grew. Megan had the right to be mad. She hadn't called like she had promised. Megan ranted all the way to homeroom, where Dylan found herself glad for the noise that drowned out the lies surrounding her. She stared past Megan, constantly watching for Jack, which only made Megan madder, and Noah smirk more.

Her phone vibrated in her pocket. Though she wanted her face to remain neutral when she saw the message was from Jack, she couldn't help frown when she read that he had stayed home and would meet her after school.

"So he's not coming in today?" Megan questioned. "Does that mean you'll actually talk to me?"

Anger was building up in Dylan. "I thought you were the one who wanted me dating people," she snapped.

Megan's jaw twitched as she gathered her books and stormed away before the bell rang.

She slouched back in her seat, unwilling to continue with the constant barrage of complaints that bellowed from her best friend. She made it all the way to lunch before she lost it.

She turned to her friend. "You have no idea what's going on."

"I would if you talked to me like you used to." To add insult, Megan turned towards Noah, effectually finishing the conversation, but Dylan grabbed her arm.

"You have no idea how hard things are for me right now and all you can whine about is that I didn't talk to you?" She dropped her voice, noticing the attention she drew. "This past week has probably been one of the hardest weeks in my entire life. What I need is a friend I can sit with without being constantly tortured by jabs about my loyalty. You're acting like you don't even know me anymore, and I can't stand it." She fought against the tears that welled up in frustration.

"I didn't think you had time for a friend," Megan spat back viciously. "You seem to barely have enough time for Jack. Maybe I don't know you anymore."

She couldn't believe what she was hearing. Megan had never been so nasty to her. She stood and walked away, sure that if she continued she would say something she really didn't mean.

"Where do you think you're going?" Megan grabbed her shoulder having followed her out of the cafeteria.

She took a deep breath before she turned around to look at Megan. "Away," she said quietly, "before I say something that I will regret." Megan took a step back. "Megan…" She drew another deep breath. "You're my best friend. I'm sorry that I didn't call you, but I can't deal with you screaming at me all day." Turning to go, she stopped. She couldn't leave things like this and needed Megan on her side if she was going to be able to handle everything else. "I will always be here for you. And right now, I need you to do the same. If you can't, then just let me walk away." Dylan hugged her. "Just know that no matter what happens, I will always be here for you. Please remember that."

Without waiting for an answer, she turned and hurried down

the hallway. Her heart broke when her best friend didn't even try to stop her. Looking back, she saw Megan crying in Noah's arms. She collapsed in the locker room shower, finally letting the pain, confusion, and uncertainty of the last week rush through her. The door moaned softly and someone walked in, but she didn't bother to see who was looking at her.

A warm hand touched her back and pulled her into a hug. She saw the blond wavy hair fall around her hand.

"Vi," she croaked around a sob. "What are you doing here?"

Vi grabbed her tighter. "Did you really think we would leave you alone when you are just learning to be a Fide? Jack called me last night after he left your place and said he wasn't coming in today. He had another lie to deal with. So I snuck in, and have been wandering around, just to make sure you were okay." Vi waited for her to look up. "And it is clear that you're not okay."

Dylan cleared her throat and forced the tears to stop. "I will be. I just need a little time." She winced as a slice opened on her thigh; sure that one had just opened on Vi's, too.

Vi muttered a curse. "When are you going to stop lying? We both know you don't believe that. We both know it will take more than a little time."

"You're right. I'm not fine." She mouthed the words unable to compose herself enough to speak.

Vi held her until she did. "It's probably good Jack isn't here today."

She rubbed her hands across her face. "Why?"

"I'm sure Mrs. Robinson would have a field day if she'd found him in here with you."

Dylan snorted but the humor quickly faded. "I can't tell Megan, can I?"

"It's hard for people to accept the truth. It's probably better that you didn't, but I'm sure Jack already told you that."

"He never explained why." She shook her head. "It's probably one of the many things he wanted to tell me but hasn't had the time." She let her head fall, momentarily feeling sorry for herself.

"When I first became a Fide, I tried to tell my best friend, to explain what was happening. She thought I was going crazy and that I lied to her." Vi sat on the floor and waited for Dylan to look at her. "She started spreading rumors about me cutting, using drugs and sleeping around. It was her way of trying to justify my sporadic behavior. It got to the point that I had to switch schools to get away from it all. I learned the hard way about truth and trust. They aren't mutually exclusive."

She thought about it for several minutes, even though she already knew what she would do. "I think I have to take that chance."

"Think about it carefully." Vi shook her head. "I know this goes against what we're all about, but not telling her may make it easier to keep her in your life."

"I hear you, but I can't live a contradiction."

Vi rubbed her shoulder. "Just think about it first." Vi reached into her pocket and pulled out her phone. "And now you have my number in case you want to talk about something you aren't ready to tell Jack."

She ran her hand through her hair. "There's so much I'm not ready to tell Jack. There's so much I'm not ready to tell myself."

"You aren't alone. There are things Jack isn't ready to tell himself, let alone you." Vi shook her head. "But you both must face it, and soon. Waiting will only things worse. The feelings you have about being stuck between you and Jack and you and Megan, I've been there, done that. And," Vi said, pulling her sleeve up, "I have the scars to prove it." Vi forced a small smile as Dylan's face fell. There were crisscrossing marks winding up her arm, from her elbow to her shoulder. "This is my reminder of what happened once when I couldn't face the truth."

"What happened?"

Vi's face fell. "I'll tell you another time. You have enough to think about right now."

She knew she would have to wait to get any real time to think. "Are you going to tell him about all this?"

"No." Vi looked at her seriously and pulled her to her feet. "You are."

Dylan headed for the door. "I knew you were going to say that," she mumbled as the bell echoed down the corridor and she was again late for class.

Chapter 14

Dylan needed to run. She needed time to herself.

The rest of her day had been painful. She could feel the small slices on her fingertips sting in the cold air, but right now, she didn't care. She thought about Jack and what she needed say to him. It was only fair. He had been nothing but honest with her. Maybe that's what made it harder for her to admit how much she liked him. Seeing him would only make everything more real for her.

But she wasn't ready yet, so she ran.

The scars on Vi's arm flashed through her mind and she knew she couldn't deny the truth. She needed Jack. It was fear that kept her from talking. She acknowledged the fear, and then defined it. The fear of admitting too much. The fear of getting too involved. The fear of loss. She was afraid that the lies would really hurt him. She was afraid that one day he would leave, but right now, she was afraid that she wouldn't be able to tell him any of this. This was why she hadn't been able to tell him before.

She thought about Megan. Could she tell her best friend about what was happening to her? She had to try. She had to risk losing her best friend to avoid pushing her away. She just didn't know when, or how for that matter. Could she really walk up to Megan and say, "I'm a human lie detector, and oh, by the way, your dad is carrying around a doozie that's threatening my life?"

That wouldn't work, but it brought another concern into her mind. Could she save Megan's father without telling her? Could she save Megan's dad period? She didn't have a choice. She had to get him to tell the truth, or she would die. And Jack would die. She couldn't let that happen. But how to talk to Mr. Lewis without Megan being around?

"What's the matter with you, Lord?" the coach yelled as she ran past him again, but still she didn't stop.

There was only one way – she'd have to go see him at work. He worked at an advertising studio down town. She'd have to skip school and hope that he would talk to her. With her thoughts finally in some sort of order, Dylan slowed to a walk. The sun was already setting over the town as she headed back towards the school. She groaned, seeing her coach waiting for her outside the locker room.

"I don't know what your problem was today, Lord, but you need to get your head on straight."

"It is now." Coach just looked at her. "I think more clearly when I run."

"Is that why you were running so fast? Today was supposed to be an easy day as you get ready for the meet in a few days; instead you ran like you were being chased by demons."

"I am," she whispered to herself and cleared her throat. "I know we have a meet coming up. I won't let you down." She walked past him and into the locker room and grabbed her bag. "Great, one more thing for me to worry about," she said aloud, and slammed the door before walking back outside.

Her foul mood instantly evaporated when she looked up and saw Jack leaning in his nonchalant way against a car. She ran over and wrapped her arms around him.

Slightly stunned, he hesitated before he returned her embrace.

"You have no idea how good it is to see you." She sighed into his neck.

He hugged her more tightly but still didn't speak. She heard the car door open and looked up to see Vi get out of the car.

Vi cleared her throat. "Well it looks like you two should talk." Vi grabbed her bag, throwing it in the car before she got in and started the car.

Jack stood, still keeping tight hold of her and took a step away from the car. She watched Vi drive away, still not ready to let Jack go.

"We have to talk?" Jack said quietly.

Dylan wrapped her hands even more tightly around his neck before finally letting him go and taking a step back. Jack took her hand.

"Lead the way."

It was only fitting that she talked to him at the first place she had heard the truth. She walked through the gazebo and headed for the swings, knowing she would have to be able to move to get all of it out. The lamps switched on and she followed them around the park. Dylan kept her gaze straight ahead, aware that Jack was watching her work through in her mind what she was going to say.

She released his hand and sat in the swing. A chuckle slipped through her lips when she saw that Jack wasn't as calm as he had appeared back at the school. She looked at the other swing and waited for him to sit. Slowly, he twisted to the side to look at her.

He started to speak, but she just shook her head. She had to be the first one to speak, and she knew it.

Dylan took a deep breath and held it until there was a tightness pressing painfully against her chest. As she released the air, she started to speak, her voice barely above a whisper.

"You are a pain in the ass, Jack, but I like you. A lot more than I feel comfortable admitting to myself. A lot more than I feel comfortable admitting to you, but you have been nothing but honest with me and I can only do the same in return. Megan was right about the walls I build to keep myself safe." She paused when Jack moved in his seat, but she kept her eyes down. "And I know why I didn't want to believe you. Even when I did, I was still afraid, but I accepted that fear. That was what had changed. I was afraid. I was afraid that you only liked me because of the lie detector connection, and that once I had learned to use whatever Jedi mind thing I have to master, you would be gone. Even though you told me you've liked me for a while, I didn't want to believe it. I didn't want to feel it. "

She fidgeted for a moment but continued. "I was afraid of

sounding stupid, and though I'm sure I do, I needed to tell you. I'm afraid of the pain that will come when the next person lies to me. I'm afraid of the pain you'll feel because of it. I'm afraid that I will lose my best friend because of this. I'm afraid that I won't be able to save her dad."

She took a shaky breath as Jack reached for her hand. She watched as Jack's thumb moved along it as it had before. She closed her eyes again, but slowly reopened them. Turning, she looked deep into his eyes. "But right now, I'm most afraid that I won't be able to save Mr. Lewis, and because of that, I'll have to watch you die."

She didn't know how, but she was standing, wrapped in Jack's arms. Tears that must have started minutes before flowed down her cheek. She buried her head on his shoulder, and let the feeling of relief wash over her.

He pulled her tighter. "You shouldn't have to carry around all these fears by yourself."

She tried to laugh through a sob. "You've seen my family. I'm by myself. They are all too busy ignoring what is happening or yelling at each other to notice me."

"I noticed you."

She smiled and hugged Jack more tightly. She heard the leaves next to her crunch and looked over.

"It's about time you told the truth." Vi smiled at her.

"Are you part ninja?" she huffed as she turned towards Vi.

Vi shrugged but wasn't embarrassed. "I needed to make sure you were actually going to tell him."

"And how would you know what I had to say when I didn't even know until practice?"

"I told you. Been there, done that."

She sighed. "This vague, stalk my shadow, cryptic bullshit is getting old."

"And it will continue as long as you hide things from us. I was afraid your lies were going to kill you before we had a chance to help others."

"Has that happened before?" She stepped away from Jack.

"My mentor told me of it happening. Sometimes a Feeder pushes a Fide too hard. Some people really can't stand the truth and it tears them up from the inside. Eventually it reaches their heart and kills them."

"Give us a minute will you?" Jack's voice hinted at impatience as he stared at Vi. She shrugged and strolled towards the gazebo.

"It's a little freaky how you guys just pop up from place to place."

Jack chuckled. "Like I said before, I'm good at not being noticed if I don't want to be. Vi taught me that trick."

She took a deep breath. "So what do we do about Megan's dad?"

Jack's smile faltered as he watched a few people walk past them.

"Jack?"

He shook his head and shrugged. "Tomorrow we'll go talk to him."

She stopped and felt her knees give out a little. "Just like that?"

He nodded. "Just like that. It's usually not a complicated business to confront someone about the truth."

"But..." She knew there was more to it and listened as Jack sighed.

"But Feeders are making it a little more complicated." Jack turned and continued to watch people walk through the park.

"Stop twitching," Jack whispered as they walked towards Megan's house Tuesday after practice.

"What if she's there?"

"Vi already checked. We're clear for another hour or two since she's with Noah."

The annoyance was clear in his voice, though he was trying

hard to hide it. He had already told her that at least twenty times. She shook her head and tried to steady her breathing. She had to trust Jack and Vi. Dylan ran her hand across her stomach, feeling the lie tighten and stretch as she moved.

"I wish you had an easier lie for your first one. Mr. Lewis's lie is definitely serious."

"What was your first lie, I mean the first lie you had to correct?"

"A kid had lied to his parents about how their car had gotten wrapped around a pole. He said someone had stolen it while he was in his room doing his homework." Jack rolled his eyes. "The hardest part was getting him to tell his parents the truth."

"We have to do that too? Not only hear the lie but get whoever they are lying to, to hear it too?"

"Not always." Jack didn't look at her as he responded. "It depends on the lie."

"Lovely." She followed his gaze and saw a car crawl slowly past. "And Mr. Lewis's lie?"

Jack rubbed her back and pushed her forward as she faltered at Megan's mailbox. "There's only one way to find out. We have to go in there." She nodded but didn't move. "You can do this." She looked at Jack. He grabbed her hand as he pulled her down the sidewalk.

"Nice timing," she muttered as she watched Mr. Lewis's car pull into the driveway. She forced a smile and waved at him as he got out of the car.

She could see Mr. Lewis fidget with his jacket and bag as she and Jack walked over to him. "I don't think Megan is here right now, Dylan. Noah took her out."

She grabbed Jack's hand more firmly. "I know. I actually was hoping we could talk to you for a few minutes."

Anxiety flooded Mr. Lewis's face as he dropped his gaze and kept fidgeting with his bag trying desperately to snap the lock on the cover in place. She stepped forward to help him and as she reached out, he jerked the bag away. Both gasped as papers flew into the air.

All three of them grabbed for the papers now sailing across the yard and down the driveway. Dylan picked up a few. She was stunned to see it was Mr. Lewis's resume.

"Why are you looking for a new job?"

"Well I don't have much of a choice." Anger and shame layered his voice. "Not that it's any of your business, but I lost my job a few weeks ago and have been trying to find a new one before I have to tell my family."

She stood quietly and watched Mr. Lewis grab the papers from Jack and stuff them back into his bag.

"Why don't you want them to know?"

Mr. Lewis flinched at the question and looked at them. "I don't want them to be embarrassed about me."

She wrapped her arms around him and studied Jack's frown from the corner of her eye. He ran his hand along his stomach, but she didn't understand why he was frowning. For the first time since Mr. Lewis lied, her stomach didn't hurt. She could feel the pain receding.

Mr. Lewis stiffened and she turned to watch Mrs. Lewis open the front door.

She smiled at her and looked back at Mr. Lewis.

"Tell her."

He nodded and walked towards his wife.

She smiled at them before looking at Jack. "That was it?"

Jack forced a smile and shrugged. "Sometimes we make the lies out to be worse than they are."

She bit her lip and thought about it for a moment. "You mean because it was Mr. Lewis and he's been like a second father to me, I made it worse than it really was?"

Jack nodded and started walking back towards the sidewalk. Dylan looked back in time to see Mr. Lewis pull his resume out of the bag and show it to his wife.

"But…" He shook his head.

"But?"

The muscles in his jaw twitched as his hand slid across his stomach again. He didn't look at her when he spoke. "Something feels off."

Chapter 15

Excitement shot through Dylan's body when she woke early Thursday morning. Her stomach was still tight, still healing from the lie she and Jack had heard earlier in the week, but she couldn't worry about that right now. She couldn't focus on why it had yet to heal, even though other lies had already healed completely.

Today was a big cross-country meet and she was ready to run. She was ready to redeem herself from the poor performance last time. Quietly, she walked to the bathroom, trying not to wake everyone as she got a shower and dressed on a rare fight-free morning.

Back in her room, she smiled when she looked at her mirror. Hanging from the corner were two small charms. One looked like a rabbit's foot and one was a winged shoe. Both were laced through a leather cord. A gift Jack had given her last night for luck. She hung it around her neck, but frowned back at the mirror.

In another corner was a sticker Megan had given her years ago. It was a simple, yellow smiley face. Megan had the same one on her mirror. It had been their symbol of friendship, a friendship that had yet to be mended.

She knew she had to tell Megan, but was glad that she had listened to Vi and waited. This conversation could not be thrown in between classes, and there wasn't enough time during the week. So she waited, knowing that tomorrow night, she would tell her best friend everything, and she prayed Megan would understand.

Jack had only nodded when she told him what she was going to do. Friday night was for Megan, whether Megan knew she was spending time with her was a separate issue altogether. Then Saturday Vi wanted to talk with her. Always, there seemed to be more things Dylan needed to learn.

She made her way downstairs. Tony was already downstairs talking to Jack, who had become a fixture in their morning routine. The three of them walked to school, bundling their jackets against the stinging air that felt more like early December than mid-October.

The day got better when Dylan reached her locker to find a green smiley face stuck to her locker. "Good Luck" was written in the shape of a smile. She turned around to see Megan standing behind her. She threw her books at Jack and ran to her friend almost toppling both of them in a hug.

She barely noticed paper cuts open on her fingers as kids passed her in the halls. Megan was talking to her again. Jack was walking with her.

But as the day drew on, she began to notice the thin red line that had been healing on her stomach was growing more uncomfortable.

"What does it mean?" she whispered to Jack at lunch.

She lowered her voice when Noah had stopped eating and was listening to her. "Does the dissimulator have a time limit? Did we do something wrong?"

"Not exactly." Jack fidgeted and avoided her question. "But that shouldn't matter if we heard the whole truth." Jack shot her a glance as he took a drink.

"If?" her voice hitched up an octave.

He shook his head and smiled. "It doesn't matter right now." She bowed her head. Jack took her hand. "I don't want you to worry about this. The only thing I want you to think about is running."

"But we heard the truth."

Jack hunched his shoulders. "Something is shielding him. He must have only told us part of it."

She stared at him for a moment. "A Feeder?" Jack didn't answer. "It's Megan's dad. How am I supposed to ignore this?"

She looked at Jack and tried to make eye contact, but he kept his gaze away. "You knew, didn't you? You knew there was something wrong when we got the truth."

"I'll called Vi. She knows about my theory and she can look into it a bit more now. This way, we are doing something about it, but you can still focus on this afternoon."

"But you still haven't told me your theory." She clenched her fists when Jack didn't answer her. "Why won't you answer me? Why didn't you tell me in the first place?"

Jack shook his head as he sent Vi a text. "It's probably going to take her a while to see what's going on." Finally, he looked at her. "But if anything comes up I will tell you."

"You knew what this meant to me." She stood, unable to remain seated any longer. "You're the one always saying I have to be honest," she whispered as she shook her head and wiped a tear away, unable to find the words.

Jack looked up at her, about to speak, but she turned away. She didn't want to hear his excuses any more than she wanted to hear her own. This is what she got from honesty. She had bared everything to him, risked everything, and he was keeping things from her.

The chill from the morning had only gotten worse as she stretched at the starting line. Her teammates huddled together, but she stood her ground, unwilling to show the other runners any weakness. Megan and Jack hunched together against the wind, trying to turn so that it would hit their backs. When he saw her look over, Jack raised his hand. She snapped her attention back towards the racecourse. She refused to let Jack ruin another meet.

Shaking her hands and bouncing in place, she willed the blood to flow through her limbs. She heard the whistle and took her place in the middle of the starting line. She nodded to each of her teammates and ignored the other runners. Slowly, the official raised the starting gun.

The wind whistled through her ears. She focused on his finger on the trigger unable to hear the pop of the gun.

She ran. Feet pounded behind her. Jack's good luck charms bounced against her throat in rhythm with her feet. She had let herself down last time. She wasn't about to do that again. She heard people yelling her name as she emerged from the woods and dashed for the finish line, finally letting a grin emerge when she crossed first.

She was winded. Doubled over trying to get her breath, she felt a new stitch of pain emerge on her stomach. Gasping for breath, she tried to straighten, but couldn't as more pain flared.

Her ribs ached in protest as a lie spread.

Megan yelled her name. Jack yelled her name.

The two yells were entirely different.

She didn't have time to wait to tell Megan the truth. She didn't have time to wait for Vi to get answers. Her coach clapped her on her back, forcing her to her knee as she struggled with the pain. Taking her hand away from her stomach, she saw blood. She had to get away from everyone before they saw.

Barely able to stand straight, she stumbled towards the school. Mr. Lewis's lie was getting worse. A car screeched to a halt inches from her. A door was thrown open.

"Get in," Vi shouted at her.

Someone behind her helped her into the car. Spots dotted her vision as the pain increased. She felt the ache in her back as another stab of pain shot through her abdomen. She could barely see Jack as he laid her across his lap and pulled up her jersey wiping away the blood with his hand.

"Hang on," he said through a grimace of pain.

His voice sounded far away and she didn't know if he was talking to her or to himself.

"What's happening to her?" Megan sounded scared.

Megan was there? She looked towards her friend's voice,

seeing her sitting in the front seat.

"Megan," Dylan croaked through clenched teeth, and she reached for her friend's hand. "I'm so sorry."

The pain subsided as Jack ran the dissimulator across her stomach and over her ribs. Dylan took a deep breath and willed her muscles to relax.

"This is getting really bad, Vi," he moaned.

Vi jammed on the breaks and spun in her seat. "Let me see." Her voice was cold. Jack moved his hands. "Let me see yours," she commanded as she slipped further into the backseat.

Megan's voice was yelling from the front seat, demanding answers. Answers that Dylan hadn't had time to tell her.

Vi spun back. "A lie is killing them, Megan. If we can't get them to hear the truth…" Vi's voice drifted away.

All Dylan could hear was the pounding of pulse in her ears. Tears pooled in Dylan's eyes. She grabbed Jack's hand.

Dylan could hear Vi as she spoke with Megan, but she couldn't comprehend what was being said.

"Jack, I'm so sorry I spent so much time not believing." She heard herself take a shaky breath. "And I'm sorry about earlier. I know you were just trying to do what you thought was right."

"No you don't." His voice was strong but quiet. He folded her into his arms, pulling her closer. "You don't get to say goodbye to me." Dylan tried to focus on the voices carrying from the front seat, but Jack pulled her attention back to him. "What did I say to you that first time we met?"

Dylan tried to laugh but the movement sent spasms through her. "Does it matter?"

"I told you there were people worth suffering for." Dylan focused on his face, seeing the calm cascade over it.

"The pain!" she cried out as it radiated through and stuck in her ribs. She could feel it leaching into her bones and spreading.

"It's going to get worse, but you fight it." He placed his hand on her cheek.

"I don't know how, Jack."

He grabbed her hand and wrapped his other arm around her back, cradling her even closer to his body. "Breathe slowly," he commanded. "Just breathe."

Dylan obeyed and felt the pain ease slightly with each breath.

"Whose lie do you need to hear? Who has to tell you the truth, Dylan?" Megan reached out and touched Dylan's arm.

Dylan cringed back from her touch and looked at Jack. He nodded and squeezed her. "Tell her, Dylan." His voice was barely above a whisper.

She looked back at Megan and swallowed. "It's your father's."

Megan stiffened in the seat and looked over at Vi.

"Look at them." Vi's voice was soft. "Does it look like they're lying to you?"

Megan finally looked back at Dylan. "There's nothing wrong with my father."

"No," Vi said. "There's something very wrong, but he hasn't talked about it."

"You're wrong. This is just some stupid trick." Megan shook her head. "If you wanted me to stay away all you had to do was tell me, Dylan," she spat. "Some friend." Megan looked at Jack before gazing back at Dylan. "But after what I've heard about Jack, I guess that's all you know now." Megan leaned towards Dylan and whispered. "I expected more from you, but I guess I was wrong. I hate you."

Dylan curled further into Jack as a new cut opened on her thigh and the car door slammed shut.

"Just hold on," Jack's voice pleaded. "Go, Vi. Get us out of here."

"Tell me something," she whispered as Vi pulled out into traffic.

The jolt of the car speeding away shot pain through her body and forced her to stop speaking until she could control the urge to scream. Slowly she cleared her throat and tried again.

"Can you tell me a truth, Jack?"

Jack bent closer, but his words were lost as she faded out of consciousness.

Chapter 16

She had no idea how she ended up in Vi's apartment. She was slumped in a chair, a towel pressed her stomach; another one wrapped around her leg. Still groggy, she tried to stand and help Vi get Jack into the apartment only to fall off the chair.

"Stay," Vi demanded after she forced her back into her seat.

She couldn't do anything but comply; the pain was mixing with increasing weakness as time passed.

Vi grabbed her dissimulator out of her pocket and ran it over her leg. Dylan's momentary relief was minimized by the pain in her stomach. Across the table, Jack was hunched forward, unable to sit up straight.

"Heal him first." She pushed Vi away. Jack shook his head. "Jack, let her heal you."

Vi slapped his hand away and grabbed his face forcing him to look at her. "She's right. Two of us can heal her more quickly that just one."

Vi stripped off his shirt and cringed, seeing the cut on his stomach had grown and a bruise ran up into his ribs. His muscles relaxed as Vi extracted the pain. Finally, Jack raised his head and held Dylan's gaze.

With a small nod of his head, Vi stopped. Jack walked over and held Dylan's hand. She could hardly see him as her vision shifted in and out of focus.

"Stay with me." He squeezed her hand harder.

Tears freely flowed down her face. "I should have told Megan sooner. I should have told her that first night." She looked on as Vi resumed her work on Jack. "She is so mad. She's not going to forgive me."

"She may." Vi tried to sound reassuring.

She shook her head and cringed as the muscles in her stomach contracted. "I don't think so."

"That's better." Jack nodded to Vi. Carefully, he picked Dylan up, carried into the living room and set her down on the floor, slowly straightening her out as she groaned with the pain. "It's easier to see the entire wound if you're straight." She could hear her pain reflected in his voice. "Just hold my hand, we'll help you." Jack watched her teeth chatter. "Grab a blanket, Vi."

Vi ran out of the room and returned with a blanket and scissors. "I'm sorry, Dylan, but we have to get your shirt off to see how much damage there is."

She shook her head. "You can't cut it." She wrapped her arms across chest. Vi nodded as she and Jack carefully pulled her running jersey over her head.

She wrapped her arms back around her chest, thankful that she had a sports bra on and not some flimsy little thing like the one Jack had seen in her bedroom.

"I'll grab another towel," Jack said awkwardly as he stood, not quite sure where he should look.

Dylan reached out for him, but Vi took her hand. "Just hang in there."

"Vi, it hurts."

"I know, but I will not let you leave him now. You just have to hang on."

She tried to focus on Vi's face. "Maybe it would be better if I—"

Vi shook her head. "Didn't you hear what he said in the car?"

She focused on Vi's face. Confusion clouded her pain.

"You didn't hear what he said, did you?"

"What did he say?" Her voice was barely above a whisper.

"It's his truth." Vi blew out a long breath. "Geez. You're both ridiculous. You're holding things inside that need to be said. These doubts aren't helping anything. They make other people's lies more painful. Hiding things makes this"—Vi waved a hand across her stomach—"much more serious."

Dylan shook her head as Jack came back into the room. She

bit down on her lip when he gently washed the blood from her skin. Dylan needed to focus on something and knew what she wanted to hear. "Tell me, Vi."

"Tell you what?"

"Tell me how you got those scars?"

Vi and Jack looked at each other for a moment. She felt the pain begin to recede as both their dissimulators ran along her stomach. She stared up at the ceiling. Vi sighed before beginning her story.

"I'd been a Fide for less than a year when it happened. It was during the time when my best friend had started spreading rumors about me. I told you about that before." Dylan nodded that she remembered and held on to her voice as she felt the dissimulators slide across her skin. She tried not to think about the fact that they were still working on her. "I had wanted to go into elementary education in college, so, after school, I worked at a day care. I love kids.

"One day, a little girl named Suzie started attending the day care. She was really shy and didn't talk to many people. I gave her a little space and waited. She watched me play with the other kids, and slowly joined our group." Vi paused. "I can still remember the way she would smile and laugh when someone would throw the ball to her on the playground, or share their snack with her.

"I started noticing that she had bruises on her arms. She tried to hide them, but it was the end of May and the weather was unusually warm, so she pushed up her sleeves. I asked her how she got them." Vi moved her dissimulator to Dylan's thigh. "Dylan, she looked me square in the face and told me she fell off a chair. I knew she was lying before I felt the cut open up just above my elbow." Vi pointed to a scar. "I told her to be more careful and gave her a hug before I went to get a Band-Aid for my arm.

"A week later, she had a new bruise. Again I asked. She told me she got that one when she tripped over a neighbor's dog. A new cut opened immediately. I talked with the owners of the day care. People were sent to her home, but nothing ever happened. She would show up with a new bruise and a new lie.

"All through the summer, she lied. On top of that, this was also the time when my best friend, Melanie, was lying about me. The cuts snaked up my arm and over my shoulder. I knew I needed to hear the truth from both of them and my mentor was getting worried. We even cornered Suzie and tried to beg her to tell us the truth. I will never forget the look she gave me. She was begging me not to ask her, but I knew I needed to hear the truth as much as she had to reveal it.

"I held her as she cried, but when she spoke, it was another lie. That night, when I looked at the cuts, I saw they were getting really close to my chest, and the bruises around the cuts were already wrapping around my body. We were both running out of time."

Vi took a moment to calm herself. "My mentor tried every-thing to help me. She was ready to have me medicated or committed, afraid that if something didn't change, I would have..." Her voice faded away as she shivered.

Dylan didn't need her to finish the sentence to know where it was going. Finally able to move, she tried to sit up but Jack held a hand on her shoulder to keep her down.

"The next day, the bruises were worse. That night, I followed her home and waited. After dinner, she came outside to play and I went over and talked to her. She finally told me the truth. Her mother was beating her whenever she got drunk. I held her and I cried for the little girl who was so strong and brave. I told her we needed to go to the police. I believed that they would help her. I told her that tomorrow when I got to the day care, we would go to the police together. She smiled at me, and I knew for the first time she truly had hope."

Silence filled the room. Jack held Dylan's hand, but she stared at Vi, who was looking off into the distance. Dylan took Vi's hand and waited.

"But we never got the chance to go. The next day, the police came to the day care. Suzie had been found dead in her bedroom. Her mother, again drunk, had heard Suzie talking to a doll and smothered her in a rage to get her to stop."

"I'd been only hours away from death myself. If Suzie had died without revealing the truth, I would have died that night. You can't live with that many unanswered lies." Vi paused and let the words sink in. "I didn't care. The pain continued to grow with every rumor Mel said, but it kept me connected to Suzie. My mentor saw me dying in front of her. She saved me, because I couldn't save myself. She forced the truth from Mel about a week later. I remember crying because I no longer felt the pain, and all I wanted to do was die like Suzie had. The next week my parents transferred me to a different school."

"Since then, I find the truths to avenge Suzie, and help others accept what they would rather not."

"Thank you for telling me," Dylan whispered as she forced herself to sit up and hug Vi. "You're right. Life's too short not to tell the truth." She felt Vi nod against her shoulder.

Chapter 17

Dylan's bruise faded back below her ribs. The wound was still red, but it was no longer bleeding. Jack forced a smile and draped the blanket over her shoulders before he wrapped his arms around her.

She tried to make her voice sound light but it sounded weak. "So Megan's dad is still lying to us."

Jack didn't respond. The silence stretched out around them before he finally cleared his throat. "Rest for a few minutes then Vi can get you cleaned up."

There was something hidden in Jack's voice, but she tried to ignore it. She rested her head on Jack's shoulder. In turn, he rested his head on hers and they sank back into silence, broken only by the sound of ice clinking into glasses in the kitchen.

"Do we need to call your parents and tell them where you are? I'd rather you weren't alone tonight," Vi called from the kitchen.

"I'll text my mom in a few minutes. I'd rather I wasn't alone right now too," she called back as she brought her hand out from under the blanket and grabbed Jack's hand, holding it tightly. "Thank you, Jack."

He shook his head. "There's nothing to thank me for." Jack removed his hand from hers, got up and walked away from her.

She sat, stunned, as Jack walked into another room and closed the door. She looked at Vi. "What did I do?"

Vi sat down next to her and handed her a drink. "Jack is like a leaf floating down a stream. It looks like a peaceful ride. But when it rains, watch out."

"I think I saw a flash of that once, when we met Jimmy's girlfriend."

Vi shook her head. "All you've seen is a pebble hit the water. Right now, I think he's afraid the rain is coming, and he won't be able to stop it, or save you."

She took a sip of her drink and thought about it. "It's a cruel fate to give the job of a Fide to a teenager."

"Don't I know it." Vi drank for a moment. "But think about it, Dylan. Who else would be able to see the lies as clearly?"

"I want to talk to him."

"Let's get you cleaned up first."

She let Vi help her to her feet. She could feel the soreness in her muscles, but the pain she had felt earlier was gone. "We don't have much time, do we?"

Vi shook her head. "I've never seen a lie only partially heal a Fide before. We're in new territory here, D. And no, I don't think you guys have a lot of time left."

Dylan rolled the elastic on the shorts Vi had given her. She felt better having showered and washed all the blood away. She stood in front of a closed door, hesitant to knock on it. Vi motioned for her to open the door before she rounded the corner and walked into the kitchen.

All she wanted was to talk to him, but he was hiding. She wasn't going to let him do that anymore. She didn't knock. Slowly she opened the door.

The only light was from a few candles burning on the dresser. Music floated quietly from the iPod on the nightstand. She took a deep breath and closed the door behind her, waited for her eyes to adjust. Jack stood on the far side of the room looking out the window. He had put a clean shirt on, but she could still see blood on his arms in the candle light.

"For someone who has been a pain in my ass since I met you, you're pretty quick to retreat into a hole when things get hard."

He tensed slightly at her voice, but he didn't otherwise acknowledge her presence.

Nothing in the room looked like it belonged to Vi. The rest of the apartment had been bright and colorful. This room, even in the dim light, was not. Pictures were hung in all the other rooms. There weren't any in here. Dylan looked over and saw the closet was littered with guys clothes.

"Do you live here?"

Jack didn't look at her when he answered, but the eerie calmness had returned to his voice. "No. This is just a spare room after her boyfriend moved out. Sometimes I crash here."

"Are you going to tell me what happened out there?"

He didn't answer.

"Or what you said in the car?" Vi had warned her that Jack would try to push her away. "It's not fair to say things when I can't remember hearing them."

Dylan slowly walked over to him, placing her hands on his back, feeling the muscles tighten under her touch. She pushed harder; refusing to let him shun her so easily and felt the moment he shifted and leaned back into her. She wrapped her arms around him. Jack took her hands and held them and she interlaced her fingers with his. His fingers tightened around hers as though he were trying to say something. She rested her head against his shoulder blade.

She waited for him to speak, but somewhere inside knew he wouldn't. They stood there, listening as cars passed by and songs faded from one to the next. He would squeeze her hand, take a deep breath, or rock on his feet, but still no words were spoken.

Finally, she backed away. Jack inhaled a staggered breath, but she forced herself to walk away from him. Her hand was on the doorknob.

"Don't go." She turned as Jack moved away from the window. "Please don't leave."

Her pulse quickened as she took Jack's hand and he pulled her into his arms.

"There are things I want to tell you, but I don't know how. I—" Jack looked up as the door cracked open. "Go away," he shot at Vi.

"Um, Dylan, it's your brother."

She blinked and looked around as Vi turned on the light. It took her a moment to realize Vi was holding her phone.

Taking a deep breath, she tried to even out her breathing. Before she even brought the phone all the way to her ear, she could hear sobbing.

"Tony?"

"Dylan? When are you coming home?"

"What happened?" Jack hurried straight over. She tried to push him away but he pulled her close and listened.

Her brother sniffled, and clearly, in the background, her parents shouted louder and more forcefully than before. Jack squeezed her in support.

"Hang on one second, Tony." She tilted her head to look at Jack. "Can we go get him? I have to get him out of there."

"You guys are still too weak." Vi walked further into the room. "I'll go get him. Tell him to leave and I'll meet him out front in five minutes."

She nodded and watched Vi leave, hearing the front door shut behind her.

"Tony?"

"Dylan, please come home."

"Tony I'm sending someone to come get you. Her name is Vi. Get your bag and throw your school stuff and some clothes in it. Make sure they're clean. If you want, bring your laptop and a game, but you have to do this quickly and quietly."

"Why can't you come?"

"I'm hurt, Tony. I can't go anywhere tonight. But Vi will bring you here. She is a very good friend. Don't be scared. She is already on her way."

She listened to the frantic movements as Tony raced around his room and stuffed items into the bag. She closed her eyes trying to tune out the screams that filled the background. Eventually, she heard Tony slowly, carefully zipping the bag closed. She waited for him to speak again already knowing what he was going to say.

"I'm afraid to go downstairs," he whispered.

She fought to control her voice. "You know which stairs are noisy and how to walk past them. Just be quiet and go outside. Vi will wait for you right in front of the house. Keep the phone with you."

She swayed as Jack pulled her onto his lap and sat with him on the bed.

"She'll be waiting for me?"

"Yes, Tony, then you can come here with me and Jack."

"Jack's there?" She smiled when Tony's voice rose slightly. She placed the phone on speaker so Jack could talk to Tony.

"I'm here, buddy. Just do what your sister said. Walk quietly down stairs and Vi will be there in just a few minutes."

"I'm scared, Jack."

"Be brave, like your sister." Jack kissed her lightly on the cheek.

Tony took a deep breath. The floor squeaked softly as he started down the stairs.

"Take your time, Tony," she whispered.

She could hear his ragged breathing as well as his sigh when his foot hit the hardwood floor at the end of the stairs.

"Now stay quiet and sneak into the living room."

"They're in the living room." Tony's voice was a frantic squeak.

"Go through the kitchen and out the back door then walk around the house."

Jack grabbed his phone out of his pocket when it chirped. "Vi's there, waiting for you, Tony. Just take your time."

Dylan dug her nails into Jack's arm as they listened to Tony's slow progression and the screaming still coming from her parents. She held her breath when the door creaked open.

"I'm outside," Tony whispered. They could hear his feet

shuffle through the dead grass and leaves. "I see a car. There's someone standing outside the car."

"She has long blond hair, right, Tony?"

"Uh huh."

"Tony?" she heard Vi ask through the phone.

"That's Vi, Tony." She sighed finally hearing Vi's voice. "Can you give her the phone?"

"I've got him," Vi said as she shut a car door before opening and shutting another one.

She relaxed her grip on Jack's arm. "Thanks, Vi. I have to call Jimmy and tell him what happened."

"Okay. We're going to make a quick stop to get some food and then we'll be home."

"Pizza!" Tony yelled through the phone.

Dylan, Jack and Vi laughed.

"I guess we're having pizza," Vi said. "Call your brother quick so he doesn't think I'm some kind of kidnapper."

"I'm on it. Thanks. And Vi? I don't know how Jimmy will take this. Tell Tony to stay in the car just in case."

"Got it." Vi clicked the phone shut.

She looked at Jack for a moment, neither of them willing to say what they were both thinking. Taking a deep breath, she dialed Jimmy's number.

Chapter 18

"You did what?"

She cringed away from the phone as Jimmy yelled.

"You should have heard them Jimmy. It was worse than ever. They're back to their old routine, and Tony called me. You should have heard him."

"Why didn't you go get him?"

"I got hurt earlier. And besides," she added quickly trying to defuse her brother, who would not be happy to hear she was hurt, "I don't have a car. And I couldn't walk there."

"What the hell is going on tonight? And why didn't you call me?"

She shook her head. "Apparently some fun Lord family disaster has swept into town. It happened at the cross-country meet, but I'm feeling a little better." She chose her words carefully. "I'm sorry, Jimmy. I wasn't thinking. Anyway, I just wanted to tell you in case Mom calls looking for him. I doubt she will. I could hear them screaming at each other with Tony in his room." The silence stretched further than Dylan wanted." It was bad, Jimmy. If she calls just tell her Tony is with me, okay?"

Jimmy sighed. "Yeah okay."

"Thanks." She ended the call.

Her hands shook. Jack grabbed and held them steady.

She cringed when she felt the cut on her leg begin to throb a little. She let out a deep breath and walked into the living room, quickly cleaning up the bloody towels and her clothes. She threw them in the bathroom hamper, not wanting Tony to see what probably looked like some scene from a horror movie. She scanned the room then walked over to the window, watching people.

She flinched slightly when Jack touched the back of her neck, but she didn't turn.

"It's not supposed to be like this," he whispered in her ear as he moved closer.

"What isn't? A life of a Fide? Based on the little bit of information you've given me, I sort of had a feeling it would be exactly like this, though I'll admit I was hoping for a little more time to adjust before someone tried to kill me."

"No," Jack breathed.

She could tell he wanted to say something more, but stopped. He took a step back. The hairs on her neck stood on end, aware that Jack was scrutinizing her.

"Tell me what you're thinking about, Dylan."

"There are too many things running through my mind, I can't focus on them clearly."

"You're going to have to try, because I'm not letting you go for a run right now."

Jack's steady breathing calmed her nerves.

"I'm worried about my parents. Something has to be done before one of them…" Her voice trailed away as she shivered and shook her head. "I'm afraid what it will do to Tony. He shouldn't have to hear that."

"Neither should you," Jack whispered.

"I'm upset at the way you reacted earlier. I don't understand what happened or why you walked away from me." She turned and looked at Jack, braver now that she had started. "Plus you hid things from me. You know how much I care about Megan and her parents, and you knew something wasn't right and yet you didn't tell me."

"Dylan…"

She shook her head; the sound of people walking up the stairs made her stop. She took a deep breath, desperate to compose herself.

"You need to get cleaned up." She took a step away from Jack, seeing the blood dried across his shirt and jeans. "Don't let Tony see you like this."

Jack headed for the bathroom. "We'll talk later," he said before shutting the bathroom door, "I promise."

She rubbed her eyes forcing the tears back, as Tony walked through the door. He dropped his bag, and ran over. Having Tony safe calmed her slightly; she nodded as Vi put the pizza on the table.

"Jimmy didn't even recognize me," Vi commented as she walked into the kitchen and grabbed plates and glasses.

"Yeah, he's not too happy with me right now." She turned Tony and marched him towards the food.

She cringed when she saw the blood on one of the chairs and pushed Tony past it to a different one.

Vi shook her head. "Don't worry. We'll clean up everything later."

Tony didn't waste any time. A plate had barely been placed in front of him before he dived into the box and grabbed the largest slice. They exchanged looks as Tony devoured his dinner.

"Whassack?" Tony asked his mouth full of pizza.

Dylan and Vi a stared at him and tried to figure out what he said. He swallowed and spoke again.

"Where's Jack?"

"Right here, buddy," Jack replied as he opened the bathroom door wearing a clean shirt and jeans. Jack brushed his hand along Dylan's shoulders as he walked around and sat next to Tony. "How you doing?" he asked Tony.

Tony shoved another bite into his mouth and nodded.

"You need to eat, too." Vi forced a slice at her.

Her stomach rumbled. Vi walked over and turned on some music, allowing the noise to drown out the silence that momentarily engulfed the room.

"Music?"

"Safer than TV." Vi shrugged. "Too many liars there."

They ate in silence. Dylan sent a text to her mom letting her know where Tony was and that she would take him to school in the morning. She sent another to Megan to apologize. She didn't get a response from either.

An hour later, Tony fell asleep on the couch. Jack picked him up, carried him into the spare bedroom, and closed the door.

She shook her head and looked around the apartment. "He'll probably freak in the morning when he can't figure out where he is."

"We'll be here." Vi nodded.

"You guys shouldn't have to deal with this." She looked at Jack for a moment before turning to Vi. "Thanks for letting him come here."

Vi didn't answer and went into the kitchen to clean up. Dylan followed, having grabbed the plates off the table. Vi yanked the plates from her hands. "Go talk to him."

"Why is it you're always pushing me to talk to Jack?"

"Because you're too stubborn to do it on your own." Vi spun her around and shoved her back into the living room.

She looked over her shoulder as Vi crossed her arms. She knew Vi would wait for her to move before she went back to cleaning. She walked slowly into the living room.

"I was dating someone when I became a Fide. Did you know that?" Jack said as he looked out the window.

She felt her heart skip a beat and bit back the question she really wanted to ask. She sighed and remembered what Megan had said about him dating someone in their grade. She tried to figure out who it was.

"How would I know that? I only just found out you existed a few weeks ago."

The corner of his mouth twitched. "I thought I really liked her, but we broke up when I didn't tell her why I was always hanging out with Vi and where I'd disappear to some days.

"After that I stopped looking at people. I didn't want to take a chance of being hurt because I had to lie to someone I liked, or hurting someone I liked because I wasn't around when they wanted me." Jack finally looked at her. "And then I saw you."

She reached out for Jack's hand, but stopped as he brought his hands up and cupped her face. "You were right before. I was pushing you away. I didn't want to see you in any more pain, knowing that there was nothing I could do to stop it."

"There is a way to stop it." Her voice was just above a whisper.

Jack shook his head. "Even if we find Mr. Lewis and get the lie, the rest of the lie, even if we convince Megan to hear the truth, even if we protect Tony... Don't you see? There will always be another lie; there will always be something else waiting to hurt you."

She sighed. "And that means there will always be something waiting to hurt you." She hugged herself to keep from trembling.

"That's not true," Vi chimed in. "What hurts you will not always hurt Jack."

"What do you mean?" Dylan stepped involuntarily towards Vi.

"Vi." Jack spoke quietly but sternly.

Vi ignored him as she walked into the living room. "I am Jack's mentor, right?" Dylan nodded her head as Vi lifted her shirt. "If I felt what he felt, and he felt your pain, then I should have a wound too, but I don't."

She heard Jack say something, but she wasn't listening. Jack reached out for her but she brushed his hand away. She walked across the room and look at Vi's stomach, seeing there wasn't a scratch on her.

The sound of a door opening didn't fully register to her as Vi smoothed her shirt back over her stomach.

"How, Vi?" Dylan whispered. "How..." but her words wouldn't come as a new voice broke her stream of thought.

"What are you guys doing?" Tony rubbed his eyes as he walked into the living room.

She turned towards Tony and quickly collected her thoughts.

"What's the matter?"

Tony yawned. "I couldn't sleep."

Vi laughed. "It looks like you were sleeping pretty soundly."

"Let's see if we can get you back to sleep." Jack walked over and took Tony's shoulder. "I think Vi needs to talk to your sister." Jack paused and looked back at Dylan for a moment before he went with Tony back into the bedroom.

She stared after them for a moment before she looked back to Vi. She felt weak as she stood there; the exhaustion from the day numbed her.

Vi walked her to the couch.

"I will tell you." Vi looked at her. "But right now you really need to sleep and give your body a little time to heal on its own. And I want both Jack and I to tell you."

She sank into the couch feeling the tiredness wash over her. "Tomorrow?"

Vi threw the blanket over her shoulders and nodded. "Tomorrow."

Her eyes closed as Vi flipped off the light and walked towards her own bedroom. She sank into a sleep on the promise of answers in the morning.

Chapter 19

Dylan woke to the feel of someone running fingers through her hair. She groaned and pulled the covers further up around her shoulders.

"Go away, Mom," she mumbled as she turned on the couch.

Her eyes snapped open when she heard Vi chuckle. Disoriented, she fell off the couch and gasped, fighting to unravel the blanket from around her, but the more she struggled, the tighter the blanked clung to her. She whipped it off and threw it, covering Jack in a heap.

"Hey!" He laughed as he removed it from his head.

She turned towards Jack's voice and saw the sun streaming in high through the window.

"We were afraid you wouldn't wake up until tomorrow." Vi smiled.

She turned around and fished through the couch cushions finally finding her phone and checked the time. "Eleven thirty! Oh my God Tony!" she squealed, rushing over and throwing open the door to the spare bedroom.

She paused and looked at the unmade bed. "Tony?" she walked further into the room.

"He's at school," Vi called. She turned and stared at her. "I took him there this morning. Coffee?"

"Thank you," she said when she finally gulped the hot coffee, feeling it burn as it went down. She stood for a moment and stared at Vi. "How was he?"

"He seemed pretty happy to spend time with Vi, actually." Jack came up behind her shoving his hands in his pockets.

"And I'm going to pick him up at the end of the day so he can come here and hang out with you until you go home." Vi took another sip from her mug.

Dylan nodded and stretched, feeling the muscles on her

stomach strain with the movement.

Vi nodded towards the bathroom. "Take your time. I put clean clothes in there. We'll wait here until you come back."

She looked over at Jack. He nodded before she took her mug and headed into the bathroom. She let the water wash over her aching muscles as she thought about everything that had happened last night, from the pain of Mr. Lewis's lie and Megan's hatred, to Tony, to Jack. She felt her muscles tense and she suppressed the urge to run away. She leaned against the wall under the water.

She had to handle all of it, somehow.

Shutting off the water, Dylan stepped out and stared at her reflection until the steam began to clear from the mirror. She took several deep breaths.

Vi and Jack talked softly through the closed door, tension clear in Jack's voice and nonchalance in Vi's. She blocked them out and willed herself to stay.

"Vi." Jack's voice floated in through the crack in the bathroom door. Dylan paused in opening the door, hearing the edge of panic as he spoke. "I think this is more than like."

Vi chuckled. "Then do something about it rather than worrying about seeing her in pain all the time." Vi snorted. "It took you long enough to admit that. Now, make sure you tell her."

"I already tried."

"What happened in the car doesn't count and we both know that."

Silence filled the apartment.

"And don't you dare use that word again unless you know it's the truth. You both have too much at stake to joke about that."

Dylan opened the door and walked into the kitchen trying to look as if she hadn't just heard the end of the conversation. She knew she failed miserably and hid her face in the dregs at the bottom of her mug. She refilled her mug before joining them at the table.

She took another long drink as she prepared herself to hear this. "Okay, Vi," she said, still grasping her mug to steady her hands. "Tell me."

She heard Jack groan but didn't look at him.

Vi sighed before she began. "Right now, Jack's your mentor." Dylan nodded. "He found you the way I found him."

She paused. "I don't completely understand how that works."

"We find each other because there is a pull between us, sort of a need to be around another Fide. You haven't experienced that yet because you are still learning to control yourself, but once you do, you will start to notice that certain people attract your attention more than others, either because they compel you to be around them, or repel you, for example if a Feeder is near." Vi took a drink. "But I'm getting off point here. With a new Fide, the pull is stronger. For Jack, who was to be your mentor, the pull, the connection between you is strongest because you are just starting out. I don't know how mentors are chosen. My mentor thought proximity has something to do with it. Regardless, your futures are connected right now. And they will be, until you get your own dissimulator. After you get the dissimulator, your connection with your mentor breaks, but you will become aware of the other pulls around you."

She nodded; a frown crept across her face. Was it really that easy? All she had to do was get a glowing piece of glass and she and Jack wouldn't be connected anymore?

"Are you listening, Dylan?" Vi's smooth voice broke through her thoughts.

"No, sorry. I was thinking." She took a deep breath. "Okay, so…is there a store or some place I get one?" Jack's chair scraped against the floor as he pushed away from the table and walked into the living room. "It's not that I want to lose the connection," she added as an afterthought as she watched Jack walk away.

"Your job is separate from everything else." Vi's voice filled with annoyance. "We told you that already." Vi leaned closer and spoke again. "He cares about you."

She stared into her coffee, wishing it would tell her the truth as easily as Vi just had. She wished life was that simple. She liked him. He liked her. She shook her head. "Okay, so where do I get one?"

"You can't just go to a store a buy one. You have to wait until the PTB decide you're ready."

"PTB. Who are they?"

Vi shrugged. "I honestly don't know. My mentor always just called them the Powers That Be. I'm not sure if they are real, but one day, when they feel you're ready, you'll get your dissimulator."

"How? When?"

"It just appears. Mine was in my shoe one morning. Jack said his was…"

"Never mind that," Jack called from the living room. Dylan could hear a slight tinge of embarrassment in his voice.

"Let's just say some things are better left to the imagination." Vi laughed. "And everyone is different. You have to prove to the PTB that you are ready and can do the job that has been assigned to you."

"And then like that? No more pain from people's lies?"

"Not exactly, Dylan. If we lie to each other, we will still cause the other person pain. That is why you get a mentor first. To learn to tell the truth so you don't hurt yourself or another Fide. As you have already witnessed, there are enough people ready to hurt us. We can't go around hurting each other too." She waited as Vi took another drink from her mug. "But yes, once you have your dissimulator, your connection with Jack will end. Just like his with me did and mine with my mentor."

"Then what? Is your mentor still around?"

Vi shook her head. "She's moved on."

"Then why are you still here? Why do you help Jack?"

Vi looked into the living room for a moment before she spoke. "It's hard to handle this and life and school. I got my dissimulator the beginning of my senior year, and I remember trying to face my senior year alone. I stay to help."

"And that's allowed?"

Vi shrugged. "No one's come to tell me it's not."

She hoped Jack would stay after she got her dissimulator.

"Wait. How many Fides are out there?"

"I only know of my mentor, Jack and you. It's not like we have a fan club or Facebook page. My mentor mentioned others she knew, but I've never met them. And I only know about that pull towards other Fides because I can feel it around you."

"You said your mentor was older, would she know more about this? Do you still talk to her?" She watched Vi's face fall. She didn't need Vi to speak to know the answer. "She died didn't she? When you said she moved on..."

Vi nodded as she got up and walked into the kitchen. Dylan ran her finger along the rim of her mug as she thought.

Jack walked in. "Vi's mentor was twenty-seven when she died trying to save a lawyer."

"When did it happen?" Dylan whispered as she glanced towards Vi who was standing by the sink.

"A little over a year ago. Just before I got my dissimulator." Jack spoke softly. "They had stayed in contact even though her mentor had moved to a new town after Vi had gotten her own dissimulator."

She looked at Jack for a minute as she processed all the information. "You don't think..." She hesitated. "...that there is a limit to how many Fides there can be? Like since you were becoming one, another had to pass?"

Jack shrugged. "I've wondered about that," Jack said even more quietly. "But I'm really hoping that's not the case."

She looked at her mug trying desperately to hold it together. "Because if it is, Vi could be next."

"Wait. Why didn't your mentor just use the dissimulator?" she asked turning towards Vi, but Jack answered her as he put his hands in his pockets.

"They aren't designed to hold every lie. You have to be careful how often you use it. You only get one, and it can only hold so many lies." The truth dawned on Dylan; Vi nodded in agreement. "If you use it too much, eventually it will turn from clear to gray and finally to black. It will reach of point where it won't be able to hold any more lies. It will crack and stop working. Then you'll be unable to heal yourself as you try to help other people. You will also get all of the lies that had been trapped back."

Her head snapped towards Jack. "Show me your dissimulator."

Jack shook his head.

"Show her, Jack." Vi stood next him. "She needs to see."

Jack bowed his head and pulled it out of his pocket. Instead of being clear, she saw a thick layer of dark gray clouding the glass.

She tipped her chair over as she stood. "So you are using your dissimulator to heal me, the entire time knowing that it is taking you that much closer to not being able to heal yourself."

Jack sighed and nodded his head. She felt the blood drain from her face, turned and walked into the bedroom, taking several deep breaths as she went. She was losing it; she could feel everything inside her begin to snap. Shaking her head, she decided she would not let them use it on her anymore. She would not let them risk their lives to try to help her. That was all there was to it. Slumping down on the bed, she tried to count the number of times in the past few weeks Jack had used his dissimulator to heal her.

She remembered that time outside Baby Bruno's when Jack had touched her with the dissimulator and given her back the lies she was carrying.

Jack walked into the room and closed the door.

"Why didn't you tell me sooner?" Her voice sounded dead to

her.

Jack tried to shrug but stopped. "The glass will clear as we hear each truth. We just have to get the truth for each lie we've heard." He sat carefully onto the bed next to her.

As the silence grew, Jack fidgeted next to her. She could carry the lies. She could hold them until she heard the truth.

"You need to give me back the lies, Jack. You need to give me back the ones you took from me."

"That's not going to happen," Jack didn't hesitate to respond.

"I can't let you carry my lies for me. You need to save the space to use for yourself."

"I can't let you carry your lies. I can't see you in pain."

She shook her head. "But if your dissimulator—"

"It won't." Jack cut her off. "I know what you're thinking, but it won't break. We will figure this out before it gets that bad."

"It's already gotten bad," she lashed out before she could stop herself. She studied Jack for a moment before speaking again. "How can you know your dissimulator won't break?"

"You, Vi and I are too stubborn to let it happen any other way. We will get the answers we need. You need to have faith in us."

She looked out the window. A cloud floated in front of the sun. Focusing on that cloud, she willed her own flight reflex to calm. They remained silent for several minutes as she struggled to relax.

Finally, she nodded. "You're right. I may not like it, but I can have faith in you."

Jack smiled and took her hand. "It's about time you agreed with me."

"Yeah, well don't get used to it." She nudged his shoulder and yawned.

Chapter 20

She heard a light knock at the door. Jack slept peacefully so she carefully inched off the bed, and followed Vi into the living room, a grin spread across her face.

"Having fun?" Vi's eyebrow went up as she spoke.

She shook her head and sat on the couch.

"I don't want to know."

"Nothing happened."

"If you say so." Vi shrugged. "I'm going to get Tony from school."

She tensed for a moment, not realizing it was already three. "Thank you so much for helping us." Vi hesitated. "But we have to do something about it." She stood slowly as her muscles ached. "I'll go with you, and take Tony straight home."

Vi shook her head. "I agree with Jack. I don't think that's a good idea."

"I can't just hide from my problems, Vi."

"But you can't face them alone, either." Vi grabbed her keys. "Stay here, and think about it. Come up with a plan. Obviously yelling at your parents didn't work."

She bit her lip, running through several options. "I'll call Jimmy and see if he has any ideas."

"That's a start. We'll be back in a bit," Vi said, and shut the door.

Dylan grabbed a mug of coffee from the kitchen and called Jimmy. He had a few ideas, but he wasn't sure if any of them would work. He agreed that something had to be fixed before it got worse. If last night was any indication, it was going to get worse, and neither of them wanted Tony anywhere near it when it did.

She grabbed a refill after she hung up with Jimmy and checked the phone for messages, hoping that Megan had sent her one when she had seen Dylan wasn't at school, but there weren't any. There wasn't even one from her mother.

She looked up when she heard the bedroom open. Jack walked out as he put on a clean shirt.

"You left me."

Dylan shook her head. "Vi needed to tell me that she was going to get Tony, and I didn't want to wake you. You looked like you could use a little more sleep."

Jack shook his head and yawned.

"You need to sleep more, and trust that I can take care of myself for a few hours." She smirked at him. "Faith works both ways, Jack. If you expect me to have faith in you, you need to have it in me." She waited for him to nod before she continued. "So, later tonight, Tony and I are going to talk to Jimmy. We're gonna come up with some plan to help our parents."

Jack sat on the couch. "That sounds like a good idea."

"Will you come with me?"

Jack smiled at her. "I was already coming whether you asked me or not."

She felt a real laugh bubble up inside her for the first time in days.

"What about you, Jack?" She sank into a chair across from the couch. "What about your family?"

Jack's face fell. "Mom left when I was ten. She lives out in Colorado somewhere with her yoga instructor."

She fidgeted uncomfortably, not sure what to say. Finally, she cleared her throat. "And your dad?"

"He drives a truck so I'm basically on my own most of the time. He stops in from time to time, but..."

"Does the school know?"

"He answers every call, and shows up for every meeting." Jack shook his head. "He's probably gotten another call since I skipped today."

"Does he get mad?"

"He says as long as I keep my grades up and I graduate, he doesn't care what I do. So since I met Vi I've been jumping back and forth between here and home." He took a sip of coffee. "Being here doesn't make me feel as alone. And Vi feels the same. We've become a family," he finished quietly. "We look out for each other."

"I wish my family was like that," she mumbled as she walked over and stared out the window.

"It looks like you and your brothers do," Jack said as he dug his phone out of his pocket when it started to beep.

Dylan didn't turn back to look at him. She knew Jack was right, but Jimmy and Tony didn't replace parents who cared, like Megan's parents.

"Text message from Vi," Jack said, tapping on the screen.

Jack went into the kitchen as he dialed the phone. She couldn't make out what he was saying, but saw his jaw clench and a vein pop out in his neck. She walked towards him, but he shook his head, making her pause.

"What is it, Jack?" she took another step towards him.

"Give me your phone, Dylan," he said calmly.

"Why?"

Jack took a deep breath. "Please just give me your phone." His voice hitched a bit as he spoke.

Jack flipped through her contacts and rattled off a few numbers. She knew them immediately. He walked over and unlocked the door.

"Why does she want Jimmy's number?"

Jack dropped both phones on the table and stepped towards her.

"And Megan's number? Why does she need that one?" She involuntarily tensed and stepped back. "Jack, tell me what's going on."

"You just can't catch a break," he whispered more to himself than to her. He finally looked at her. She could see he was struggling to control his emotions. "You need to sit down first, Dylan."

"No."

Jack walked towards her slowly, barely managing to keep his voice calm. "You told me that when I had to tell you something important to tell you, to make sure you were seated before I spoke. Do you remember asking me that?"

She replied weakly. "Even if it means holding me down."

Jack grabbed her and together they spun around until she was sitting on his lap on the couch.

The air caught in her throat as she tried to speak. "You're scaring me, Jack. Please just tell me what happened." She gasped as a thought dawned on her. "Did something happen to Tony?"

Jack shook his head and tightened his grip as he squirmed. "He's fine. He's with Vi. She has to get a few things before she comes back with him."

"Get a few things? From where?"

Jack didn't answer. He held her to him as she struggled to get up. She could hear him murmuring things, but couldn't make out what he was saying.

"Jack, please just tell me." She dug her nails into the back on Jack's arm. "Isn't this the opposite of trust and faith? Weren't we just talking about that?"

"I will always tell you the truth, but I can't tell you this one."

He buried his head in her neck as she continued to plead with him to speak. She fought to free herself, but Jack just held her tightly to him and continued to murmur things she couldn't quite catch.

She stared at the clock, feeling herself shatter with each second that passed. She fought to free herself, feeling the pain in her arms from being held so tightly. Feet pounded up the stairs and Megan flew into the apartment. Megan's eyes were rimmed red and her mascara was smeared down her face. Dylan tried to get up, but Jack held her tightly in place. Megan ran over and hugged her around Jack's hands. She watched Noah walk slowly into the apartment as Megan released her.

"I am so sorry. I don't hate you. I love you. You're my best friend."

She felt her eyes sting as the throb in her leg died. She struggled to hold back the tears she didn't know why she wanted to shed.

Megan looked at Jack, still holding Dylan tightly. "You didn't tell her?"

Jack shook his head. "She needs to hear it from someone she has known for a long time and trusts completely."

"Jack, I trust you." She tried to turn in his lap. Her heart raced as panic kicked in as she looked from Jack to Megan. "What happened? Someone needs to tell me." She choked on the words.

Megan sat next to them on the couch. "I'm glad you weren't home last night, and that you were able to get Tony out of the house."

She struggled to hear Megan. "What happened?" Her voice was a whisper.

Megan looked at Jack. Dylan felt him nod, but she didn't look away from Megan.

"Dylan"—Megan took a ragged breath—"your mother was found this morning in your living room." Her ears rang as Megan's voice began to fade away. "She's dead."

Chapter 21

The words sank in and washed over her. Megan couldn't be telling the truth. Noah leaned against the wall. Dylan locked eyes with him. She shook her head and tried to clear her thoughts. Her mother couldn't be dead. She floated to the floor with both Megan and Jack still holding her.

They were wrong.

That's all there was to it. It was someone else. There was no way her mother was dead.

Her parents had fought for years, but it had never become physically violent. Maybe it was a heart attack, or she slipped and fell. She slowly shook her head back and forth. Megan was still speaking as tears streamed down her face, but Dylan couldn't hear it. She knew Jack was still holding her, but she couldn't feel it. She tried to think, but was trapped in her own mind.

"You know she's telling you the truth," Jack whispered. "You can feel it."

Putting her hands over her ears, she refused to believe it. It had to be a trick. She had met people who were really good liars, and there were Feeders out there. There were ways to beat her.

She tried to wiggle out of Jack's grasp, but he held her firmly against his chest. She scratched her nails down his arms, feeling the skin break as she went, but he didn't move. He wouldn't let her go. Megan and Noah turned their attention towards the door. Dylan followed her gaze as Tony walked in. Behind him, Vi carried several bags and dropped them in the doorway.

She pushed away from Jack, who finally released her, and ran to Tony. She could see the same shock registering across his face. He cried and wrapped his arms around her.

"Maybe if I'd stayed there..." Tony sobbed, but she buried his head in her shirt and refused to hear any more.

It had been a thought that had been crashing around her mind since Megan first spoke, and she would not let her little brother blame himself. She felt a light touch on her back, but ignored it. She heard more feet running up the stairs and looked up to see Jimmy and Rachel trip over the bags still in the doorway. Jimmy wrapped his arms around Dylan, smothering Tony in the process.

"It's not true." She pulled back and looked at Jimmy. "It's not true."

"It is. The cops called right after I hung up with you. They didn't find her until this afternoon when her coworkers called the cops and insisted they go check on her because Mom was never late for work." Jimmy rubbed his eyes. "Rachel and I just came from the morgue." His voice faltered. "I had to identify her body."

She could hear the truth. Their mother was dead.

She swayed for a moment, and again felt the hand at her back to steady her, ready to catch her. Jimmy knelt down and hugged Tony. Rachel placed her hand on Jimmy's shoulder. Vi moved some of the bags out of the doorway so she could close the door.

Dylan sighed. She rocked back again, and felt Jack's hand stop her. She looked over as Noah nodded at her knowingly while he hugged Megan. She looked over at Tony, still wrapped in Jimmy's arms. Tears welled up in her eyes as she felt Jack's hand placed protectively on her lower back. Biting back a noise trying to escape from her throat, she leaned forwards a bit further and he took a step back for balance.

"Don't do it," Jack whispered as he grabbed her shirt. "I know what you're thinking but right now isn't the time."

Her shoulders slumped in defeat. She waited for Jack to lighten his grip and looked over to Noah one more time. She saw him grin and nod.

With a slight bow of her head, she ran.

Jack yelled down the steps after her, and Tony cried in the kitchen. The cold November air hit her face when she threw open the door. People shouted behind her, but she didn't stop. She didn't care she was only wearing a shirt and an old pair of shorts. She didn't care that she didn't have shoes on. She ran, feeling the broken glass and stones cut her feet, but she didn't slow.

Tears stung her eyes as a harsh wind blew, but she bowed her head and kept running. Only when she reached her house did she slow. The police were still there. Tape stretched across her yard. Neighbors called her name. A cop looked up from what he was writing and began walking towards her. She took a step back, turned, and again was running. The cop shouted after her, but she didn't stop.

She ran to the bank and threw open the door, expecting to see her mother smile at her from behind the counter. All she saw were red-rimmed eyes. Someone grabbed her arm but she yanked it back as she walked to the counter.

"Where's my mom?" she asked Lydia, a woman who had worked with her mother for years.

Lydia broke into tears and tried to reach over and hold her hand. She shook her head and headed back towards the door. People pleaded with her to stay, but she wouldn't.

The cold numbed her as she ran. She passed Baby Bruno's. Bruno was behind the counter. He met her gaze through the glass and was around the counter coming to her. She shook her head. She couldn't hear him call her name as the wind whipped past her ears.

Dylan didn't know how, but she slowed to a walk when she passed the gazebo. The cold consumed her, but she didn't shiver as she walked towards the swing set. She brought her foot up, placed it on her lap, and pulled a stone and a piece of glass out, before putting it back on the ground to rub against the frozen dirt.

She didn't hug herself for warmth. She rested her head against the metal chain that held the swing and thought.

It was all her fault. She should have gone home last night. If she had, her mother wouldn't be dead.

"You're probably right." An older man stood in front of her.

She cringed back in the swing, wary at how easily he crept up on her.

The old man smiled and repeated his statement. "You're right."

"What do you mean?" Her teeth chattered, though she didn't pay attention to how cold she was.

The man smiled and a fog swirled in her head. "If you had been home last night, your mother would be alive right now."

Dylan shook her head. "You don't know that...how could you know that?"

"You don't know it's not true." The man cocked his head.

They stared at each other for a moment. Out of the corner of her eye, someone else approached. Dylan turned as Noah walked up and nodded to the old man.

"And that's not the only thing we're right about." Noah smirked.

"What?"

Noah's smile grew into a sneer. "Jack."

The old man clicked his tongue. "You think he cares about you."

She tried to doubt the pity in the old man's voice. She turned towards Noah for support. "You know he cares about me." She heard the unsteadiness of her voice.

Noah looked at her. "You're a job, something he is forced to do."

She shook her head repeatedly, trying to remove their words. The vile way they spoke caused goose bumps to crawl over her skin. She was not just something to be bought, used, and then discarded. "You're wrong." She wouldn't look at the old man. "You have to be," she said more quietly, almost pleadingly.

Noah and the older man shrugged before they walked away. Their words played continually until she was ready to admit they were right.

The light by the swing clicked on, but she didn't immediately register that she had been there long enough for darkness to fall. She couldn't feel her feet, her hands or her nose anymore. The wind rustled the leaves and the sky darkened as the first drops of wet snow fell.

She didn't move. She didn't care. She hadn't stopped the yelling. Her mother was dead. Her father was... Dylan shook her head, trying to remember if Megan had mentioned her father.

Two people walked towards her. She wondered if Noah and the old man were back to tell her she was wrong again. She tried to get up, but couldn't. She didn't want to hear that man again, didn't want to know anymore. The cold had taken her further than she thought it would, and now she couldn't move.

Jack moved out of the shadows. His mouth moved, but she couldn't hear what he was saying. Megan carried something, and although she was still crying, looked relieved to see her.

Dylan flinched back from the heat of Jack's hand. He knelt down in front of her and pushed her wet hair back behind her ear. She stared past him as he placed his hands on her face and forced her to look at him.

Her body sagged as she released the swing.

He shivered when her cold skin brushed against his.

Jack spoke to Megan. "We need to get her out of here."

Megan helped Jack wrap a blanket around her. Megan held it tight while Jack picked her up and carried her out of the snow. She was unable to help or resist.

Had it only been a few days ago that everything in her life made sense?

Dylan had a family. She had after school pizza rituals. She had running. Right now, she had nothing.

"We found her," Megan said. "We're bringing her back now. She's going to need a hot shower, some warm clothes and lots of blankets."

She stared through Megan as she spoke. She heard the words, but couldn't understand who Megan was talking about. Megan walked around and got in the driver's side of the car as Jack held Dylan and climbed into the back. His warm breath caressed her cheek as he rubbed his arms up and down the blanket.

"Just be careful with Vi's car or she'll kill us."

Megan pulled in a deep breath as she sped away from the sidewalk, popped a u-turn in the middle of the busy street and flew back to Vi's apartment. Dylan tried to shake her head. She had to be dreaming. Megan didn't have her license. None of this made any sense.

And then several hands pulled her from the car. In the apartment, she was passed over to Vi, Rachel and Megan who stripped her and held her in the shower, watching her skin go from a pale blue to pink as the water heated her slowly. She shivered. That small action brought a smile to Vi's face.

"Can you hear me?" Vi asked quietly.

Nodding almost toppled her. She grabbed Vi's arm for balance.

"Why did you do that?" Megan's voice came from behind her.

She tried to turn, but her feet were still frozen. Six strong arms grabbed her before she fell. Tears fell down her cheeks as she tried to speak, but the words were stuck somewhere inside her. Megan's arms wrapped around her and both girls cried with the shower pouring over them.

Chapter 22

Dylan panted in the heat of the blankets and the arms that were holding her firmly on the couch. Light streamed in and the murmur of voices carried softly from the kitchen table. A finger lightly brushed along her cheek and she turned in its direction.

"What were you thinking?"

It took her several moments to respond. "I just needed to get away." Her voice a hoarse whisper.

"That's not good enough, Dylan. You weren't just trying to get away." Dylan stared past Jack not ready to answer him. He brought her face back and made her look at him. "Why?"

She didn't want to answer but she knew she had to. "I needed to see for myself. I wanted to see her, but the cops were there—"

He cut her off. "We know." He took a deep breath and closed his eyes. Anger radiated off him. "An officer told us when we got there. Then a lady, who worked with your mom, called Jimmy when you left the bank. Then Bruno called. We were searching for you, with no idea where you would go next. Do you realize it was only by luck that Megan thought to check the park?"

If they had called Noah, they would have known. She shook her head, knowing that someone had found her a long time before Jack had.

She shivered. "I just needed to time to think."

Jack pulled his arm away from the blanket the shoved it in front of her face. Blood trickled down his arm. An identical cut on her own arm opened.

"When are you going to stop lying to me, Dylan?" She bowed her head as he continued to speak. "We both know you weren't there just to think." Jack walked into the kitchen.

Jack threw his jacket on and slammed the door behind him. She worked to control the tears she knew were coming. Was Jack right? She shook her head. She hadn't wanted to kill herself. She had just wanted to understand, she had wanted to know what it felt like to be cold, and alone, as her mother had been. Did that mean she wanted to die? Maybe things would have been easier that way.

A chair scraped across the floor and she cringed. Someone was walking towards her, but she kept her head down. She didn't want to face more of what she had seen in Jack's eyes. She wondered if it would have been better if they hadn't found her. She sighed as someone carefully sank onto the couch next to her. If she really was thinking that, Jack had been right.

"That's not true," a quiet voice to spoke to her. She looked over at Rachel, not sure what she meant. "I can see what you're thinking." She started to speak but Rachel just shook her head. "Now you need to listen to me. Everyone in here cares about you."

"Sorry," she whispered.

Rachel shook her head. "That isn't good enough. Your mother is gone. And you felt like it would be a good idea to go for a run in freezing weather. Did you even think what that would have done to Jimmy or Tony if you hadn't been found?" Dylan cringed. "What about Megan, Noah, and Vi?" She felt a shiver pass along her spine. "And what about Jack?"

She took a ragged breath and shook her head. Over at the table Megan sat on Noah's lap. She shivered, remembering the old man in the park but held on to the fact that the old man wasn't alone. Noah had been with him. He whispered to Megan before kissing her on the head and walking out the door.

"I know how you feel. It's how I felt when I watched two men kill my parents." Dylan stared at Rachel who looked back towards the kitchen. "I told Jimmy. Not the whole truth, but enough that he knows why I wasn't honest with him." Rachel nodded to herself. "Your brothers need you right now. You have to pull it together."

Rachel walked away as tears rolled down Dylan's cheeks. She

wiped them away with the sweatshirt she was wearing and pulled the blankets up around her shoulders, sinking further into the couch.

People were still talking, but she wasn't concentrating. All she could think about was how quickly everything had changed. The lie still etched on her stomach began to sting. She took a few deep breaths and steadied her heartbeat. She didn't know how she could do all this and not implode with the force of her pain, and now she had one more thing she needed to do. Questions rolled through her mind, jumbling her thoughts. One kept creeping back regardless of the direction of her thoughts: Could she beat a Feeder?

She heard the door open again, and bags land on the table, but she didn't look up. Through the window as the first rays of light lit the town, and snow stuck to the glass for a moment before it melted. How she wished she was one of those snowflakes. Wished that when things got too close, she could melt away. But melting away wouldn't help anyone right now, except for herself, and Jack was right. She was stronger than that.

Another sting radiated through her stomach, but she ignored it and sat up as Jimmy and Jack walked towards her.

"It's my fault." She shivered and looked at Jimmy. "If I had gone..."

Jimmy put his hand over her mouth and refused to take it away. She shook Jimmy's hand away from her mouth.

"If you had gone home, Tony would have been in that house when Mom died."

"If I was home, it wouldn't have happened."

"You don't know that."

"You don't know it wouldn't have," she replied to Jack before she looked back at Jimmy. Dylan tried to shuffle through her own thoughts and compare them to what that old man had said in the park. "Was it Dad?"

He nodded. "They believe so, but the cops haven't found him

yet."

Jimmy knew what she was thinking without her saying a word. "You can't see him, Dylan."

"Why not?"

"Because if he lies to you about this..." Jack worked at keeping his voice level but stopped speaking. Jimmy nodded in agreement. Jack followed Dylan's gaze. "They know, Dylan. Vi and I told them."

Vi cocked her head to the side as she took in Dylan's gaze. She could see Jack narrow his gaze at her from beside her.

"What do you know?" Jack asked.

She looked around at her family and friends. "What about Tony?"

"I know, too." Tony walked out of Vi's room and over to his sister.

She listened to the blare of the TV carry from Vi's bedroom before looking at Jimmy. "What do we do now?"

"We'll figure it out." He ran a hand through his hair.

"And we'll help you." Rachel put her hand on Dylan's shoulder. "You won't go through this alone."

The sting that had earlier risen in her stomach began to radiate and she sucked in a deep breath. She closed her eyes and forced her face to remain calm in spite of the pain she felt climbing through her ribs. Wrapping her arms around her stomach, she waited for Jimmy to walk into the kitchen with Tony.

"I thought we couldn't tell them," she whispered, knowing Jack would hear.

He sighed. "It would be better if we didn't, but with everything going on, it's safer if they know." Jack slid off the couch and knelt in front of her.

"What did you tell them?"

"Just enough, about you being a new Fide."

"Did you tell all of them? Like all all?"

Jack repeated his question from earlier. "What do you know?"

She tried to sit up as another shot of pain flashed through her side. "I know who the Feeders are." Jack whistled, grabbing Vi's attention. Dylan waited for her to walk into the living room. "I've met two of them," she said in a quick whisper when Vi was close. "They came to pay me a visit in the park earlier, though I didn't realize one of them was a Feeder, even though I guess I should have because he has played havoc with my thoughts a few times before."

"You aren't making sense." Vi raised a hand.

She stopped babbling and focused. "They've been messing with my mind, making me second guess things that were already hard for me to deal with. Such as liking you, Jack, or at least I think they were. I see how easily they can manipulate the truth." She looked at him. "They make it so easy to believe what they want you to."

"What did they say last night?"

She blew out a deep breath. "It's weird. I know I talked to them, but it feels like my own thoughts, not a conversation I had with other people."

"That's their specialty." Vi nodded. "But now think, what did they say?"

She was quiet for a moment, closed her eyes and thought about last night. "First, that it was my fault that my mom is dead."

"But it's not," Jack cut in.

"Part of me knows, but part of me believes them. I can't make sense of it." She opened her eyes and looked at him. "And it was something I had already thought, and something Tony repeated as his fault as well."

"What else?" Vi asked, getting her to focus.

Dylan looked from Vi to Jack. "That Jack doesn't care about me. That I'm a nuisance and he's only here because he has to be my mentor."

She dropped her head and listened to both Vi and Jack deny

it.

"Look," she huffed, getting annoyed. "I know it's not true, but both things they said had already been in my head, so it was easy for them to make me believe they *were* true. I know you both have tried to convince me again and again about…things." She stumbled and refused to looked at Jack. "But you have to see how hard all this is."

Vi took her hand and smiled. "You'll figure it out."

Stunned, she stared at Vi. "That's it? I'll figure it out?"

Jack carefully wrapped an arm around her. "You're telling the truth. You'll figure everything else out as you go."

"So who were they?" Vi said after a minute of silence.

"I don't know who the old man is. I've never seen him before." She hesitated and tried to focus. "It was dark. I know he was bald and wearing black, but beyond that, I'm not sure I could describe him. I was a little less than coherent. But I know the other one. And so do you." She watched Vi and Jack exchange a look, and she nodded along with what she saw pass between them. "And based on that look, I would bet you both already know who it is too."

"Noah."

She nodded at Jack. "He was in the park long before you and Megan were. So he knew where I was and didn't call you guys to help." She paused for a moment. "He also showed up there the night I yelled at my parents. Does he want me dead?"

"Apparently," Vi said quietly.

The apartment was eerily silent for a moment. "Does he know you know?" Jack finally asked as Vi paced around the couch.

She looked at him. "Does he know I know I'm a Fide?"

"No," Vi said quietly. "We told them all individually. Only your brothers, Megan and Rachel know."

She sighed quietly, happy for a little break of luck.

"Does he know you know he's a Feeder?" Jack asked quietly.

She shook her head. "I honestly don't know." She giggled.

"Honestly…that's funny."

Jack and Vi shot each other glances as she continued to chuckle.

"Okay," Vi said, drawing the word out on a long breath, "someone apparently needs to eat and get more sleep."

"Oh, come on, that was funny! I'm just being honest with you!" She chuckled for a moment before her laughter died.

"You okay?" Vi reached out and touched her.

She shook her head. Jack grabbed her, pulled her off the couch and held her. She felt the tears coming. Tony laughed in the kitchen as someone got him breakfast.

"I don't want to cry where Tony can see me," she cried into Jack's neck.

"Just hang on." Vi walked them into the spare room.

She waited until Vi shut the door and left them standing in silence.

"Jack, I know you feel it too. He's lying again." She paused. "And I'm not trying to say this to make you angry even though I'm pretty sure you will be, but right now I really don't care."

Jack grabbed her face as she sat on the edge of the bed. "I am upset that you would think that, but I am also relieved that you are finally telling me the truth." They stared at each other for a moment.

"Why didn't you tell me about Noah?"

Jack wiped a tear from her face. "I wanted to be sure."

She crawled further onto the bed as the tears came. She worked to keep quiet, but it wasn't working. Jack turned on the radio and turned the volume up.

"You're stronger than this," he whispered as he reached out and tentatively stroked her hair.

The door opened and she bit back a stronger retort. "It doesn't feel like it."

"Get her to eat this," Vi said. It wasn't a request.

Jack placed the food on the dresser, came and wrapped his

arms around her, and let her cry through the pain and loss.

"What am I going to do, Jack?" she squeezed him tightly.

He spoke calmly. "You're going to eat and rest. Then we're going to get to the bottom of Mr. Lewis's lie, and then deal with the Feeders."

She choked on a sob. "You make it sound so easy."

Chapter 23

Dylan didn't sleep when the tears stopped. She let the pain spread as the late afternoon sun broke through the clouds. She rested her head on Jack's chest and found comfort in the fact that he was there.

"Are you awake?" Megan's voice was soft as she walked into the room.

Dylan sat up as Megan walked around and sat next to her. They stared at each other for several minutes, neither one quite sure what to say. Megan clicked her tongue and looked over at the plate of uneaten food.

"Vi said you really need to eat something."

She pretended she didn't hear.

"I tried," Jack said quietly.

Megan sighed. "Vi also said you needed to get your strength up."

Dylan fought the urge to say she didn't care. She knew it was a lie before Jack squeezed her hand. She did care, and clenched her teeth as a new wave of pain swept through her.

"Let me see." Megan flipped on a light next to the bed.

Dylan wrapped her arms around her stomach.

"I want to see what my father's doing to you."

"Why?"

"Because I have to." Megan slowly raised Dylan's sweatshirt and T-shirt.

Jack leaned into her. "Let her see," he whispered. "We may need her help."

Megan gasped at the long cut that stretched across Dylan's stomach. She saw the bruise that spread cross her skin and had begun snaking its way over her rib area. Megan watched as blood oozed from the wound and slid slowly towards her pants. Megan fought for composure and finally looked into her eyes.

"We're going tomorrow to get the truth."

Dylan shook her head. "I don't know if I can face another lie."

"Oh, he won't lie," Megan said.

"You don't know that," she pleaded with Megan. "Just give me a few days. I don't know how to do this yet."

Megan shook her head, "You don't have a few days."

"You've done it a few times already," Jack said quietly into her neck.

She turned her head towards Jack. "You're not helping, and this one's different."

"How?" Megan beat Jack to the question.

"It's your dad."

"And?" Megan and Jack asked simultaneously.

She sat forward, wrapped her arms back around her stomach and stared past Megan. "I was lying to Jack and Vi without even realizing it. When I heard the lie on the street the other night, it wasn't a big deal. He was just some jerk from school. And I thought Rachel was hiding something from my brother, so I was determined to find out. As a matter of fact, it was Jack who heard that truth. Not me.

"But this is your dad," she pleaded. "I'm afraid of what he may say."

Megan nodded. "So am I, but you don't have the time to wait and worry about the 'what if's.'"

She started to speak but Megan cut her off.

"We aren't going to fight about this. We aren't going to debate the pros and cons. We are going to do this so at least some of your pain is gone." Jack chuckled behind her and she ground her teeth together. Megan stood. "Now, I'm going to get you something to eat, and you will eat it, or I'll have Jack here"—she pointed at Jack, as if Dylan wasn't already keenly aware of him—"hold you down, something I'm sure he is just waiting to do anyway. And I'll force it down your throat."

She didn't speak when Megan left. She snapped her jaw shut

and felt Jack quietly laugh behind her. Absently, she pulled at a loose thread on the blanket.

Finally she couldn't help herself. "I'm not ready for this, Jack." She felt the panic rising. "For any of this."

Jack didn't respond and Dylan's panic threatened to overwhelm her. "What if I can't do it?"

Jack shrugged. "You don't seem like the kind to give up before you even try."

She played with the loose thread wrapped around her finger. Knowing he was right, she glanced up, stared into his eyes, sighed, and looked back at the blanket.

"No." She knew she sounded defeated. "I just run when it gets too bad."

Jack leaned forward, wrapped a hand around her neck and tilted her face up towards his, but his response was cut off as Megan walked in.

"Okay behave, you two." Megan balanced a bowl of soup, a sandwich and a cup of coffee as she set them down on the bed. "Now, will you eat or is Jack going to get to have a little fun?"

She looked at Jack. The smirk that slid across his lips told her he was daring her to resist. Megan crossed her arms.

"Okay." Dylan raised her hands in defeat as the smell of the food hit her and her stomach growled. She gathered her legs under her and took a sip of the coffee.

Megan smiled. "That's better." She walked towards the door. "Oh and Jack…" She turned and looked back into the room. "I'm sure you'll get your chance before long."

Jack laughed even as Dylan spat her coffee. "Was that one of those staged things like you and Vi pulled on me a few times?"

He grabbed the coffee from her and took a sip. "Nope."

Snatching the mug back, she shook her head, feeling the blood rush to her cheeks. "I'm not ready for that either."

He brushed his knuckles along her cheek and waited until she looked up at him. "I will never make you do anything until you're ready."

"You didn't give me a chance when you talked about being a Fide."

He waited for her to look up at him. "That was different and we both know it."

Shrugging, she took a bite of the sandwich and washed it down with the soup. She placed the food down.

"I'm scared."

He only nodded his head. "We'll get through this together. But I need you to stop running and talk to me."

She heard the concern and urgency in his voice, bit her lip and thought about it. "I can't stop running."

"I'm not talking about exercise."

"I'm not good at this. I don't have much to give. But I will try and talk to you before I fly out of a room." She studied his reaction. "It's the best I can do, Jack."

Jack reached out and tucked a strand of hair behind her ear. "Then it's the best I can ask for."

There was something lurking in his eyes, but shook her head, refusing to ask. Picking up her sandwich, she ate in silence.

With the food gone, she felt a little better. Her wound still throbbed but at least now, she didn't feel weak. She slid off the bed, taking the empty plate, bowl, and mug with her. Jack followed behind her. Vi slept on the couch. Tony played a video game on the TV. Megan, Jimmy and Rachel sat at the table.

Neither she nor Jimmy knew what would happen. Best case, since Jimmy was of age, was that he would be their guardian. She didn't want Jimmy to drop out of college to take care of her or Tony. Whether their father was guilty or not, they didn't want to go back there and were momentarily glad that Vi had been able to get a bag of clothes for each of them the night before.

Slowly, the group dispersed. Megan went home and Tony was finally coaxed to bed. Jimmy and Rachel joined Tony in the spare room as Dylan finished washing the cups and plates from the day. Jack watched her, but eventually he turned and headed into the living room.

Dylan stood at the kitchen window long after the plates had been dried and watched the stars shimmer in the night sky. She wrapped her arms around herself and let the wishes she had been holding out.

Vi walked into the kitchen. "I put a pillow and a blanket back on the couch for you. I hope that will be okay." Vi stopped when she saw the look on her face. "What's the matter?" Vi stepped closer and leaned against the counter next.

Dylan continued to look out the window and watched another star appear in the sky. "I heard you and Jack talking this morning." From the corner of her eye, she saw Vi nod. "I only heard a little at the end of the conversation." Biting her lip, she waited for Vi to understand she hadn't been intentionally listening in. "Was he serious?"

"He's always serious."

Dylan rolled her eyes. "About liking me?"

"You really haven't noticed?" She finally turned her gaze as Vi let out a little laugh. "That boy is in serious like with you." Vi paused. "And I wouldn't be surprised to see it's more than that."

Dylan turned away. "I don't know what to do about it."

"This is one of those times I can't help you. If it had to do with being a Fide we'd be golden and I would know how to help you. But this"—Vi shook her head—"only you and Jack can figure it out." Vi cocked her head. "Do you like him?"

She felt a shiver pass through her. "Yeah, I do." She frowned. "But he hasn't done anything."

"He's done exactly what you needed." Vi's stare had her blushing even though nothing had happened between them. "He's doing what he thinks will help most. And that isn't to be a boyfriend, at least not yet. It is just to be *that* friend that you can depend on." Vi smiled for a moment. "You are going through an insane amount of stuff in a small period of time, Dylan. And right now Jack is struggling because he is trying to be everything you need without making you uncomfortable or being pushy."

"That's too much pressure."

"It's his pressure and he can handle it. But sooner or later he will push." Vi shrugged. "Fair warning."

Vi squeezed her arm before heading to her own room.

Dylan looked back at the stars and watched them disappear behind and bank of clouds. Slowly, she clicked off the lights in the apartment as she made her way to the couch. She didn't think she would be able to relax, but the gentle rhythm of people breathing around her soon lulled her to sleep.

Sun streaking in through the window woke Dylan much sooner than she had expected. Her hand, which she had draped over the edge of the couch, entwined with Jack's and she wondered when that had happened. Looking down, she watched him sleep peacefully. She didn't move, instead soaked in the noises of the apartment. She could hear someone snoring from the spare bedroom. It seemed like days since anyone had gotten a decent night sleep.

She stretched carefully on the couch, not wanting to let go of Jack's hand, and could feel pain radiate through her stomach and sighed, knowing that if Megan had her way, today they would uncover the rest of the truth her father was afraid to admit.

Unable to deny it anymore, she slowly freed her hand from Jack's and made her way to the bathroom, then quietly, to the kitchen to make coffee. She grabbed the counter and stifled a groan as a new wave of pain swept through her. She knew she would suffer until this was resolved. And since she had to, she would do it as silently as possible.

There was no point in bringing her pain to the surface. She could bear this. If Vi had been able to shoulder the loss of that little girl, she could bear this. Breathing deeply she focused on the sound of the coffee hissing and sputtering as it filled the pot. She let her mind wander away from the pain to the things she needed to do.

She could hear others stir as the aroma filled the apartment. A spoon clanked onto the counter as she realized half the things she had wanted to do no longer existed. She wanted to talk to her mom about school, and about Jack. She took in a deep breath knowing she would never see her mom again, or that flash of recognition on those rare moments when her mom wasn't yelling. Those moments when her mom saw clearly what was happening around her daughter. She remembered the way her mom had smiled at her when she spoke easily with Jack. There had been that knowledge. Even before she had admitted it to herself, her mom had known she liked Jack. Now her mom would never see her run again, or help her pick out a dress for prom, or watch her graduate...

She drowned the emotions in the mug as she poured the coffee. She stared out the window that over looked the sink and watched cars roll by lazily. She hadn't heard him approach, but felt him lean against the counter next to her.

She focused outside as she spoke. "You're still supposed to be sleeping."

Out of the corner of her eye, she saw him shrug but he didn't speak. She didn't need to look over to know he was staring intently at her. Dylan locked her gaze on the window, and hoped Jack couldn't tell how she was feeling. She knew him. He would be that pain in the ass. He would be relentless until she spilled it out and let the pain wash over her. Hadn't she had enough already?

She heard him sigh, but she didn't inquire as to why.

The cup, half brought to her lips, fell suddenly from her hands and shattered against the counter, breaking and sending pieces everywhere. The coffee burnt everywhere it touched, dripping from the counter and splashing on her foot, but she didn't react. She watched in shock as the man walked slowly down the sidewalk, a hat pulled low over his head and a coat wrapped tightly around his body.

She didn't have to see his face to know his walk. She didn't have to hear his voice to know how it would sound. He stepped out of the shadow of a building, looked up into the sun, and for a moment, she wondered if her father was looking at her.

Jack tried to turn her but she wouldn't budge. He tried to make her speak, but she wouldn't. Her father took a deep breath and head further down the street.

Dylan yanked her arm away and headed towards the door before even she knew what she was doing. Spinning quickly, she knocked Jack over without even noticing he was there, marched into the living room, and grabbed her shoes and the first jacket she found.

"And where do you think you're going?" His voice was controlled.

She cocked her head to the side for a moment. "I figured it would be obvious with what I was wearing. I'm going out." She threw her hands on her hips to keep them from trembling.

"Why?" Jack drew out the word and watched her.

She would not lie to Jack. She remained silent and waited for him to move. He answered her silent protest.

"I'm not moving until you answer me."

Behind her, a door opened. She hoped it would be Jimmy. He would let her go. He would be able to keep Jack here as she raced down the street, but the voice she heard shattered her resolve.

"Where are you going?"

Tony rubbed sleep from his eyes, and stepped towards her. She forced her pulse to slow and looked at her brother, taking a deep breath. With a sigh, she took off the jacket and threw it on a chair.

"Nowhere."

Dylan went back into the kitchen grabbing a bowl and some cereal for Tony. Chairs scraped across the floor as both Tony and Jack sat. After plopping breakfast down for Tony, she returned to the kitchen and cleaned up the spilt coffee. Jack's eyes narrowed. It did not escape her notice that he sat away from the table, in a seat closest to the door.

She ran a hand through Tony's hair before heading for the bathroom. Turning on the cold water, she splashed some on her face taking deep, though not calming, breaths.

This was crazy. She shuddered and cursed herself. She didn't hear the door open, but she heard it shut and the lock click as she looked into the mirror and saw Jack.

"What is it with you and bathrooms?" She huffed as she splashed her face again before grabbing the towel from the rack beside her.

His eyes were still narrow. "Seems like the best place to talk to you without a chance that you'll escape." Tears stung her eyes and she fought them back. Jack stepped towards her and spun her around, forcing her to look at him. "You can't talk to your father, Dylan."

He took another step forward. His face was inches from hers as he waited for her to speak. She winced when a new strike of pain spread through her stomach. Jack didn't flinch. He waited for her speak.

"Let me out, Jack."

"Not until you stop running away from everything."

"If you will remember correctly, I was just heading towards something."

Jack grabbed her arms and shook her slightly. "I don't care how much pain you're in. I don't care if you won't admit it to yourself, but we aren't leaving this bathroom until you tell me the truth."

"I tell you the truth."

"When I force it out of you."

In the silence that followed the yelling, doors creaked opened and people stepped lightly past the closed bathroom door. A smirk spread across Jack's face and she watched him fall back into the calmness that made her stomach churn and heart leap.

"You are the most stubborn, strong-willed, temperamental, beautiful person I've ever known." He stepped closer and wrapped his arms around her. "But I won't let you see your father."

He released her and stepped towards the door.

A shaky whisper escaped when she reached for him. "Wait."

Jack offered a sad little smile. "I'll be right back. Stay here."

Chapter 24

Dylan's jaw clenched as she leaned against the sink. Jack spoke just beyond the door, and she was pretty sure he was holding the doorknob. She tested it, and was right. The doorknob turned back against her as she tried to open the door. Like a caged animal, she spun around in the small room, feeling the walls close in on her. She needed to get out. Jack was barely back inside before she spoke.

"Let me out, Jack."

"Nope."

The lock clicked as he looked at her. Everyone in the apartment moved around. The front door shut, and then there was silence. The walls seemed to collapse a little more around her.

Jack sat on the floor with his back to the door. "I'm not letting you out until you calm down."

A chill crawled up and down her spine at how calm Jack was. She slowly slid down the sink, letting go of the air trapped in her lungs. Dylan felt like he was a million miles away instead of a few feet.

"Can I ask you something without you getting mad?"

She huffed. "Probably not, but ask anyway."

"It didn't seem like you were that close to your mom." Jack hesitated. "What changed?"

"The old cliché is true. I guess I didn't realize what I had until it was gone." She stared at the pattern in the tile walls, picturing faces in them as she spoke. "I was thinking about her this morning. There were these times when she would flash a look and I would know."

"Know what?"

"That she knew me better than I knew myself." She struggled for control. "And now I'll never…" The words fell away and she shook her head. "She'll never..." She ran her hands over her face. "I just wanted to know why. And if he did it on purpose..."

Jack let out a deep breath. "When my mom left I wanted to know, too."

"Did you ever find out why?"

He shook his head.

"But he's out there and I have a chance to know the truth."

"If he lies to you." Jack leaned forward. "If he really intended to kill her but tells you it was an accident, on top of Mr. Lewis's lie, you will die. Not could, not might, but will. The body can only take so much. That would be the proverbial straw."

"He wouldn't lie," she insisted, shaking her head.

Jack stared into Dylan's eyes. "I'm not willing to risk your life on that." She looked away from the intensity of his stare. He waited for her to look back. "And you shouldn't either."

A tear rolled down her cheek, followed by another and another. "I just want to know," she murmured, and slumped back against the sink.

There was silence. Finally, she looked up to see Jack holding out his hand to her. She took it and allowed herself to be pulled into his arms. Resting her head on his chest, she didn't speak, but wrapped her arms around him and listened to his slow, steady breathing.

When she finally spoke, her voice felt small in comparison to the voice she heard radiate from herself earlier. "You told them what I saw, didn't you?"

Jack nodded. "They went to the police station to file a report."

"Why didn't they just call?"

"To give you time to cool off."

A new jolt of pain leached through her side. She shifted and looked up at Jack. "We have to go see Megan's dad today."

He nodded. "I know, but you won't be alone."

Dylan blinked several times. "I'm not sure what that means. I'm not used to not being alone."

"I know." Jack nodded as he leapt to his feet and helped her stand. He pulled her into a hug.

"Thanks, Jack."

When he spoke, there was again something more in his voice. "That's what I'm here for."

She turned the lock on the bathroom door. "No," she started, not brave enough to look at him as she spoke, "you're here for more than that."

They walked back into the kitchen and each grabbed a mug of coffee. She tapped the counter top as Jack stared intently at magnets on the fridge.

"Should we go back into the bathroom where we can talk?"

He forced a smile that quickly faded. She looked down and traced the rim of her mug.

A guy she wanted to be with was right there, and yet he felt miles away. She couldn't tell if it was her fault or his. Slowly she drank, afraid to move away from Jack. Just being near him was comforting. She heard him exhale loudly, but resisted the urge to look over at him.

If he wasn't willing to take the next step, then she wasn't going to do it.

Both turned as the others walked slowly back into the apartment. Tony ran and hugged Dylan. She looked up to see two cops enter the apartment behind Vi. Rachel grabbed Tony and took him into Vi's bedroom. Everyone else sat at the table. A wave of nausea swept over her.

"This will only take a few minutes." One pulled out a notepad and paper. "I'm Detective Larson and this is Officer Brown. We're heading the investigation into your mother's death. We are very sorry for your loss."

Jack grabbed her leg. She brought her hand down and held his hand for strength. Looking at the men who sat across from her, she nodded.

"We just have a few questions we weren't able to ask you

yesterday," Detective Larson continued. "Are you feeling better?"

She nodded again and tried to smile.

Officer Brown started. "Where were you Thursday afternoon?"

"I had a cross-country meet at school." She watched them scribble the information.

"And then?"

"I wasn't feeling well at the end of the race so my friend Vi brought me here. I stayed here with her and Jack." She looked over and watched Jack nod. She could see Jimmy squint across the table at her. She wouldn't lie to the detectives. She would just withhold anything that would turn her into either a crazy person or a toy.

"Then what happened," Larson chimed in.

She took a breath. "Tony called me. He was really upset and asked if I could come pick him up, but I still wasn't feeling well, so Vi went."

"And what time was that?"

She reached onto the table and grabbed her phone looking at the call log quickly. "He called me at 8:27."

Dylan told them about the yelling she could hear and the fear in her brother's voice. She also talked about how they had persuaded Tony to sneak out the back and how Vi had brought him back here.

"I couldn't leave him there. He was so scared."

Both men nodded as Detective Larson spoke. "It was probably the luckiest thing that neither of you were there."

She nodded but didn't agree, instead looked down at her phone, fighting to maintain her composure. "About an hour later I sent my mom a text to let her know I had Tony, but she never responded."

"How did he get to school yesterday?"

"I took him," Vi said calmly. "Dylan still wasn't feeling well so I woke him up and took him. We met when I picked him up as well."

Officer Brown nodded. "And this morning? What happened?"

She blew out a deep breath before looking to the two men. "I was standing over by the sink, looking out the window waiting for the coffee. I looked down and watched him walking down the sidewalk."

"By him," Detective Larson asked, "you mean—"

"My father." She cut him off. "I'd know that walk anywhere. But, as he reached the edge of the sidewalk, he looked up into the sun and I saw his face. There's no doubt in my mind it was him."

"What was he wearing?" Officer Brown asked.

She closed her eyes trying to recall the details. "He was wearing a longer khaki colored jacket and a ball cap."

"I know that jacket," Jimmy chimed in. "I bought it for him for Christmas. I don't think he'd ever worn it. It's been hanging in the hall closet."

Dylan watched the detective and officer jot down notes. She looked at Jimmy and could see her questions in his eyes as well.

"Did it hurt?" Dylan's voice didn't sound like hers as she asked the question.

"Tell us the truth," Jimmy interjected. "We don't want lies."

Detective Larson sighed and rubbed his forehead.

"We're still collecting evidence," the other jumped in.

The cops shot each other looks and fidgeted in the silence that surrounded the kitchen.

"Still collecting evidence?" Jimmy's voice was shaky.

Jack chimed in. "What evidence?"

"Finger prints and muddy footprints that don't match members of the family."

Larson placed his notepad in his jacket and cleared his throat. Both men headed for the door. The officer turned back and looked at Dylan.

"If you or your brothers think of anything else"—he walked back to the table and placed his business card in Jimmy's hand—

"don't hesitate to call us."

Jimmy nodded but no one else responded. She watched the door close behind them. Silence surrounded the kitchen.

"Does that mean..." Her voice sounded far away.

Vi nodded. And felt Jack squeeze her leg harder.

She pushed away from the table and walked into the living room. She paced by the window and let her mind wander. When had she begun believing her dad had killed her mother? It was an assumption, even though she knew they had never struck each other. Hadn't she said that? So what happened? What made her believe her dad was a killer? What made everyone believe her dad was a killer?

She swung around to stare at Vi and Jack who were still sitting at the table and watching her. Vi frowned solemnly. That small recognition almost broke her heart because in that frown, she knew what had happened.

It only took one word of confirmation whispered across Jack's lips. "Feeders."

"Is it safe?" Everyone looked over as Rachel peaked out of Vi's room, her question overlapped Jack's word. "Someone wants to play video games."

Rachel and Tony walked into the living room. Tony smiled and promptly plopped down in front of the TV to play his video games. Dylan smiled over at Vi, glad that Vi had been able to grab Tony's games when she stopped to get clothes for them from the house. The thought made her squirm. She walked over to Vi.

"Was there anything out of place when you went there Vi?" she whispered, shooting looks and Jimmy and Tony.

Vi shook her head. "A few plates were broken on the ground, but I didn't get to see much. After I flirted my way in, they actually shielded me from the living room so I couldn't see. Tony's room was a mess."

She snorted. "It always is."

"And your room was pretty clean. I'd never been there before so it's hard for me to tell if something was wrong."

She turned to Jimmy. "Could you and Rachel give us a few minutes?"

"If this is about Mom—" Jimmy started.

"I don't know what this is about," she interrupted. She looked towards Tony. "Just keep him in there for a few. Please?"

Jimmy walked into the living room.

She looked back to Jack. "Could they do that? Could they make all of us believe?"

"Oh that's just evil." Vi huffed and walked away.

Jack looked towards Jimmy. "We all knew your parents fought. It's not a huge leap to take verbal abuse to physical."

"But Dad never hit any of us."

"That should have been our first clue, but instead we all jumped to the conclusion that he murdered your mom," Jack said.

"Why?" she started, but stopped when she realized the truth. "Because someone wanted us to," she whispered. "Someone made us."

"It wasn't that hard of a leap given they were fighting earlier that night," Vi said.

Dylan shook her head unable to process this. "But why?"

"We don't know what this means." Vi shook her head. "It could still be your dad."

Jack muttered something about a wild goose chase before he cleared his throat. "Dylan, you need to go get ready. We have the other thing to take care of." He glanced at the clock. "And Megan expects us there in about an hour."

He was purposely changing the subject.

"Why can't you tell me what you're thinking?" Jack looked away from her. "Yet again, you're keeping something from me." With a long look at Vi she pushed away from the table, rattling coffee mugs and tipping chairs. "You want transparency, yet every time I get close to being able to do that, there's something else you aren't quite saying to me. And you wonder why things are so hard for me."

Hunching his shoulders, Jack wouldn't look at her. Feeling defeated, she went to get ready.

Chapter 25

Megan waited on the porch of her house. Dylan saw her own nervousness mirrored in the restless fidgeting of her best friend.

"He's inside," Megan said in a small, unnaturally quiet voice that didn't seem to belong to her.

Jack walked past with a stiff smile on his face, stopping when he realized both girls were frozen in place.

"We aren't going to get the truth out here."

She nodded but didn't step forward. A car, moving slower than normal, drove by. She forced herself to remain calm as she saw who was in the passenger seat. Taking a deep breath, she looked back at Jack who has still staring at her. He hadn't noticed the car.

"We need to hear the truth, very soon," he said softly, "preferably now."

She remembered the darker gray color Jack's dissimulator became after more of the lie had been leached from each of them before they left Vi's. There was still a dull throb, but the more acute stabs of pain were gone for the moment.

"I'm afraid, Jack." She walked towards him. "What if we can't get the truth?" It was at least the hundredth time she'd asked in the last hour. She continued in a panicked whisper, shooting Megan a glance. "What if Noah is in there?"

The muscles in Jack's jaw clenched. "Then you'll have to deal with Mr. Lewis while I keep Noah occupied."

"And what about Megan? We have to tell her about Noah."

"We will." Jack grabbed her face and forced her to look only at him. "Remember one obstacle at a time. You can do this. You know you can. You have to stop doubting everything and believe in yourself." He dropped his voice. "And believe in me."

She took a deep breath and Jack spun her around. Holding her by the shoulders, they marched towards the front door. She gasped when Mr. Lewis opened the door. Jack pushed her inside with Megan right behind him.

Mr. Lewis smiled at Dylan but she could tell it was forced. She worked hard to control the panic that ripped through her. His expression fell when he looked at her more closely.

"I am very sorry to hear about your mother. Megan told us. If there's anything we can do to help, just let us know."

She only nodded not trusting herself to speak.

Mr. Lewis hesitated for a moment. "I know this will sound silly, but are you okay?"

Dylan shook her head, but still didn't speak. That would inevitably lead to her asking a question, and she didn't want to hear another lie float carelessly from his mouth. She gasped when Mrs. Lewis grabbed her into a forceful hug. She hadn't seen Mrs. Lewis walk in just behind her husband.

Mr. Lewis twitched nervously as she stared him down. Trying, through sheer willpower alone, to get him to speak without having to demand the truth. She moved further into the house. Mrs. Lewis still had an arm wrapped protectively around her, as Jack and Megan closed the front door. Mrs. Lewis released her grasp and turned quickly into the kitchen to hide a sob. She followed Mrs. Lewis's escape, and saw Noah standing in the kitchen. Dylan narrowed her gaze and watched Noah smile stiffly.

Coughing uncomfortably, Mr. Lewis followed his wife, glancing back as he rounded the corner to see Dylan still staring at him.

Megan grabbed Dylan's arm and forced her up the stairs and into her room. Jack shadowed them up the stairs. Dylan took a deep breath and sank on the bed.

She could almost hear Megan roll her eyes as she plopped down on the bed next to her. Dylan looked at Jack and saw the vein in his neck throb. She held his gaze and watched his temper slowly fade.

Jack opened the door and waited, unceremoniously, for Megan to leave. "When are you going to stop and listen to me?" Jack spoke to the closed bedroom door.

"I heard every word." Her voice was cool and calculated.

"Damn it, Dylan, you have to listen to me." Dylan was caught by his quick turn towards her. "Mr. Lewis's lie is different and we both know that. You can't just stare him down and think that will solve anything! He's not some fucking kid who just stole money from his mommy's purse. Jeez!" Jack paused when both his and Dylan's phones began to ring at the same time. "This isn't the first time"—his voice was dangerously low and controlled—"that you and I have had to talk about trust and faith." She watched Jack dig out his phone. "Maybe I was wrong about this," he spat as he looked at his phone and not at Dylan.

Neither of them flinched when identical cuts opened on their forearms.

"You're not the only one," she whispered, not even trying to get her phone out of her pocket. "It's not just you who is realizing that something is wrong." Her phone stopped ringing when Jack answered his. She glanced at him. "And maybe, for once, it isn't just me."

She sat there and stared at her hands, feeling numb and guilty. Jack was angry and he had every reason to be. He was right. She didn't have the trust in him she needed to, the trust that he deserved, but she also knew he was keeping things from her. More confused than she was before, she tried to force the frustration to ebb.

Jack turned slightly away from her when he had answered the phone. Megan walked back into the room, but she continued to stare at Jack. His face paled and he closed his eyes. When he opened them, his expression change several times before he willed it back under his control.

"That was Jimmy on the phone." His voice was too calm.

She turned her head towards Megan, as Noah hesitated in the

doorway. Megan looked at Jack. He stepped towards Dylan and knelt in front of her, holding her hands tightly in his. She tried to squirm but was trapped on the bed with Jack holding her in place and Megan stationed right next to her.

She gulped loudly, and tried to speak but Jack silenced her with a look.

"Jimmy, Rachel and Tony went out while we came to talk to Mr. Lewis. Jimmy wanted to get Tony out of the apartment and try to get his mind off everything that happened."

Dylan glanced over at Noah but Jack quickly forced her attention back with a small noise from the back of his throat. Dylan gave herself the time to remember everything Jack and Vi had said. She had spoken with Jimmy before leaving for Megan's. Vi had gone shopping and was probably already back at her apartment. She shook her head and forced herself to remain in the moment. She looked back into Jack's eyes and silently pleaded with him to tell her what had happened, the anger and aggravation of a moment ago already buried beneath a new and growing terror.

With a staggered breath Jack spoke. "It's Tony." Dylan stopped breathing. "He ran away."

Chapter 26

Calm swept over Dylan. Jack's words echoed in her head and she waited for the panic to come. A new stab of pain radiated through her stomach. Mr. Lewis was lying right now.

Noah wrapped his arms around Megan. Slowly she stood and faced Noah. His concerned expression disappeared as Megan buried her head in his chest. He winked at Dylan, and nodded at Jack before he pulled Megan into the hall and shut the door.

Dylan listened to the door click. She took a deep breath and felt Jack take her hand but she was already moving forward.

"Please wait." The need in his voice made her turn back to him.

"I'm going, Jack," she said matter-of-factly. "You knew that before you even hung up the phone."

He nodded. "But we need to hear Mr. Lewis's lie first." Dylan started to speak but Jack put a finger to her lips and waited for her to stop. "I know you're going, and so am I, but we need to remove this lie." He pulled his dissimulator out of his pocket and brought it up to Dylan's eye level. The dark gray glass swirled in his fingers. "And now there's no doubt that Noah knows who we both are. We can't continue to hope for the best scenario here. We don't stand a chance against him or any other Feeder with all these lies hanging around us. We've waited too long to try and hear the truth as it is. We're out of time, in almost every respect possible."

Dylan shook Jack's hand away from her mouth and stood there. She knew he was right. Slowly he relaxed his stance.

"I know you won't listen, but when we're done here you can't come with me, Jack."

"The hell I can't."

Dylan gulped down the moan she felt rising in her throat.

Jack cupped her face and whispered. "I know what you're

thinking, Dylan." He brushed a tear away from her cheek. "We don't know where Tony is. Maybe he isn't with your father." She cocked her head. "We both jumped to that alternative pretty quickly. Isn't that a little odd to you?"

She grabbed Jack's hand still on her cheek.

"Did Noah do that?" Dylan watched Jack shrug. She rubbed her thumb across the back of his hand. "There's so much we don't know." Her voice was barely a whisper.

"There's so much we do," Jack replied. "Just focus on the truth, Dylan. Don't let Noah control you."

"What is the truth? I'm so confused..." She looked over as the bedroom door clicked open and watched Megan enter the bedroom.

She released Jack's hand. Jack lowered his hands and shoved them in his pockets.

"After this"—she lowered her eyes, indicating Mr. Lewis downstairs—"I will let you come—"

"I'm not asking for your permission." Jack grinned.

Dylan kept talking as if he hadn't spoken. "As long as you use your dissimulator on yourself first." She watched him shake his head.

They turned and looked at Megan. They stood silently and looked at each other.

"We will get to the bottom of your dad's issue first. That will heal the biggest lie we've been carrying." She felt Jack grab her hand tightly. "Then we'll find my brother."

She didn't wait for Megan to respond as she opened the door. She nodded at Noah as she passed him in the hallway. Dylan followed the voices and found Mr. and Mrs. Lewis sitting comfortably in the living room watching TV.

Mrs. Lewis looked up as everyone walked in. "Is everything okay? We heard a lot of noise up there."

"No, Mrs. Lewis," Jack said first. "Everything is not okay."

Megan and Noah came around the corner and looked at her

mother. "Can I talk to you for a minute in the kitchen?"

Dylan watched Mr. Lewis squirm as Mrs. Lewis stood and followed her daughter out of the living room. She followed Jack's lead and sat in front of Mr. Lewis, pulling a table over so she was eye level with him.

"What's going on, kids?" The nervousness in his voice gave her a little confidence.

Jack focused his attention on Noah. Taking a deep breath, Dylan nodded for him to leave and smiled as Jack easily maneuvered Noah through the living room by twisting one of his arms behind his back.

Megan and Mrs. Lewis's voices carried from the kitchen. The front door clicked shut and she watched some of the denial float out of Mr. Lewis's expression.

"The time before we were last here" — the words flowed out of her smoothly — "you said that you were fine." She paused for a moment and watched a bead of sweat form on his brow. "I know that was a lie."

Mr. Lewis shifted in his seat and looked over his shoulder for someone to help him. His breathing sped up slightly and he wheezed.

"I need to know what is really going on, Mr. Lewis." She spoke calmly but forcefully as Jack had with Rachel.

"How do you know something's wrong?"

She turned towards the kitchen and listened to pans clatter to the floor. "I know because of this." She pulled her sweater and T-shirt up. Mr. Lewis gasped as he looked at the gash and bruises that spread all the way around Dylan's torso, through her ribcage, and towards her throat.

"Your lie is killing me," she said quietly as Mr. Lewis stared at her.

"Impossible." He shook his head and looked towards the kitchen. "How?"

"Because" — she lowered her shirt — "I feel pain when people around me lie, or when people who have lied to me continue to lie."

"But everything's fine." He chuckled.

Dylan gasped as a new slash formed. She pulled off her bulky sweater and waited for blood to seep through the white shirt she was wearing. It left a jagged trail from her collarbone to her navel.

"Can't you see you're killing me?" There was fear in her voice.

She dropped to her knees and took Mr. Lewis's hands. "Please," she pleaded through the pain that spread closer to her heart, "please tell me what's wrong. Why are you lying?" He shook his head. "You have to let me help you." She forced the words out. "You've been like a father to me for so many years. Please. Let me help you now."

"If Joan knew…" Mr. Lewis's words were barely above a whisper when he finally spoke several minutes later. His eyes continued to watch the blood spread across Dylan's shirt and a new bruise begin to radiate out from her neck.

"Your wife will still love you and probably be able to help you," she whispered back, still clutching his hands. His resolution faltered. "I have never seen two people love each other more."

His lip twitched. "But I already told you about losing my job."

She nodded in agreement. "Then there is something else you are lying about. It is obvious that you are not fine." She paused. "Is it your health?"

Mr. Lewis shook his head.

Dylan looked past him, wishing Jack would come back in. She took a moment, closed her eyes, and pictured him sitting next to her. He would know how to talk to Mr. Lewis, and be able to calm her at the same time. She needed to remain calm and focus on the task, not the fact that she could feel her strength draining. His gaze darted to the kitchen before it fell to the blood streaking through her shirt. She tried again to get him to tell the truth.

"Please," she whispered, swallowing a weak moan. She fought to remain kneeling and not lower herself to the ground.

Tears came as he struggled for words. "It was a stupid mistake. Seven years ago at a conference..."

She just had to hang on long enough to hear the truth.

"...apparently she wasn't so honest about using birth control." Mr. Lewis fidgeted and looked past Dylan. She waited for him to continue. "And she left him. He's only a child, even if I didn't know he was mine until Child Services called me. And even then I didn't believe it until I saw the DNA test." She found herself wondering if Feeders had manipulated what Mr. Lewis believed. "I've been trying to do the right thing, but how do I tell my wife that I have a child with another woman? A child who was abandoned by his mother and I now want to take in?"

She let the silence fill the room as she waited for him to say more. She could feel the pain receding and knew he was telling the truth, she just hoped she was hearing all of it.

Still weak, she spoke softly. "What's his name?"

Mr. Lewis looked at her and cracked a little smile. "Davey." He took a deep breath. "David Michael Lewis."

"What are you going to do?"

"I don't know." Mr. Lewis shook his head. "I guess that's why I'm not fine." He stared at her for a few moments. "I lost a job and this landed in my lap in the same week. I haven't been eating well, which Joan has noticed, I'm sure. I can't sleep." He shook his head. "I've ruined everything."

"You've only ruined it if you refuse to fight for what you care about. You've only ruined it if you refuse to fix it." Her words were not only for Mr. Lewis but also for herself. "You need to tell your family."

He nodded.

"The sooner the better."

He nodded again. Slowly, he stood and pulled her into a bear hug.

"Thank you." His voice wavered. "You're right. I need to tell them." Mr. Lewis pulled back and looked at her. "There were moments when I wanted to, but it felt like something was stopping me."

She knew exactly how that felt and exactly who was to blame. She pulled herself away from him and looked him in the eye.

"What's stopping you now?"

She picked her sweatshirt off the floor and forced herself to stand straight. With a grim nod, she walked to the door, looking back in time to see Mr. Lewis head into the kitchen.

Closing the door, she turned towards Jack. She wrapped her arms around his waist and let him support her as her strength slowly continued to return.

"That's my girl," he murmured, and wrapped her more tightly in a hug.

Jack's color returned. They had been so close. Her smile faded and she traced a finger along his jaw.

She opened her mouth, but the words she wanted so desperately to say; the things she really wanted to tell him wouldn't come out.

"I know." The smile didn't quite touch his eyes. They stood there and stared at each other for a few moments. "And I'm still coming with you."

"I know."

Chapter 27

"Where's Noah?"

Jack took out the dissimulator and spun it between his fingers. Momentarily distracted, she could see it was almost clear. Mr. Lewis's lies, which had clouded it, were fading away.

Dylan narrowed her gaze. He heard her and chose not to answer. He led her into the park and took out his phone.

"Why won't you answer me?" Her steps faltered. "Again and again?" The second part she said more for herself than for him.

"Because I want to talk to you about this with Vi"—he turned towards her—"in person and in private."

"Do we have time to wait?" She looked around anxiously expecting to see a Feeder behind one of the trees.

"We don't have time not to." Jack voice hinted at an agitation that was not typical for him. "We need to talk the others. We need to search for Tony. We need to know where they've looked so we don't go there too."

She stood silently as Jack made a call.

"Vi." He sighed with relief and looked at Dylan. "Yeah, we're clean. But we have a situation." Jack held out his hand for her. She leaned in and listened to the phone call, shifting even closer as he wrapped his arm around her waist.

"Noah right? Well, you and I knew that was coming." Vi shut a door. "And I knew she could do it."

"That makes one of us, Vi," Dylan muttered. "Hey, where are you?"

She could just about hear Vi's eyes roll. "Oh will you please stop underestimating yourself. You were born to be a Fide." She huffed. "And I just walked into my place. Jimmy and Rachel should be back in a few minutes."

"What do we know, Vi?" Jack picked up the conversation.

"Not much, I'm afraid." The disappointment was evident in

her voice. "We've been over a lot of the town and haven't found either of them, though I'll admit we really weren't looking for your father. We stopped by Bruno's and he's keeping an eye out, as well as Lydia at the bank. And we called the officer who was here earlier to let him know what happened. The police are out patrolling the area as well."

Dylan felt panic rise. "Vi, he has to be in town. I mean it hasn't been that long since he ran away. Right?"

"You need to get a watch. That was more than two and a half, almost three hours ago."

"Was it really that long?"

Jack nodded at her. "Getting the truth causes you to lose sight of time."

A door opened and closed and a muffled conversation started. "I still think he's here." She said to no one in particular.

"What?" Vi's voice was distant. She was no longer speaking into the phone.

Dylan answered anyway. "My father. I think he's still here, and I think Tony running away has to do with him. I saw him this morning at your place, and later at Megan's."

"You saw Tony?"

"No." Dylan refused to look at Jack.

"You saw him at Megan's?"

She didn't have to look at Jack to hear the hurt in his voice. "I didn't want it to be him after what happened this morning at the apartment, but I can't deny it was him." She squirmed under Jack's gaze and tried to step away only to have him hold her more tightly. "And he wasn't alone. That guy from the park was with him. But I think he wants to talk. Maybe if I just wait somewhere, he'll come to me."

"Absolutely not," Vi answered at the same time Jack spoke.

"How's that going to help find Tony?" Jack demanded.

"Maybe he can help us find Tony."

"That is not going to happen," Rachel said. Dylan didn't

realize she was on speaker.

"I think you're right," Jimmy said, "but I am not going to allow you to be bait for that psycho."

"We don't know he is a psycho," Vi chimed in calmly.

Jimmy and Rachel argued with Vi and Dylan looked up at Jack.

"We'll be back soon." Jack ended the call.

She shook her head and sat down, rubbing her hands up and down her thighs. She could feel the residual irritation as it faded from Jack.

"This sucks." She drew out the words. "There are too many things I'm not sure of." She looked up at Jack. "Too many things I don't think I can trust anymore. Can Feeders do all this?"

"Feeders work better with a closer proximity. So if you're right, there would have to be multiple Feeders in town to mess with not only you, but the rest of your family as well." He sat down next to her. "This is unlike anything I've dealt with before, which is why I wanted to wait and figure all this out with Vi. All I know right now is the longer we are away from them, the easier it is to know the truth. Even though Noah is a newer Feeder, with both of us weak, it's relatively easy for him to manipulate the environment."

Slowly she reached out and traced the back of Jack's hand. "Will it ever not be confusing?"

"Will what?"

"To know the truth."

"Nope." Jack's lip twitched again. "Sometimes maybe we just have to go on faith…" He looked at her. "And hope we're right."

She grinned. "I hope you're right."

Jack chuckled and held his hand out to her as he stood. Together, they walked out of the gazebo. Her steps faltered on the path. Immediately she knew she wasn't alone. Jack squeezed her hand and urged her to keep walking, pulling her away from the park.

Dylan turned towards Jack, but looked past him. "You feel that?"

"We're being watched." He shook his head. "Don't look back."

She shivered. "What a creepy feeling." The muscles in Jack's jaw tense. "Is this about Noah?"

His only answer was to walk more quickly.

"Why won't you answer me?"

She tried to pull her hand from his grasp, but he wouldn't let her go. Admitting temporary defeat, she walked next to him, her irritation building with each step. Paper cuts appeared on her fingers as she passed a few girls talking. She tried to ignore them, but she paused, succeeding in tugging her hand from Jack's grip.

She walked over to the girls, annoyed at their lies. "The truth is easier." The girls stopped and stared at her. She shrugged. "Maybe give it a try and see if you can be better friends to each other than you're pretending to be now."

Jack grabbed her shoulders and spun her back. He shook his head as they walked away. By the time they reached Vi's apartment four blocks later, her fingers no longer throbbed.

Jack pulled her into a hug before he opened the door of the apartment building.

"What's this for?" she asked, stunned, before he released her.

"For being yourself." He squeezed her tighter. "I hadn't seen a lot of that girl lately."

She cocked her head. "Which one?"

"The one that does her own thing." His voice was thick and quiet. He waited for her to look up at him. "The one that doesn't take anyone's shit." He bent and brushed his lips lightly across her mouth. "Is that okay?" he whispered when she opened her eyes.

Losing her ability to speak at the light touch, she nodded as she leaned in and kissed him harder.

"I've wanted to do that since the first night we talked." He kissed her again. "I want to be with you, Dylan. I don't just want to be your mentor."

"Why are you telling me now?"

Jack look to the window that overlooked Vi's kitchen. "Sometimes it's easier to focus on the lies and forget life. I don't want to just exist."

She leaned in and kissed him again.

"Just don't start spilling things on me again."

A grinned spread across her face. "If you'll remember correctly, I don't believe I've ever stopped."

He laughed remembering the coffee she choked on yesterday and the mug she broke this morning.

"Looks like I'll have to get more clothes," he joked.

Her face fell. "If we make it through this."

The humor faded but his smile didn't. He reached down and took her hand. "We will."

Chapter 28

"We can't give up," Dylan said calmly. She sounded like Jack, cool and collected but inside the panic built.

Jack grabbed her shoulders tightly but forced her to lean back into him.

"I don't know where else to look." Jimmy shook his head.

"You don't get to be defeated right now," Rachel snapped before Dylan had the chance.

He slammed his hand on the table. "Don't you think I know that? We searched almost everywhere."

"Almost." She narrowed her gaze as she took a seat. "That means there are still places left to look."

They sat and ran through all the places they had looked, and argued about splitting up to search more. In the middle of the conversation, Megan barged in. Her face was red and puffy as she hugged Jack tightly.

"What's the plan?" she asked, pulling a chair up and squeezing in next to Dylan.

She stared at her brother. "I think Jimmy and I should be the only ones who go out looking for Tony."

Protests and raised voices followed.

Jimmy nodded in agreement. "You guys have done enough."

"Tough," Jack said calmly as Rachel, Megan and Vi agreed.

"We don't give a shit what you believe," Vi said as heads turned towards her. "Tony may be your brother, but we are a family. You aren't going out there alone."

Jimmy shrugged in defeat. Silence filled the room as everyone thought. There had to be a place he would go. She traced the grain of the table's wood as a thought started to form in her mind.

"I need to do something." Jimmy jumped to his feet.

Everyone jolted with Jimmy's sudden movement. She watched something pass between Vi and Jack. "You take Megan and

Rachel and go," Vi agreed. "We'll keep working on things here."

Dylan rounded the table and hugged her brother tightly. She faced the door after they left not wanting to turn and have Jack and Vi see her crying again. She didn't know what had happened, or why she could no longer hang on to that careful mask of peace she had just minutes ago. She heard Vi move into the kitchen.

"I can't grab this bowl from the top shelf." Vi's voice was quiet and tentative. "Jack, come help me." Chairs shifted and scraped. "Dylan, why don't you take a minute to clean yourself up and change? We'll wait to talk."

She rushed into the bathroom, quickly turning the water on to cover the sniffling. She buried her face in a towel and sobbed harder, unable to control the rush of panic and sorrow that was filling her with every breath.

"Can't I even cry in peace?" she whispered when the door opened, not taking her eyes off the towel draped over her hands.

She didn't look up as the door closed, but flinched when thin arms wrapped around her.

"You can cry in peace," Vi whispered, "but you don't have to cry alone."

She cried even harder. "Why can't I stop?" She finally got the question out between choked sobs.

Vi forced Dylan to look at her. "You'll stop crying soon. Take a shower. Change clothes. Then we'll talk."

She followed Vi's gaze to the clean clothes on the shelf next to the sink.

Dylan closed and locked the door quickly. Steam poured from the tub as she stepped into the shower. She let the water wash away the blood still on her skin. She let the water wash away her tears.

She barely recognized herself when she finally wiped the condensation off the mirror. Her skin, usually sun kissed and glowing, looked fragile and her eyes haunted. She quickly turned away to finish towel drying her hair and changed into the warm leggings and oversized sweatshirt Vi had left for her.

When she emerged, Jack jumped to his feet. She was wrapped in his arms before she had taken a step.

"Are you okay?"

"I'm not sure," she whispered. "Nothing is making sense."

A cough snapped her head towards the table. "I think we should all be sharing this discussion."

"Not this part, Vi." Jack strained to keep his voice even. He lowered his head slightly and looked deep into her eyes waiting until Dylan looked back at him to continue. "This part has to be just me and her."

Vi sighed. "Can your part wait until after my part?"

Dylan watched Vi and Jack glare at each other, neither speaking a word for several moments.

"Is someone going to share any part of this?" she snapped as she stepped slightly away from Jack. "I feel like a ping pong ball in a game I didn't sign up to play."

"We're sorry. We are being pretty controlling here."

"Ya think?" She stepped further back. "I feel like I should be looking for the remote control running me lately." She shook her head. "I don't know how to explain it. Sometimes I feel like myself. Sometimes I feel like something mechanical, and I hate it." She watched Vi and Jack exchange glances. "And then you guys do that creepy quasy-mind reading thing you do and I about lose my mind. One of you needs to tell me what the hell is going on here. Or both of you. I really don't give a damn who starts, as long as one of you does." They exchanged looks. "Now!"

Vi gently placed her hand on Dylan's shoulder. "You're going through withdrawal."

"Oh. Is that all? Well since you put it like that." She walked away. "Everything you say sounds so cryptic." She turned and looked first at Vi before speaking to Jack. "I don't understand."

Jack motioned Dylan over to the table.

"Withdrawal is probably the easiest to describe, and Jack basically told you all this already." She looked to Jack as he nodded. "The longer you are away from a Feeder, the easier it is to see lies. Their personalities and influence are powerful. When a person walks away from a Feeder, they feel disoriented or confused, sometimes emotional and jittery. As a Fide, these feelings and the withdrawals are enhanced because you are so attuned to finding lies."

"Why aren't you and Jack affected?"

"We are," Jack said quietly. "But we know what's happening since we have faced it before. And we are focused on helping you. We are trying to ignore the withdrawal. And we are carrying less lies than you are. Each lie makes it easier for a Feeder to control what we're thinking and in some cases feeling."

"Not to mention that you've had more exposure to the Feeders than we have," Vi added.

She took a deep breath. "So all I can do is wait?" She rolled her eyes. "Lovely."

"With time comes practice." Vi shrugged. "I know that sucks as a response, but it's the only one I can give you. But..." She paused until Dylan settled down again. "There are other things that we can discuss in more detail."

She pounced. "Such as."

Vi smiled and looked over at Jack. "Look closely at the dissimulators." Vi placed hers on the table and waited as Jack finally set his down next to it.

Dylan stared at the two pieces of glass and waited for something to happen. She started to look away but out of the corner of her eye she saw something. She grabbed Vi's and held it in the fading evening light. She could see a fine gray string, nothing more than a strand of hair, swirling in her glass. She looked over at Vi, who nodded.

"That lie was one I heard earlier today while I was out

looking for your brother. I didn't bother to hear the truth and just healed myself and kept moving." Vi shrugged. "I'll go back later and clear it up, but I needed you to see it."

She replaced Vi's and picked up Jack's dissimulator. She did the same thing and saw more fine wisps of light grey smoke floating in the otherwise clear glass. Though she couldn't tell how many were in there, it was clear Jack's dissimulator was carrying more lies than Vi's.

"I believe most of those are all related to you." Vi waited for her to look up before continuing. "Jack's holding lies that either one or both of you have heard and haven't corrected yet, only healed. There are things you still haven't been honest about or heard the truth about yet."

"Is there a way to know which lies?"

"Vi, we aren't doing this," Jack said in an eerie calm. She could see his jaw clench with each word. He ran his hands through his hair and stared at Vi, though his words were for Dylan. "I wanted to talk to you before we got to this point." He looked at Dylan. "I had hoped to clear up some of these lies sooner, so I didn't feel like I was forcing you." He grabbed her hand. "I never want to force you," he whispered with an urgency in his voice she didn't understand.

"I do get it, Jack. But we can't wait." Vi looked at Jack. "And you can't give her half the story. As a mentor you have to be willing to do everything and teach everything."

Jack slouched back in his seat and finally nodded. Dylan turned her attention back to the wisps.

"There is a way, but I'm not happy about it," he snapped at Vi. "Dylan"—he leaned toward her, trying to pull her attention away from his dissimulator—"did you notice sometimes that the cuts you received would throb more?"

"How could I forget? Every time Mr. Lewis spoke I'm pretty sure it throbbed."

He shook his head. "That was a bigger lie and a bigger cut is prone just out of nature and location to throb independent of the lie. But I'm talking about the little ones that you got on your fingers. Did you notice when they throbbed?"

She thought back to the cuts on her fingers and tried to remember. Finally she nodded, "I remembering them throbbing, but it doesn't make sense to me why they did."

"They would throb for one of two reasons. Either you were in the proximity of the person who said the lie, or you were close to a Feeder propagating the lie."

"You mean..." She tried to work through what Jack had just said.

Jack nodded. "The lies do more than tell us who is lying. They become beacons that help us return to the liar and get the truth."

"So I can still fix those lies?"

Vi nodded, but she didn't notice if Jack responded as her mind started to replay some of the lies she knew she would have to face, some of them being her own.

She snapped her head towards Jack. "Is this why you wanted to talk to me, I mean before?"

"Partially."

"We don't have time for a long and drawn out explanation," Vi said quickly. "But I'll give you a bit of time while I get a shower and change."

Vi stood, but Dylan's attention was drawn back to Jack.

"How do we know who each lie belongs to?"

"That's the hard part." Jack slid his chair closer to her. "We don't. But if we can figure out most of them, and figure out the truth, it'll make it easier when we face the Feeders. And"—he smiled—"it'll make the withdrawal a little bit easier."

"I don't even know where to start."

Jack smiled. "There are a few I remember."

"A few? Of mine?" She fidgeted. "From when?"

"The first night." Jack rubbed his hands together and took a deep breath. "Ready?"

She stared at the dissimulator. "No."

"Great! Here we go."

Choking on a laugh, she said, "How do you remember that night?"

"Because I had waited a long time to talk to you." He paused. "But we've already talked about that. Now. Why did you lie to me that first night?"

Dylan shook her head. "I don't even remember what I said."

"It doesn't matter if you remember the lie. What matters is the truth."

It took several moments for her to realize he was trying to teach her how to clear up lies that weren't healed immediately.

"I still don't understand."

Jack sighed. "When most people lie, it isn't original. The little lies, the little slices on our fingers, are simple lies. If you can pinpoint the liar and talk to them, they will probably lie again. If you continue talking to them you can usually get the truth."

She thought back. "Is that what you did that one day after school with those girls from my homeroom?"

"Yup." An evil little smirk danced across his mouth. "Of course it is easier to confront people when they don't know who you are. Carrie and Stephanie didn't even recognize me. All they saw was some cocky, confident guy who wanted to talk to them." She snorted. "Do you know I said hello to them the next day in the hall and they didn't even recognize me? They actually acted like I was some type of walking plague."

She shook her head as Jack took her hands.

"So that first night you met me"—his voice dropped to a whisper—"why did you lie?"

She thought about that first night at Baby Bruno's, a little smile tugged at her lips. "It scared me a little that I turned and you were there. It unnerved me that you were"—she took a shaky breath, and looked at Jack—"so unfalteringly calm. And it freaked me out that you wanted me to come with you when I didn't know who you were."

As she spoke, the glass dissimulator glowed, and finally faded revealing a few less wisps inside.

"That did help." She took a deep breath and felt steadier.

"We told you it would." She heard the sarcasm in his voice.

Jack still watched her. He leaned closer. "Now, I have another question I need to ask." She nodded slightly and licked her lips. "Do you care about me?"

Dylan blinked twice. She couldn't believe she needed to answer that question. "Yes," she whispered. "I thought you knew. I thought it was clear."

Jack shook his head. "At times I thought I did, but then I was never sure."

"I could say the same about you." She watched him bow his head for a moment. "There were times I felt like there was something, and then there were nights it felt like you were pulling away from me." She waited until he lifted his eyes to her. "Why didn't you ask sooner?"

"I tried, but it never seemed like the right time."

"But."

Jack shook his head and stood. She could see he was nervous. "We never discussed this." He waved his hand at her. "And I didn't want to assume things any longer. I just wanted to know the truth."

Finding courage, she wrapped her arms around Jack's neck, and pulled him closer. "How's this for truth," she said with her lips a whisper from his.

A cough had both grinning. In unison, they turned their heads to the side to see Vi saunter towards them. "Glad to see you two have worked everything out."

"You need to take longer showers." Jack wrapped his arms tightly around Dylan.

Vi only shrugged as she walked past them. With only a quick peck, Jack and Dylan followed Vi to the table to work out what other lies they had heard. Carefully, they created a list and divided the lies into groups. Vi, with more experience, would go with Dylan to clear up some of the harder lies.

She traced the grain of wood in the table, lost in thought. A tear rolled down her cheek.

They waited for her to speak.

"I can't fix them all." Her voice cracked. She stared at the dissimulator unwilling to look at Vi or Jack. "Two of them were from my mom."

Chapter 29

"They got him."

Dylan, Jack and Vi all snapped their heads toward the door as Jimmy flew in with that simple sentence.

"What?" Dylan managed as she wiped her eyes, cleared her throat, and grabbed for Jack's hand. "Who? Tony?"

Jimmy's smile spread shrank before he spoke again. "No." Jimmy ran his hand through his hair. "Detective Larson called me."

Dylan watched him fidget for a moment.

"And?" Vi jumped on the word.

"Larson said Dad just walked into the precinct a little while ago."

"Just like that?"

Jimmy slumped into the seat. Exhaustion crept into his face. "That's all I know. Larson said he would contact me later after they talk to him about what happened that night." Jimmy looked at his watch.

"But you don't think he killed Mom."

Jimmy nodded. "But I don't think he killed Mom."

"Where are Rachel and Megan?" Jack asked.

"What about Tony?" Vi asked at the same time.

"Oh." Jimmy looked back and forth from Jack to Vi. "I didn't even think to call them." He sighed before looking at her. "We don't have anything new on Tony."

"But he's been gone all day." She bit her lip.

"Why aren't they with you?" Jack's question snapped her out of her thoughts.

Vi was on the phone before Dylan could process her brother's unusual mood.

Jack squeezed her hand. "We'll give you two a minute." He motioned Vi to follow him into the living room. He leaned over and gave her a quick kiss before leaving.

She stared at her brother for a long moment. "What's the matter with you?"

Jimmy choked on a nervous laugh. "Nothing."

Taking a deep breath, she rounded the table to sit next to him. "You remember what I am, right Jimmy?"

He nodded.

"So you know that lying to be is beyond pointless?"

He nodded again, weakly.

She pulled up the sleeve of her shirt and showed him the newly forming cut on her forearm. "So are you going to tell me what has you so jumpy or am I going to have to beat it out of you?"

"Noth—" Jimmy started but cut himself off as she raised an eyebrow. Slowly he shook his head. "I don't know what's wrong."

They both watched the cut on her arm healed. She grabbed a napkin to dab the blood that had seeped out before the wound closed.

"Then tell me what happened. Why would you split from the girls?"

Jimmy shook his head slowly and looked away from her. "Because he told me I had to."

"Who did?" she asked, even though she was fairly certain who had.

He shook his head. "I don't know. Some bald guy." Jimmy slumped back in his chair and she stiffened. "And I had to believe him."

Her nails bit into her palm, making her realize she had clenched her hands into fists. "Vi," she called in a tight voice, "did you get a hold of Megan and Rachel?"

"Uh huh," Vi called from the living room. "They're on their way back now."

She let out a breath and sat back giving herself the time to calm down.

"We'll get to the bottom of this." She gently placed her hand on her brother's arm. "And we *will* find Tony."

Dylan walked into the kitchen and away from her brother. She wrapped her arms around herself and looked out the window. "Where are you Tony?" she whispered into the growing darkness.

Involuntarily she cringed when Jack put his arms around her. "I didn't hear you," she said.

"I know." She could hear the smile in his voice. "So lost in thought a bomb could have gone off and you wouldn't have heard it. What are you thinking about?"

She bit down on her lip. "I don't know what to do."

"One step at a time."

"We need to find Tony," she said, still looking out the window.

"We need to find those lies," he reminded her. She groaned and leaned back into him. "And we need to do that before we face the Feeders."

"Do we have to?" she whined.

"We have to. We have to be at our strongest if we are going to face them."

"And we have to face them, right?" She waited, but he didn't answer. "Is that the 'what else' you wanted to talk to me about?"

"Yes," Jack said quietly, the word barely escaping his throat.

"Is that why Noah left? Because he knew there would be a next time."

"Exactly."

She wrapped Jack's arms around her more tightly. "I'm scared."

She felt Jack's lips at her ear. "I won't let anything happen to you. Vi and I will be right there. You will not face them alone." Jack pulled away, spun her around, and looked deep into her eyes. "I promise."

She took a deep breath and shook her head. "Please don't

make promises you can't keep."

"I never will."

"They're back," Vi said as the door to the apartment opened. Jack started to walk back towards the table.

"Wait a sec." Dylan reached out and grabbed Jack's arm. She pulled him back. "We need to keep an eye on them." She nodded towards Jimmy, Rachel and Megan. "A Feeder separated them. That's why Jimmy was acting so weird when he got here. That's why the girls weren't with him." She took a deep breath. "Should we tell them about the Feeders?"

Jack frowned. "They already know more than they should." He rubbed the back of his neck. "Let me talk to Vi and ask her." He walked away, grabbed Vi by the arm and headed into the living room.

Megan and Rachel forced smiles as they walked into the kitchen. "You guys look as tired as I feel."

"I think we are." Rachel leaned against the counter.

"Coffee?" Megan pleaded.

"Coffee," Dylan replied and started brewing a new pot.

A few minutes later, Vi walked into the kitchen, grabbed her jacket, hugged Dylan and left the apartment. No one spoke as they sipped the coffee and lounged around the table.

Everyone at the table jumped when Dylan's phone rang, shattering the silence. Slowly, she reached across the table for her phone, but Jack hit the speaker before she could answer. They listened to breathing on the other end.

"Dylan?" Everyone gasped hearing Tony's voice, but no one had a chance to respond before another voice began to speak. She saw her own confusion mirrored in Jimmy's face. She swore she could hear some of her father's voice in the phone, but also heard an edge of something more sinister.

"It's not your father," Jack whispered as he leaned into her ear.

She knew it wasn't her father. He was in jail, but she was having a hard time making herself believe that as the man on the phone talked.

"I just wanted to let you know he was fine. I would never hurt my own child." She heard the mock astonishment in the voice as a long cut opened along her thigh. Her ears rang, and she tried to focus and listen for any clue as to where he was. "I am looking forward to seeing you again Dylan." She cringed but didn't speak, not sure she could trust her voice to be strong and confident.

She shooed Jack's hand away from her leg. She would not let him use the dissimulator on her again.

"It really was too bad you and Jack didn't stop in the park. We could have" — the voice clicked his tongue — "talked. All of this nasty business would already be over, but I guess we will have to draw out the inevitable."

"What's inevitable?" Megan whispered. She looked nervously from Dylan to Jack.

"Megan is that you? Oh it's so nice to hear you. You know, Noah has told me so much about you."

She saw the look of confusion on Megan's face and knew why. Everyone else believed they were talking to her father.

"But why not ask Dylan. She already knows what's happening." Dylan refused to speak and silence spread through the room. She listened as the man clicked his tongue again. "Well, when you're ready."

They sat in silence as the line went dead. Slowly, a murmuring started around the table, but she didn't pay attention to it. She sat there and thought. She knew everyone was staring at her, but she didn't look at any of them. Dylan felt Megan squeeze her hand, but she didn't acknowledge it. In her mind, she rewound the phone call and listened closely, but she wasn't listening to the voice.

The man had been walking around. She could hear his feet shuffle along a carpeted floor. He had walked into a room. She had heard a subtle moan of a door's hinge swinging slowly open.

He had opened and closed something.

Dylan closed her eyes. She knew that sound. The sound echoed through her mind. It was the sound of metal hitting wood and thudding into something. A sound she had heard almost daily since her tenth birthday. Taking a deep breath, she opened her eyes and looked around at her friends.

Their voices were drowned out by the mocking voice that had claimed to be her father.

She squeezed Megan's hand, and watched Rachel kiss Jimmy before pulling him closer. Jack's hand on her leg anchored her in place and she sighed when he kissed her right below the ear. She controlled herself as she looked at each of these people, and knew, without a doubt, that she had to do everything she could to save them.

She would find a way to save Tony.

She would find a way to save Jack.

She had to get out of here without them. She would confront the Feeders. That tiny sound of echoed in her mind again, and she knew without a doubt she was supposed to go.

She stood and took Jack's hand. Everyone watched, but she didn't care. She led Jack into the bathroom and stared into his eyes as the lock snapped into place. Jack pulled out his dissimulator but she stopped him, placing a hand on his arm.

Turning slowly, Dylan grabbed the small tub of supplies from under the sink, pulled down her sweats, and sat on the edge of the bath rub. She wiped and cleaned the wound, then put several butterfly Band-Aids across it to stop the bleeding.

Jack stood against the door, watching, shifting weight from one foot the next. A soft smile crossed her lips to see him slowly, tentatively put the dissimulator back in his pocket. She walked towards him, turned him around and backed him against the sink.

With nothing more than a nod and a raised eyebrow, Jack undid his belt and let his jeans fall. He stood awkwardly as she cleaned and applied Band-Aids to his wound in the same, slow, meticulous manner she had attended to her own.

He stared at the wall, trying to focus on anything other than Dylan kneeling in front of him.

"This is wrong," Jack said through clenched teeth as she applied the last Band-Aid.

She let her finger trail down Jack's leg and heard his staggered intake of breath. Slowly she wiped the last of the blood off his leg and stood.

"You know we can't waste the dissimulator. And since that was a Feeder, it's not like he is just going to tell us the truth." She put the supplies away as Jack pulled his jeans back over his hips.

"*Everything* about what just happened is wrong." Jack spat, working hard to control the emotions that raged through him. "I hate seeing you in pain."

"Then help me." She took his face in her hands and kissed him. When he opened his eyes and looked at her she spoke. "A truth?" Jack nodded with a quick jerk of his head. "If I ask you to do something for me, will you?"

He cleared his throat. She could see he wanted to say yes, but shook his head slightly. "It will depend on what it is."

"What if I asked you to stay and keep Jimmy here? Would you?"

His expression shifted. She kept her hands on his face. He would not turn away from her.

"I will not let you go searching..." She raised an eyebrow halting Jack's statement. Jack pushed away from the door and grabbed her hands, trapping them between their bodies. She bumped up against the sink as Jack continued to step even closer to her. She didn't break eye contact. "You know where they are, don't you?"

She nodded. "At least one."

"And you want to go without me?" His whispered response did not hide the hurt. Jack bent and rested his forehead against hers, shaking his head back and forth. "Why? Are you giving up? On me? On us?"

"No," she said. "I'm not giving up." She wrapped his arms around her. "Jack, please listen to me. I think I have a plan, and I think it's already started. I need to know you will do what I ask."

"Maybe."

"Please, Jack." She pulled him closer. "Trust me."

They stared at each other for several long minutes until Jack finally submitted.

"Thank you. Now, we have a few things to discuss." She took a deep breath. "Can I take Noah by myself? Feeder versus Fide?"

Jack stepped back and lowering himself to the floor, and pulled Dylan down to sit in front of him. "Yeah." He sounded defeated but continued. "I think there is a way."

Chapter 30

Everyone had moved into the living room and eyed Dylan suspiciously as she led Jack out of the bathroom and into the bedroom. Outside, a light snow fell. It was going to be cold, but she had hoped it wouldn't be snowing. With her luck, she knew better.

"Is there anything else I need to know?" she asked as she stripped off the sweats and searched for warmer clothing. She turned towards Jack as she threw on a pair of leggings before hopping into a pair of jeans.

Jack blushed but kept eye contact with her. "I think that's about it, but please remember, I haven't had to face a Feeder as experienced as the one here now."

"Has Vi checked in?"

Jack checked his phone. "Looks like five down."

She pulled the sweatshirt over her head. "That means at least ten more, right?" she questioned as she yanked her T-shirt off. Any embarrassment she thought she would feel changing in front of Jack had disappeared the night he saw her lying on the floor in nothing but a pair of running shorts and a sports bra. She barely hid the smile that threatened to expose her as she watched Jack's neck redden with each article of clothing she removed.

"If we were correct with the number of lies still out there, yeah that will be about right."

Digging into her running bag, Dylan found her Under Armour running shirt and threw that on before adding a few more layers.

"And you think you guys will be able to get those in the next three hours?" She shot a look at the alarm clock next to the bed. She tossed a hoodie on the bed and pulled her sleeves up, already beginning to sweat.

"That's the plan." Jack frowned, clearly not thrilled by the plan.

213

The unease in his voice shook her resolve, but she couldn't focus on that right now. She couldn't let doubt cloud her mind. With a deep, calming breath, she drew on two pairs of socks and her sneakers.

"Let's do this." She set her game face and walked past Jack.

He grabbed her arm and spun her back towards him. He opened his mouth to speak but no words came out. Slowly, he ran his hand through her hair and tucked a strand that was hanging in front of her eyes behind her ear.

"Jack," she started.

"This is wrong." He repeated the mantra he used multiple times in the bathroom. "I can't let you do this."

"You have to."

"No," he spat, and pulled her tighter. "We will do this together."

"We are," she said quietly, hoping to disarm him with sincerity instead of volume. "Have faith in me to do what we discussed."

"What if something goes wrong?"

Dylan could feel him tense even as he spoke. "What if it doesn't?" She took a deep breath and forced herself to calm down. "Jack," she whispered, "please."

He traced her jaw with the tip of a finger before pulling her into a kiss that left her knees shaking.

"Promise me," he said, and lifted her chin. "Promise you'll be careful."

She couldn't look at him. Though his words were calm, his eyes were pleading. She gave him the hoodie, and headed into the living room. She sank on the couch next to Rachel and listened to their discussion. They all believed Tony was close, thanks to the phone call. Now, they were even more determined to find him. They would head in opposite directions, check every house, back alley, hotel, bar, restaurant, and store in their path.

No one liked the plan. Nobody liked the idea of searching

randomly, but they didn't feel there was another way.

Dylan willed everyone not to ask what she thought. The attention slowly turned away from her as she sank further onto the couch. No one was concerned when she got up to get a drink. All she had to do was grab the hoodie Jack had draped across the back of a chair, and sneak out of the apartment.

Jack promised to keep everyone there long enough for her to disappear, even though it almost broke him to make that promise. But he had, and she knew he would do it. Looking at him one last time, she hoped that she would see him again when all this was over. She bowed her head and knew it took every muscle he had to hold him there.

Outside, she put on her hoodie. She left the hood up and tucked her hair behind her ears as she took a deep breath, glancing around the street. Her pace quickened even though she told herself not to run. She needed to walk. She needed to give Jack and Vi time. Laughter echoed off the buildings as a group of kids tried to have a snowball fight with the light, fluffy, snow. Their voices faded quickly when she passed. No other sounds replaced theirs. She willed herself not to let the eerie silence that accompanied new snow let doubt set in.

She walked past Megan's house just as a car door opened and a little boy got out. Mr. and Mrs. Lewis walked across the yard and met the boy. Mrs. Lewis bent down and hugged the boy. Their eyes met and Mrs. Lewis waved while still hugging the boy. She waved back but kept walking.

Shoving her hands deeper into the hoodie, Dylan took her time and walked into the park. The wind started to pick up, and even with all her layers, she felt the cold. She shoved the cold out of her head and focused on what she had to do. She sat in the gazebo where Jack had first told her about being a Fide.

So many things changed that day.

So many more had changed since.

When the lights came on, she walked over and sat on the

swing where she had told Jack the truth, and where the older Feeder had first confronted her. A few stray flurries lazily floated by.

She closed her eyes and listed every truth she knew. That was what Jack had told her to do. She needed time to work through her list, and in doing so, hopefully she gave Jack and Vi the time they needed. A yawn stretched through her, but she shook the sleepiness off. There would be time to sleep later, hopefully.

She swayed back and forth and continued to list truths from small details like the color of her hair and her age to her feelings for her family and friends. She focused each truth, making sure that she knew exactly why each was true as well as how much it meant to her. She thought about how long she and Megan had been friends, the night she had met Jack at Bruno's, and where Jimmy went to college. She thought about Tony's favorite video game, the pictures tacked beside her bed, and her favorite teacher at school. A shuttered breath escaped her as she thought of another truth she needed to admit.

She loved Jack.

On a groan, she fought the urge to rush to Tony and finish this. She had to have faith in her own plan. She pulled out her phone to check the time but quickly shoved it back in her pocket. It wasn't time yet, and she couldn't run away from the truth anymore.

She had to face the fact that she didn't just like Jack; she didn't just want to work with him as a Fide. She loved him.

A chill ran down her spine as she forced herself to admit the truth. A smile quirked the corner of her mouth as she looked forward to telling Jack for the first time. That smile quickly faded when she realized just what she would have to survive in order for that to happen.

A clock in the distance began to chime and she made her way out of the park. There was one more list she had to create. She needed to acknowledge the lies. She needed to be prepared in case Vi and Jack couldn't get all of them. She listed the lies in Jack's dissimulator before she had convinced him to give them back. Dylan looked down at her fingers, and watched another small cut heal.

Jack and Vi were doing it. They were finding the truths.

She rounded the corner and saw her house.

The yellow tape surrounding her front steps swayed in the breeze. Carefully, she walked towards her house, the snow shifted with each step she took.

Gunfire and death echoed off the trees and surrounded her. She could just barely see a light through the blanket that had been thrown over Tony's window, but knew by the sounds of the game he was in there. She narrowed her gaze to her own window. Barely recognizable against the darkness, a shadow moved back and forth.

Taking a calming breath, Dylan moved forward. She would not let lies bring any more harm to her family.

She needed to finish this alone.

Chapter 31

The backdoor moaned when she opened it; the sound echoed into the darkness. She paused for only a moment before she stepped into the house.

"Nicely played, Dylan."

She spun around, hearing the voice coming from every corner of the kitchen, but unable to find the source.

"I'm glad to see you were able to come alone."

A smile twitched at the corner of her lips. "So," she whispered to herself, "they can tell the truth." She checked the corners and shadows for the voice.

"Of course I *can* tell the truth," the voice replied. "But what fun is that?"

Dylan spun around, expecting to see him standing behind her. She had spoken so quietly, she didn't know how he could have heard. She cleared her throat but continued to speak quietly. "When you said earlier that you were looking forward to seeing me…"

Laughter boomed through the house. "I guess see you one last time. You know you should really stop walking so slowly. It's just wasting time."

The throb in her leg died away. She fought to keep her face neutral. One more lie was gone. She paused, and knew Jack would know she had reached the house as that lie closed. Glancing down at her hands, she saw a few thin bleeding cuts still etched into her fingers. Dylan mentally repeated things she knew were true, as she inched closer to meeting the man who wanted her dead.

Jack and Vi needed to hurry because right now she was alone with a psycho.

"How can you see me?" she called, knowing there was no point in trying to hide.

All her care in approaching slowly and quietly had been for nothing.

"You'll see." The mocking tone grew more menacing.

She closed her eyes forcing herself to calm down. When she opened them, a small, barely visible red dot drew her attention. She knew there wasn't anything in the kitchen that made that light. Walking over to it, she saw a small video camera sitting in a potted plant by the kitchen sink. She held back the urge to stick out her tongue as she smashed the little device under her foot.

Scanning the rest of the kitchen, she saw two more. She unhurriedly took off the hoodie and tossed it on a chair as she moved past the table. Several more lights dotted the living room and dining area.

"You've been busy."

"Lots of time to get things set up after the cops left. And Noah's been a big help getting everything ready. I guess most people wouldn't think I would return here, but why wouldn't I? This is my house."

The cut on her leg reopened but instantly sealed itself again. She smiled. Jack had been right. Knowing the truth, truly believing in the truth was the only way she would be able to beat a Feeder. Mentally, she checked off items on her list as the man spoke. She balled her hands into fists and held onto the truth.

"It's not. You may sound like him, but I know you aren't my father." Dylan looked directly into the camera. "And this isn't your house. You can stop pretending now."

The guy clicked his tongue before responding. "Fair enough."

The voice had changed. He no longer sounded like her father. His voice was somehow deeper than her father's had been, and carried an accent she wasn't familiar with. A muffled chuckle rumbled through the speakers followed by the same sound that drew her there, the sound of metal thudding against wood.

"So who are you?"

"Come and find out."

Nodding, she climbed the stairs, cursing herself for walking into the lair of the monster so easily. Each step moaned under her step. At the top, she pressed her ear to the door to Tony's room. Tony cursed at his video game. Trying the handle, Dylan noted a padlock on the door. She pulled out her phone and sent a message before she shoved it in her back pocket.

It was time to find out who wanted her dead.

As she approached, her bedroom door opened and a shadow, cast from a small lamp on her desk, slithered across the hallway.

"It's too late to turn back now." Several voices spoke at once.

One came from her bedroom. One from the bathroom down the hall behind her. The last, extremely familiar voice echoed through the empty house.

She clamped her mouth shut to keep in the scream that threatened to escape. She had thought assumed there would be one Feeder, possibly two.

To know there were at least three greatly reduced her confidence.

"Hurry, Jack," she hissed, unable to stop herself from speaking the words that were echoing in her mind.

She hadn't prepared for this.

Three Feeders tipped the odds.

She could only delay things for so long. If she didn't go in, they would come out. Right now, she was just one Fide.

"Yes it is too late." She wasn't able to hide the fear vibrating through her as she walked forward and stood in her bedroom door.

As the lights flicked on and her eyes adjusted to the light, she found herself looking at the man who destroyed her family. He smiled easily as he lowered the hood hung low on his head. He was bald, as she had remembered, but appeared younger than when she had seen him that night in the park. His eyes remained cold and his slow smile was wicked.

"I'm here." She took another step forward breaking eye

contact. "Will you let Tony go?"

"You know," he continued as if she hadn't spoken, "I'm surprised at how easily you came." His eyes shifted towards her desk. "I guess you were right, Noah."

She turned her head in the direction the man spoke and took the last step out of the hallway and into her bedroom. Noah straddled her desk chair. Casually he flipped through all of the camera angles in the house. She wished she had destroyed more. Now, even if Jack managed to get into the house quietly, they would know. Noah raised his head, and shrugged as their eyes met.

"What do you think I've been doing all these months, Steven?" Noah cocked an eyebrow at her, a grin danced on his face. "Just wasting time with her friend?"

She looked back at the man who stood in front of her. He turned to face the window. She stepped further into the room, and even though Jack had told her not to, she looked at him closely.

The light played with his face until the profile and crooked smile she had seen every day since she was born came into focus.

His features shimmered again, shifting from one identity to the next. Each shift was subtle, but pronounced enough to leave her confused. When his features settled, she was again looking at her father.

She leaned against the doorjamb forcing herself to think of Jack as the man smirked at her.

They had sat on the bathroom floor. She had seen Jack thinking what to say.

"You have to find the truth," Jack had said. "You have to find it between the lies. These Feeders will use any information they can to make the lies more believable. You must..." he had said. "You must believe the truth, no matter how convincingly they lie. Remember what you know. List what you don't. You cannot let them fool you."

She stood there, as the man gloated. Jack's words continued to echo through her mind as she struggled to hold on to the truth. She looked down at her hands and wiped the dried blood off another finger. She turned her gaze back to Steven. Something flickered across his face.

Her mind raced back to Jack's instructions.

"You can't take on both an experienced Feeder and a new one."

She had rolled her eyes at him. "Okay, I won't take on both of them at the same time."

"Dylan, I can't let you do this."

"You have to. Noah lied to me a few times. I need to clear those up while you and Vi are clearing up the rest of the lies. This way, we will be three…well two and a half strong Fides when we face the other Feeder."

Jack clenched his jaw. "Stop underestimating yourself."

"I'm only giving myself a half because I don't know what I'm doing."

"Then give me a half too because I've never faced someone strong enough to manipulate people over a phone."

Chairs scraped outside the bathroom but she stared at Jack.

"I can do this," she whispered. "I need to do this."

"I know." Jack had leaned over and kissed her softly. "But you can't just barge in there. You have to prepare…"

She blinked slowly and turned her gaze on Noah. She concentrated all her energy on only him, eliminating Steven from her consciousness. "And you're here because…"

"What better way to teach than by doing," Steven answered.

She kept her gaze locked on Noah, remembering Jack's instructions to focus only on one Feeder. "So you have no feelings for Megan. Everything you have done was to get closer to me." She watched his mouth twitch slightly as he nodded. She bit off a snort. She studied him for another moment. "You're lying. And do you want to know how I know?"

Fear crept into Noah's eyes.

"Because the Noah I know really does care about Megan. The

Noah I know loves her, and no amount of on the job training is going to make it possible to hide those feelings." She took a step towards him. "You are a talented liar, Noah. But it's easy to lie convincingly when your opponent is at a low point. Not so much when they aren't."

She squared her shoulders. "So..." She slowly put her hands in her pockets. "Let's try this again, and this time, see if you can make me *believe* you."

Noah's eyes darted back and forth between her and Steven. A trail of perspiration ran down the side of his face. His muscles tensed as fear flooded his system.

Noah stood, grabbing the back of the chair so tightly his knuckles were white. "She means nothing to me."

Dylan nodded her head as a cut formed on her cheek and stepped forward. "You sure about that? You are awfully tense for someone who doesn't care." Noah took a step back and bumped into her desk. "And you started dating her months before I became a Fide." Dylan raised an eyebrow. Noah's Adam's apple bobbed as he swallowed.

She knew what had brought fear into his eyes. The cut on her cheek began to heal on its own. "Okay, so Megan's a touchy subject, and you are obviously not able to handle that. Let's clear up a few other things."

"We don't have time," Steven interjected.

"Oh, we have all the time in the world." She waved a hand as she flung him a casual look. She knew she needed to buy as much time as possible. With a silent prayer that Jack would get here, she brought her attention back to Noah.

"Where was I?" She returned her focus to Noah, and prayed that her voice wouldn't betray the nervousness ricocheting through her. "That's right. You've said some not so nice things to me, and I think it's time to clear them up."

"You can try," Noah sneered, but there was uncertainty in his voice.

"Why, exactly, is it my fault my mother is dead?" she whispered at him.

Noah smirked. "Because you weren't home."

"Um hum." She dropped her gaze. This was one lie she was ready for. Jack knew they would lie about this, and had helped her prepare. When she looked back at Noah, he flinched at the ferocity in her eyes.

"And how would it have been different if I had been home?"

Noah swallowed loudly.

"Are you saying I would have been able to stop her death?"

"Absolutely." Noah spoke with absolutely no confidence.

For the first time since she started talking to Noah, she turned and really acknowledged Steven. With a subtle twist at the waist, she turned and raised an eyebrow. His response was immediate and intense. Dylan returned her focus to Noah, sure that if she looked at Steven for even a second longer, all of her confidence would be gone. He was livid. Dylan had to keep Noah going. She had to stall him for a long as possible. Her life depended on it.

"This is all part of the strategy," Noah burst out. "Lulling you into a false sense of security."

"Well…" She shrugged taking the time to refocus. "I am sufficiently lulled. Time for round two? Would you like to convince me I am the reason my mother is dead or would you like to move onto another lie?"

She held up her hand and watched as two more cuts closed. In the distance, sirens flared out of the night, and she knew her time was running out. She leaned into Noah effectively trapping him between herself and her desk.

"Do you see these," she whispered, showing him two thin pink lines on her hand. "These are from lies you gave me. Do you see how they are healing?" She waited for him to speak and repeated her question more forcefully, throwing her nerves into anger and raising her voice. "Do you see, Noah?"

He nodded, but she could see by the look in his eyes he

already knew what had happened. He knew what the healed lies meant.

She had conquered his lies. He was no longer a Feeder.

Dylan turned to Steven again, hoping her careless retort would shift his wrath to Noah and away from her. "I think this one's broken."

Noah pushed past her and ran from the room. She caught her balance and took a deep breath. She stood for a moment, jamming her hands into her pockets to cover the trembling, trying to prolong this part as long as possible. They listened as Noah cursed in the hallway and stormed down the stairs.

"You've dragged me all the way down here," she said, when she was sure her voice wouldn't tremble. "Care to explain why?"

Amusement danced in his eyes. "I knew you would be strong, and if you became a Fide, you would pose big problems for me." Steven took a step towards her. "It's still not too late. You can become my apprentice, since I recently obtained a vacancy. We can travel the world..."

Dylan cut him off. "I'm not going with you, Steven. I have no desire to be like you."

"Everyone wants to be like me."

"Apparently not everyone." She nodded towards the window. "You hear those sirens? They're for you, and I would really like to clear up a few things before they get here, which gives you, oh, maybe two minutes."

"You're stronger than Noah was. But you aren't stronger than me."

She looked down as another cut on her finger closed. She wiped her hand on her pants. She took a deep breath and recited some of the things she knew were true.

Steven's features began to shift. His lips thinned and eyes narrowed slightly. His bald head was coated with a light layer of short, dirty blond hair. The crooked nose straightened out.

"Probably not, but something has definitely shifted." She

cocked her head, and grabbing an object from her desk, stepped forward. "I can see the truth."

She held a small compact mirror up for him to see.

With those words, the rest of the lie Steven was using faded away.

She took a small step forward and watched the transformation complete itself. Standing in front of her was a middle-aged man with dirty blond hair, goatee and mustache. His features were sun beaten and windblown and the wrinkles around his eyes hinted at a lifetime of smiling. Had she not known he was there to kill her, she would have thought he looked kind. Impending death changes one's perception.

"Jack never told me about this," Dylan whispered to herself.

He smiled and those wrinkles met his eyes just the way she thought they would. "There's a lot Jack doesn't know. There's a lot Vi doesn't either." He shrugged. "Maybe if her mentor hadn't died so tragically."

His feigned concern told Dylan he had something to do with that death. Dylan took a deep breath and tried to focus. She couldn't afford to relax.

"Don't lie to me." Dylan spoke quietly, not trusting her voice to be strong. "I can see you clearly now."

"You sure about that?"

Four simple words and Dylan hesitated. Steven saw that and lunged.

Her head spun as it connected with a right hook. She heard a door slam and knew Jimmy and Jack were coming. She heard glass break as Tony's window smashed open.

Steven heard them too. He grabbed her arm, threw her across her room and slapped the door shut. A bolt slid into place on the door.

Dylan listened to the sound of feet running up the stairs, and someone yelled in the hallway. The other Feeder jumped out in ambush.

Voices carried up the stairs. The scuffle in the hallway died, but she didn't take her eyes off Steven.

His face contorted in pure anger. "It appears I don't have as much time with you as I wanted. You really have been a menace since I showed up in this town. Do you realize how much effort I had to put into you?" He paced the room, offering no chance of escape. "First with Mr. Lewis's lie layered one on top of another and spiced with pity and self-loathing. That was some of my best work. I'm sure Noah botched the lies a bit, but I thought that would take you months to uncover, if you ever had the courage to face them. Courage has always been your nemesis, Dylan.

"Then I orchestrated your mother's death and your father's fall for the crime. That should have been enough to break your will. I really thought they would slow you down. I really wanted you to have a slow, painful death if you weren't smart enough to join me." He reached over picking up a trophy she had received last year at the awards ceremony for MVP. By the look in Steven's eyes, she knew that the long, triangular, crystal award would be used to kill her. "I wanted to lie to you and watch you bleed, knowing that it would also kill your mentor, but you had to go and break Noah."

Jimmy and Jack pounded on her door, but it wouldn't budge.

"I'm glad I spent a little extra time reinforcing your door, Dylan." He tossed her trophy back and forth in his hands. "Maybe I won't be able to kill you with a lie, but I'll still enjoy watching you die. Do you know I sat there and watched TV as your mother bled out?"

"Why would you kill my mother?"

A slow sneer curved his lips. "You were going to be a powerful Fide, one with the ability to change the game between Fides and Feeders. I had to stop that by any means necessary. It was conveniently suggested to your father that he go for a drink after the fight with your mom. Of course, their fighting had increased in the last few weeks with my help, not that it took much. Unfortunately, I underestimated the other two Fides and the influence they had over you as well as way they supported you." Steven clicked his tongue. "But it's a solid plan. Destroy a Fide before they get too powerful. I'll have to try it again."

"No you won't." She rushed him, grabbing for the award as she slammed into him.

She was not going to go down without a fight. He pushed her away easily and lunged, using the trophy like a bayonet. She moved out of the way a little too slowly and felt the edge of her crystal award slice through the skin at her side. She grabbed her side and brought her gaze back up to see Steven's fist coming towards her face. Unable to stop her fall, she crashed to the floor.

Helplessly, she watched Steven lunge again and her trophy embed itself in her leg. She cried out and kicked up, dislodging the award. She tried to crawl away, but the award pierced her back. Curling into a ball on the floor, she listened to the banging from the other side of her bedroom door.

Steven stood over her. He kicked her in the face and sent her onto her back before he went down, driving his knee into the wound in her leg.

She screamed. Her head spinning as she struggled with the pain. She tried to remain conscious and hold on to Jack's voice yelling from the hallway.

"I'm sorry, Jack," she mouthed through the blood that bubbled in her mouth.

Steven raised the award over his head. She stared at the tip smeared with her blood.

Glass shattered over her face as three loud bangs rang through her room. She waited for the pain to end and the cold to come.

There was chaos. People shouted.

Jack bent down, and gently cradled her head in his arms. Bringing her hand up she cupped his face, attempting to open her mouth to speak. She had to tell him she loved him, at least once.

But the words wouldn't come.

On a staggered breath, she closed her eyes.
And the cold came.

Chapter 32

"Did we have to move into a third floor walkup?" she grunted as she tried to maneuver her cramping hip and stitched leg up the last flight of stairs.

Jimmy chuckled and he kept a hand on her back for balance. "Bitch, bitch, bitch."

"It was the best I could do," her father mumbled at the same time.

She huffed half-heartedly; glad to be out of the hospital. The stitches in her back and side tightened as she moved, but at least she could move. Jimmy bumped past her when she finally reached the landing and paused to catch her breath. Half way down the hall, he opened a door and smiled.

"Welcome home." Her father placed an arm around her shoulders awkwardly.

She and her dad walked into the apartment together. She looked at Tony, Jack, Vi, Megan and Rachel all smiling at her. A bouquet of flowers sat on a coffee table and balloons hung from chairs around the kitchen table. Tony ran and hugged her, almost knocking her over, but Jimmy and her dad were there to steady her.

Tony pulled her around the apartment, determined to show her everything. She hobbled painfully after him on her crutches. She could feel a pang of sorrow when she recognized some of the items were from their home, but she realized she needed them. She touched the kitchen table and remembering how her mom would make cookies there with her when she was sick.

Nothing in the living room looked familiar. Dylan was glad for that. She didn't want to sit on a couch and remember *him* sitting there watching her mother die.

She let out a little gasp as Tony pulled her into her bedroom. Her trophies, minus the one that almost killed her, lined a shelf over her bed. Her dresser and mirror were against the other wall. Megan's sticker was still in the corner, and hanging from the other was the necklace Jack had given her.

A framed picture of her mom sat on the dresser.

"I knew you always liked that picture," her father said from behind her. She turned and watched him shuffle his feet and clear this throat before he spoke again. "I hope that's okay."

Dylan hugged him tightly. "Thank you," she whispered.

Her father cleared his throat again as he walked out of the room.

She went to the window, and took a deep breath.

Jack wrapped his arms carefully around her. "You will get through this."

"I know." She rested her head back against his chest and closed her eyes. She would get through this.

"Hungry?" she heard Vi call.

"All I've eaten is that slop they pass for food for the past few weeks." Dylan kissed Jack and headed for the kitchen.

"We know Thanksgiving isn't for another week," Megan said when she came into the living room and saw food spread around the table, "but we sort of wanted to have it early."

Tears blurred her vision as she watched Megan's parents as well as Davey carry plates and silverware from the kitchen, followed closely by Vi and Rachel with different dishes full of steaming food. She could barely see by the time her father walked forward with a large turkey on her mom's old carving platter.

The table was too small for so many people, but no one cared. Everyone squeezed in and spent their time talking and laughing.

Dylan made her way back into her room once Megan and her family left. Jack helped her lie on the bed before he wrapped his arms around her.

"The third one got away, didn't he?" Dylan didn't need to look at Jack to know the answer. They had avoided the topic since she woke in the hospital.

"Yes. He never even made it officially into custody," Jack said as he pulled her closer. "The police had him. I saw them put him in the back of the police car as I got into the ambulance with you, but the police car arrived at the precinct empty. He'd disappeared. I checked on that the next day after I knew you were stable and out of surgery." He ran his hands over his face. "I just had this feeling something had happened." Dylan didn't respond. He softened his expression. "I don't want you to worry about that right now. Just get better. We'll deal with him when we have to."

"But we will have to deal with him, won't we?" She squeezed his hand as much to comfort herself as to comfort him. "And we don't even know who he was."

"He'll be back," Jack said as he tucked a strand of hair behind her ear and cupped her cheek for a moment before continuing. "Steven was a powerful Feeder. And he said he was responsible for Vi's mentor's death?"

"He implied it," Dylan mumbled, distracted by the memory of that night.

"You took out two Feeders in one night. They will not take kindly to that."

She cringed and silently prayed she wouldn't have to worry about that third Feeder for a long time. "What did Steven mean when he said 'I could change everything'?"

"I don't know, and that's why I'm sure the third Feeder will return," Jack said softly. "You aren't alone. Vi is already trying to track down some information. We will find out what Steven meant. Together. I promise."

She squeezed his hand, trying to control her emotions. "Thanks, Jack."

She drifted in and out of sleep, comfortable and safe for the first time in a long time.

"What am I going to do about school?" Dylan asked later with a smile twitching her lips.

Jack shrugged. "Looks like now you have an excuse for running late."

She nudged his shoulder.

"And," he continued, "if someone gets in your way, you'll have to hit them with something other than your foot."

Dylan chuckled. "That could definitely be a lot of fun."

"Well take advantage of it while you can. Doc said that cast will be off and stitches out by Christmas."

Jack was right; she could make it through this.

"Will you be here when I wake up?" she mumbled on the edge of sleep.

He kissed her lips. "You know I will."

Chapter 33

Dylan walked slowly down the slick sidewalk, her leg still stiff and uncooperative after being in a cast for almost two months. Since she left the hospital, she had gotten better at finding the truth. Even with the cast and the crutches, she discovered she did have a talent for sneaking up on people and laughed on several occasions as people's eyes widened when she would appear next to them.

She looked around. All the houses were bright and festively decorated with snowmen and twinkling lights. People arrived with presents and packages. Laughter rang through the snow. She winced, feeling the lies that accompanied family gatherings flow easily from open doors.

Jack grabbed her hand. "It's harder around holidays with everyone on their best behavior, isn't?"

She shook her head. "Part of me wants to storm every house and demand the truth."

"And the other part?"

"Wants to let them have their moment of bliss." She offered a small smile. "We'll get the truth out of them after Christmas."

Jack laughed and wrapped his arm around her. "No wonder I love you."

They walked through the park, taking a path that led to the other side of town and the cemetery. Jack didn't say anything as they walked. She knew he would go with her, even if she hadn't been aware that she wanted to go herself.

"I'll let you two talk." He kissed her at the gate and stepped back.

Dylan nodded and headed in. She hadn't been here since the funeral. She brushed the snow from her mother's headstone and carefully kneeled in front of it.

"I wish you were still here, but I'm sure you already know

that." She looked up as it began to snow. "I know how much you loved the holidays, so we're trying to be festive...kind of. Dad's doing okay, though there are times when everything feels awkward between us. Vi says we just need time. She's probably right, though sometimes I think time is her answer for everything." She looked back towards the entrance and saw Jack leaning against a street light. "I wish you had gotten to know Jack. He's still a pain in the ass, but I love him, Mom. And I think you already knew that." She paused and brushed the snow away again. "Tony's doing really well, not that you were ever worried." She took a deep steadying breath. "You always knew Jimmy and I would take care of him. And Dad's there too, more than he used to be.

"We finally finished unpacking all the boxes in the apartment. I can't really say I miss the house. On good days, Dad says he wants to start looking for a bigger place in the spring, but I don't know if that will happen." Dylan bit her lip. "I don't even know if I want a bigger place."

"So I'm cooking Christmas dinner for everyone tomorrow night, even though the apartment really isn't big enough for everyone. Dad, Jimmy and Rachel, Jack and Tony, Vi and her new boyfriend Ethan will all be there and Megan and her family are coming too. I'm not sure if I'll be able to get the apple pie to taste as good as yours, but I'll try."

A dog's bark echoed off the gravestones. She looked deeper into the cemetery sure she heard footsteps slowly making their way towards her. She clenched her jaw and forced herself to calm down. All she could do if Feeders came for her was beat them. "Honestly, I'm just hoping I don't burn down the place trying to cook the turkey and ham."

Suddenly, she felt much older than she was.

"There are so many more things you needed to tell me. There are so many more things you are supposed to be part of in my life." She bowed her head as the wind picked up. "I know you will still be part of my life. I will come here as often as I can and let you know what's going on, and as soon as my leg is better, I'll run by every now and then.

"I love you. I miss you." Dylan leaned forward the kissed her mother's headstone.

She looked up. A few flakes of snow were falling. A low humming noise drew her attention back to the headstone, and she watched as out of the stone, a glass cylinder appeared. It glowed black, progressing to gray and finally bright white, forcing her to shield her eyes. When the glow faded, a crystal-clear dissimulator remained.

Her hands shook as she picked it up. Curling her fingers around it, the dissimulator pulsated as it removed the lies from people she had passed earlier on her walk to the cemetery.

"See you later, Mom," Dylan whispered.

Jack waited for her at the entrance to the cemetery. She smiled, and then felt it falter as she walked towards him. His expression turned to concern as she approached with her head bowed.

"Okay?" he stepped towards her.

Dylan opened her hand and showed him the dissimulator, but she didn't want to look at him. She gasped as Jack pulled her into his arms.

He shook his head and waited for her to look up. "What did I tell you before, Dylan?" She blinked twice trying to figure out which "before" she was supposed to remember. "Do you still love me?"

"Yes." She shook her head. "I just didn't think it would be that fast."

"I didn't either."

Jack grabbed and spun her until she was laughing. "I love you, Dylan," he said as he kissed her. "A dissimulator won't change that." Still dizzy, Dylan hung on as he set her back on the sidewalk. "You ready to head back?"

She wrapped an arm around his waist as they walked back to

Vi's apartment. "You know," she chuckled, "you never did tell me where your dissimulator showed up."

"Maybe one day I will." He laughed. "I think some things are better left to the imagination."

New cuts opened on her fingers as she passed more people on the street, but they would wait, she told herself.

She would enjoy Christmas with her family and friends tomorrow. Then she and Jack could head out to uncover the truth that so many people were determined to ignore.

Acknowledgements

Huge thanks are definitely in order to so many people who inspired, encouraged, or motivated me to complete this novel.

First, to my critique partner of awesome! Kris: This book would not have existed without your motivation, support, and criticism during the writing and the editing. From the first crazy draft, written in a whirlwind during NaNoWriMo, and through rounds of edits, you have been a rock that I could always depend on to stay true and honest.

To my friends and family: thank you for listening to me talk about the writing world more than was probably acceptable, and believing that I could do this. Thank you for your patience and encouragement during every stage of the writing process. Writing this novel has been an amazing journey, one that I would not have been able to finish without each of you.

To my production team at Lodestone Books: thank you for your time, patience, and expertise in helping me share *Etched in Lies* with the world.

Lastly, I want to thank you. Yes. I'm talking to you. You took a chance, and picked up this book, and for that, I am grateful.